and her books

"Rita Herron blends pulsing romance and knife-edge suspense so effortlessly, you'll be gasping for more."
—Stephanie Bond, author of *Party Crashers*

"A fast-paced, romantic thriller that captivates readers from the first page. This is a masterpiece of multilayered plots and memorable characters. With its romance, suspense, supernatural undertones and brilliant dialogue...this novel will make the hairs stand up on the back of your neck."
—*Romantic Times BOOKreviews* on
Last Kiss Goodbye

"Ms. Herron weaves a lovely romance into a world of chaos, mystery and angst-ridden souls trying to find the power to live again."
—*Romance Junkies* on *In a Heartbeat*

"A psychologically frightening novel... complex and compelling."
—*Romantic Times BOOKreviews* on
A Breath Away

RITA HERRON
DON'T SAY
A Word

HQN™

ISBN-13: 978-0-373-77217-9
ISBN-10: 0-373-77217-3

DON'T SAY A WORD

Dear Reader,

Welcome back to New Orleans. In *Say You Love Me* you met the Dubois family, a family that includes three tough men who all work in law enforcement. All are devoted to fighting crime and protecting the citizens of The Big Easy. And all are loyal to their parents, who suffered during the aftermath of the hurricanes, but who pulled together to rebuild their home, business and lives.

The brothers have a soft spot for a woman in trouble, but each has vowed that no woman will ever come between them.

In *Don't Say a Word,* the youngest brother, police officer Antwaun Dubois, is arrested for murder. The middle brother, FBI agent Damon Dubois, steps up to spearhead the investigation and exonerate his brother. But the case grows more intriguing when he discovers that the woman his brother is accused of killing might still be alive.

Brotherly ties and family loyalties are challenged as Damon finds himself falling in love with the mysterious woman. Complicating matters more, she has undergone plastic surgery and lost her true identity.

Hints of paranormal, the sultry New Orleans setting, deadly secrets and a killer bent on revenge add to the twists and turns and mysterious flavor of the story.

At the time I first came up with the idea for this book, the innovative cutting-edge medical procedure of performing a facial transplant was mere talk. But during the course of writing *Don't Say a Word,* research and the reality of this procedure became more public. Still, I thought the idea of a faceless person, especially one who might not know her identity, was fascinating and that it would make a terrific backdrop for my mystery.

I think you'll find it does, and I hope you enjoy the story!

Sincerely,

Rita

To all the soldiers fighting for our country
and our freedom—you are the real heroes!

PROLOGUE

May, New Orleans

THE WOMAN HAD NO FACE. No voice. No name.

Dr. Reginald Pace studied her near lifeless form as it lay on the shiny surgical table. The harsh fluorescent lights glared off her charred skin and raw flesh, painting an inhuman picture.

Her silent, vacant eyes begged for mercy. For death.

But the voice inside his head whispered that he could not fulfill her wish. It proclaimed that her body craved the transformation only his gifted hands could offer.

As a plastic surgeon, he saw the ruins of people's faces and bodies on a daily basis. But never had he beheld a sight like the one before him—the very reason he'd made a deal with a demon to get her. She was the perfect one for his experiment.

Mangled, charred skin had peeled away from the severed tendons. Lips that once held a feminine smile now gaped with blisters and raw flesh. Bloodshot eyes, blinded by pain, had flickered with pleas for death before he had swept her under with the bliss of drugs.

His healing hands would piece her back together.

His healing hands and time…

Layer by layer he would rebuild her. Repair severed nerve endings, damaged cartilage. Replace tissue. Mold the monster into his beauty.

Without a face, a name, a picture, he could shape her into whatever he chose.

The woman of his dreams, God willing. She would be his creation. His to keep forever…

He gently brushed the remnants of her singed hair from her hairline. She would be in agony for a while, but he would be there with her every step of the way to offer her comfort.

And she would recover; he wouldn't rest until she did.

A smile curled his mouth as he picked up the scalpel to get started. Yes, she would thank him in the end.

CHAPTER ONE

A year later, New Orleans

DAMON DUBOIS WAS A DEAD MAN.

As dead as the soldiers who'd fallen and given their lives for the country. As dead as the ones who'd lost their lives during the terrible hurricane that nearly destroyed New Orleans.

As dead as the woman he had killed.

His own heart did still beat and blood still flowed through his veins, forcing him to go through the motions of life.

A punishment issued by the gods, he was certain.

He could still see the flames licking at her skin, see the smoke swirling above her face, hear the crackle of the house as wood splintered and crumbled down upon her body.

For although his head hadn't yet touched the pillow this dreary evening, nightmares already haunted him with the cries of that anguished woman screaming in pain.

And the *bébé*'s ghostlike cry…

"*Tite ange,*" he whispered. "Little angel, you did not deserve to die."

Perspiration beaded on his neck and trickled down into the collar of his shirt as he opened the French doors to the hundred-year-old bayou house and breathed in the sultry summer air. The end of May was nearing and already the summer heat was oppressive. Sticky. The air hung thick with the scent of blood and swamp water. Eerie sounds cut through the endless night. The muddy Mississippi slapping at the embankment. A faint breeze stirring the tupelo trees. The gators' shrill attack cry in the night. Insects buzzing for their next feed. A Louis Armstrong blues tune floated from the stereo, the soul-wrenching words echoing his mood.

Though a thick fog of blessed darkness clouded the waning daylight, forming morbid images to bombard him. A hand outstretched, begging for help. The fingers curled around the tiny *bébé*'s rattle. The accusing, horror-stricken eyes.

He blinked to stop the damning images, but they flickered in his mind like flashes of lightning splintering the sky.

The scream tore the air again, and he swallowed back bile. Its tormenting sound refused to stop, pounding against his conscience with a will he couldn't defy. Reminding him of his past. His sins. His vow of silence.

So many secrets… Tell and you die.

Inside his pocket, his cell phone vibrated, jarring him back to the present. Hauling him away from the pain and self-recriminations clawing at his mind.

He connected the call with sweaty fingers.

"Special Agent Damon Dubois."

"Damon, thank God you answered."

His little brother Antwaun's strained voice rattled unevenly over the line. Something was wrong. What kind of mess had his youngest sibling gotten into this time?

Hell, not that he had a right to judge anyone.

But the family knew nothing of his secrets. Or his lies…

"You have to come meet me. We found a woman…at least part of one."

Holy Christ. "I'll be right there. Where are you?"

Antwaun relayed the GPS coordinates and Damon snapped the phone closed, grabbed his badge and weapon and strapped it onto his shoulder holster. Fifteen minutes later, he parked and headed through a dense stretch of the swamp. The scent of murk floated from the marshy water as the mud sucked at his feet. The voices and faint beams of flashlights ahead served as his guide through the knot of trees, and when he reached the crime-scene tape, he identified himself to the officer in charge.

Through the shadows, he spotted Antwaun and strode toward him. His brother's forehead was furrowed with worry, the intense anger in his dark eyes warning Damon that this was not an everyday crime scene. Something personal had entered into it.

"What's going on, Antwaun?" he asked quietly.

Two uniforms frowned and muttered curses at his arrival, already the thread of territorial rights adding tension to an anxiety-ridden situation.

Antwaun leaned in close, his voice a conspiratorial whisper. "Hell, Damon. I think I know the victim."

Damon's gaze shot to his brother's, his pulse racing. "*How* do you know her?"

"I can't be sure, but…" His gruff voice cracked. "But if it is who I think it is, we dated."

The heat thickened, causing a cold clamminess to bead on Damon's skin. "You recognize her or what?"

Antwaun scrubbed a hand over the back of his scraggly hair, his face as pale as buttermilk. "Like I said, we only found part of her."

Damon sucked in a sharp breath, then followed Antwaun over to the edge of the swamp. The murk chewed at Damon's shoes, the stench of blood and a decaying animal hitting him. Somewhere nearby the hiss of gators warned him that hungry creatures lurked at the edges of the rivers. Yellow eyes pierced the inky darkness, scaly predators hiding beneath the water's surface, taking stock of their prey. Biding their time. Waiting to strike.

Then he saw her. At least the part that was visible. Her hand.

Just a single hand sticking up through the quicksand.

Brittle, yellowed bones poked through skin that had been gnawed away. The fingertips were half-gone. Blood dotted the remnants of mangled flesh, revealing exposed veins that had been sawed away by the jagged teeth of animals now watching nearby in silent reverie.

"How…" He had to clear his throat, push away the mounting fury and choking bile. No woman deserved to end up like this.

Had she been dead or alive when the gators got her?

"If this is all they found, what makes you think you know her?"

Antwaun's hand shook as he pointed to what was left of her third finger. "That ring…"

"Yeah?" Damon squinted, moved closer, knelt and caught the thin thread of silver glinting through the mud and debris. Amazingly, the simple silver band still clung to the bone.

"I gave it to her," Antwaun said in a low, tortured voice. "Right before she went missing."

SHE LIVED IN THE DARKNESS. Had known nothing but pain for months.

And all that time, she had been missing, but no one had come looking for her. Why?

Clutching the sheets of her hospital bed between bandaged fingers, she begged for relief from the agony of her tormenting thoughts. Time bled and flowed together, sometimes nonexistent, sometimes slipping through the hourglass in slow motion. Sometimes chunks and days, even weeks gone by without notice.

Isolated, starved for human contact, she lay waiting for the doctor's visit.

The bleep-bleep of hospital machinery became her music. His voice, her salvation.

Gruff. Soothing. Coaxing her to sit up. Eat. Fight for her life. Heal.

His touch offered comfort, compassion. It murmured promises that she might recover one day. Be human. Even beautiful.

His miracle.

Yet as much as his manner evoked concern and care for her, even growing feelings, the scent of medicine and hospital permeated his clothing, reminding her that he was her doctor, she his patient. She was only one of many he had helped. But she'd heard the rumors. The hushed voices. And she had yet to see her reflection because he had stripped the hospital rehab facility of mirrors.

She was the woman without a face. A human monster.

He had repaired what he could. Endless, countless surgeries over the past few months. Bandages and medication, hours and hours of mind-control techniques to keep from going crazy. Sometimes she feared she walked a tightrope to insanity.

And when he left her room for the night, another man came. A monster like her who whispered in the shadows. The man with the scalelike skin.

Her one and only friend here. Lex Van Wormer.

He seemed to sense when she was teetering on the edge, and reeled her back in, sewing the tethered strands of her mind together with some fanciful story. Silly dreams of a future she had to look forward to.

One he dreamed about as well, but one that eluded them both. Instead they had become prisoners of the darkness.

A gentle knock sounded at the door, and the heavy wooden structure squeaked open. A sliver of light from the hall sliced the black interior, causing her to blink. Slowly over the past months of her imprisonment, her vision had adjusted and returned to near normal, though she still preferred the shadows. Whether this was to shield herself from having to face others and see the disgust or pity in their eyes, or because she'd begun to view the darkness as her best friend, she wasn't certain.

Her breath lodged in a momentary panic in her throat as she listened to the approaching footsteps. One of the nurses with another round of injections? Dr. Pace with his soothing voice and promises that she would get better? Or Lex, somehow sensing that she had suffered another nightmare?

Nightmares or memories—she could no longer distinguish the difference. She only knew that night after endless night, some fathomless, sightless, black-hearted devil chased her. That he waited around every corner, watching, stalking, breathing down her neck. That she had to escape. That he wanted her dead and would stop at nothing until he achieved his purpose.

The door closed, blanketing the room once again in the gray fog that offered her safety.

It was always twilight in her room.

"Crystal?"

"Lex." She exhaled a sigh of heartfelt relief. Still, the name felt foreign. The first time he'd seen her, he'd commented that her eyes reminded him of sparkling crystal cut glass, so he'd called her Crystal, and the nurses had latched on to it.

That she'd been blind at first and hadn't been able to see him hadn't mattered. She'd relished his company.

Then, finally, on a pain-filled admission to prove to her that she wasn't alone in her world of shadows, he'd allowed her to touch his hand. She'd felt the scaly dry patches of leatherlike skin and had understood his reason for withdrawing from the world.

The condition, caused by exposure to an unknown chemical he'd been exposed to in the war, had disfigured him and eaten away at his body like battery acid. For a brief time before the bandages from her eyes had been removed, she'd feared she would react to his impairment.

But she had grown accustomed to the sound of his voice as he read her poetry at night, to the cadence of his laugh as he fabricated stories of journeys he'd taken, and his looks hadn't mattered. In fact, she hadn't even cringed when she'd finally rested her eyes upon him.

Apparently, he had adjusted to seeing her without a face, and covered in bandages as well. Who else would be so accepting?

He dragged the straight chair against the wall near her bed, then reached for her hand. A light squeeze, and her breathing steadied.

"Thank you for coming." Heavens, she hated the choked, childish quiver of her voice. But she had been so lonely.

"I'll always be here for you, Crystal. Always."

She closed her eyes to stem the tears threatening. Theirs was an odd relationship. Two misfits thrown together, two survivors hanging on to life by a severed thread. Yet they weren't really living either.

"I've missed you since last night, Crystal," he said in a low voice.

She tensed. She'd sensed that his friendship ran deep, that he wanted more from her. She loved him in a platonic way.

Too many pieces of her past lost. Too many questions unanswered.

Another man…maybe waiting.

The sound of Lex turning his harmonica over in his hands with fingers brittle from his disease forced her to open her eyes again.

"Our quote for the day," he began, "is from Ecclesiastes 49:10. 'Two are better than one, for if they fall, the one will lift up his fellow.'"

A sliver of unease tickled her spine as his words washed over her. Lex was her friend, but if she healed as Dr. Pace promised, and she had to hold on to the hope that she *would* recover, she couldn't imagine Lex as her lover. And she knew that he wanted more from her.

He lifted his harmonica and began to wail out a blues song that gripped her with sadness. Regret fed the flames of her emotions. She loved Lex, and she didn't want to hurt him.

But she had to find out who she was. Where she'd come from. How she had ended up here.

If she had a family, a husband, other friends. A lover.

And why in the past months, not a single person had cared enough to hunt for her.

DAMON STUDIED HIS BROTHER'S face as he drove toward their family's house. Of all the confounded nights to have a homey get-together…but his mother had refused to take no for an answer. She'd hinted that his oldest brother, Jean-Paul, a detective with the New Orleans Police Department, had to see them.

God, he hoped that didn't mean more trouble. Their family had been through hell the past two years. Katrina had nearly destroyed the family home and business—Jean-Paul had lost his first wife during the ordeal—and only a few months ago, their baby sister, Catherine, had almost died at the hands of a serial killer they'd dubbed the Swamp Devil.

Tonight—after witnessing the extraction of the woman's mutilated hand from the swamp, listening to conjecture about the cause of death and the perp from the officers at the scene, and watching his brother sweat bullets for three hours—Damon's head throbbed with anxiety.

But his mother insisted the Dubois family needed to celebrate Jean-Paul's marriage to Britta Berger, the editor of a secret-confession column for a local magazine called *Naked Desires,* a woman who had drawn the serial killer to New Orleans a few months ago and given his brother the chase of a lifetime.

And the woman of Jean-Paul's dreams.

Granted, Damon had been suspicious of Britta at first, and with good reason. Britta had a shady past, a traumatized upbringing, had lied and had secrets. But when the truth had been revealed, he'd realized she had been an innocent victim of a sinister cult that had sacrificed humans to a god they called Sobek. Not only had she survived and escaped the cult, and the leader who'd tried to kill her, now she helped teenage prostitutes get off the streets. She also loved his brother dearly.

Lucky bastard.

Damon pulled down the drive to their parents' house, weaving through the maze of giant live oaks and the moss sweeping downward like spiderwebs. "Tell me about this woman, the one you think is our victim."

"Her name is Kendra. Kendra Yates."

"And how did you meet her?"

"She was a dancer at a casino bar. I...didn't ask questions until later."

Antwaun coughed into his hand. "Much later."

So they'd slept together. No big surprise. His brother was quite the ladies' man, in a hellion, take-me-as-I-am kind of way. "Dammit, Antwaun, when are you going to stop picking up chicks in bars?"

"Look, Damon, not everyone's the sainted ex-marine that you are."

Damon gritted his teeth, guilt plaguing him. "I'm not a saint. Never claimed to be."

Antwaun scowled. "The folks and people in town sure see it that way."

Damon narrowed his eyes. He didn't have time for this bullshit. "Just tell me what happened between you and this woman."

Antwaun flexed his fisted hands and stared at the blunt tips of his fingers. "We saw each other for a while. I…thought we were getting close."

"You gave her a ring?"

"Yeah."

He cut his eyes sharply to the side. "And its significance?"

"I didn't propose, if that's what you're asking. But I did think about it, although the ring wasn't expensive. I bought it from one of those artists on the streets." He cleared his throat. Hesitated. Looked almost sheepish. Then a frown pulled at his mouth. "Later that night, she disappeared."

"You reported her missing?"

"No. I thought she'd just left. Me." His eyes darkened with hurt. "Figured I'd scared her off, or the ring wasn't expensive enough."

Damon contemplated his brother's declaration. He sounded serious.

"I've never known you to fall for a woman, Antwaun."

Antwaun shrugged his blue denim-clad shoulders. "Never thought I would either."

Damon's neck tightened as he parked the black FBI-issued sedan in the drive of his parents' antebellum home. Since his last visit, they'd painted the house a pale yellow, the trim white. Huge ferns swung from the awning, and his dad had built a porch swing at one end and staged rocking chairs between pots of geraniums. Such a domestic setting.

So at odds with the Dubois men and their jobs. And now this trouble...

His mind spun back to Antwaun's admission. If his little brother had actually fallen in love with Kendra Yates, she must have been pretty damn special.

But now the woman was dead. Murdered—and they both knew that Antwaun's relationship with her meant he would be interrogated.

"All right, Antwaun. Now tell me the truth. Do you know why someone would kill her?"

"No. Like I told you, I have no idea what happened to her." His brother shifted, chewed the inside of his cheek, then stared at the woods that backed his parents' property. A shadow caught Damon's eye, and he watched a gator slither up onto the bank and settle in the dark bed of weeds, hidden.

Damon's gut churned. The cops called Antwaun a chameleon. When undercover, he could change colors to blend in with any background. Like the gator who hid in the spiny shadows of the weeping willow.

But Antwaun also had a temper, and a habit of being in the wrong place at the wrong time. He also liked to break the rules and push the limits. And sometimes he played the role of undercover bad guy a little too convincingly. His hotheaded temper had landed him in jail a few times when he was younger, and Damon and Jean-Paul had bailed out his ass, although they hadn't been happy about it. And even in the service, he'd walked a fine line between fighting the enemy on the field and ending up in the brig for insubordinate conduct.

Damon studied the rigid set to his jaw as Antwaun climbed out. There was more to the story than he was telling. Something Antwaun didn't want him to know. Something about Kendra Yates? Or was it about himself and their relationship? What else had happened between them?

LEX VAN WORMER WATCHED her sleep.

Crystal, he called her, because she had no name. Not that she knew of anyway.

Still, in spite of the way she had come into his life, she was an innocent angel shining light on his darkest hour. Like a rare piece of cut glass or a precious gem he'd discovered buried in graveyard dust.

At a time when he hung in limbo, he'd found a kindred soul.

Restless, tortured sounds erupted from her throat, drawing his aching eyes to the pale column of her neck. Whispers of fear echoed in her cries. Moments of reliving such horrid pain that even he felt like weeping from the misery.

He had known misery himself.

He had also caused it some, for which God would never forgive him.

He tucked the sheet gently around her slender, quivering form, then laid a hand against the silky hair that fanned across the hospital pillow. His breath caught in his throat as he waited for her to turn and scream, then jerk away from his touch. Yet she nestled farther into the bedding and turned to press her cheek against his scaly hand.

Tears of joy dampened his eyes. She trusted him. Needed him. And had accepted that he was grotesque from the disease that chewed away at his flesh. And not with his birth as a dark soul. One that had allowed him to push aside his conscience. One that had allowed the seeds of wrong to fester inside him. His diseased body now bore witness.

And so he lived in a world between heaven and hell, fighting the demons that wanted to take his soul.

Crystal was his salvation. If he could hang on

long enough to save her, he just might escape the wrath of Satan....

Yet, even as regrets for the evil he had done burned his throat, the thrill of the blood hunt still seized his soul.

CHAPTER TWO

ANTWAUN DUBOIS HATED THE way his brother was looking at him. As if he didn't trust him enough to confide the truth.

Dammit, trust had nothing to do with his silence.

If anything, Antwaun had to keep his secrets to himself to protect his brother. Every aspect of undercover police work involved putting up fronts. Pretending to be something you weren't. Lying.

Sometimes he told so many lies he didn't know the truth himself.

As the Chameleon, he could change his appearance to blend in anywhere. No job was too dangerous or too edgy for him to tackle. The risks be damned.

Unfortunately, the fact that he melded with the dregs and crooks of society meant it would be easy for him to cross the line, and almost as easy for him to hide his indiscretions. His poker face kept him alive. It could keep him from revealing his motives if needed.

He silently cursed as sweat trickled down the side of his face. He'd been warned how enticing the other side of the law could be, and he had been tempted more than once....

Hell.

How could he blame his big brother for scrutinizing him when Antwaun had a reputation as a troublemaker?

Anger churned in his belly as he and Damon walked up the clamshell-lined entry to his parents' house. How the fuck could he ever live up to his older brothers?

"Bon à rien, toi, 'tit souris," Jean-Paul had said to him when he was younger, meaning "good for nothing, you, little mouse."

It had been true. But he'd tried to change that reputation since he'd been on the force.

Jean-Paul and Damon had always been good. As a detective, Jean-Paul had been decorated for bravery and saving lives during Katrina. Damon, the special agent in the mix, had received commendations from the military and goddamn president for bravery and heroism.

Antwaun...he was the screwup.

A rookie on the police force, and now that position might be in jeopardy.

The door swung open, and his mother squealed as if she hadn't seen them in years. God, he loved his boisterous family. Just wished he fit in better and didn't disappoint them so much.

Damon, quiet, methodical and intense as always, bent to hug their mother, Daniella, a short, roundish woman who ran the show at home and at the new restaurant they'd opened in New Orleans. She and their father made the best Cajun cuisine in the state.

All the boys were over six feet, and towered over Daniella, but she boasted that she would turn them over her knee if she needed to, and Antwaun believed her.

Damon finally released her from the bear hug, and his mother yanked Antwaun close, enveloping him in the heavenly scents of her spicy jambalaya, fresh bread and sinful chocolate cake. He leaned into her, allowing her to rub his back and pat his cheek, but his stomach clenched when she looked into his eyes with a fine sheen of tears.

"It's so nice to have all my wonderful boys here together."

Wonderful? If she only knew…

But neither he nor Damon would discuss the mutilated corpse of the woman they'd discovered earlier, or the implications of his involvement. The unspoken rule—they left their weapons and gritty police talk at the door and didn't bring either to the dinner table.

Yep, act like a chameleon. Put on a pretty coat.

Smile as if the world wasn't all gray. Pretend not to have seen the monsters encountered in the bayou and on the streets.

Damon cleared his throat, looking almost as uncomfortable as Antwaun felt. For the past year, he'd been even more solemn. Brooding at times. Almost distant.

Daniella beamed with pride and ushered them into the homey kitchen. Already Jean-Paul and his new wife, Britta, his baby sister, Catherine, her daughter, Chrissy, and his other sister, Stephanie, had gathered. His father wore a chef's hat and stirred the bubbling stew while Jean-Paul popped the cork on a bottle of cabernet sauvignon and poured them all a glass.

Antwaun would have preferred a beer, but Jean-Paul wanted to make a toast.

"Let's all sit down." Daniella Dubois waved her hands, shooing them to their places as she hoisted bowls full of the Cajun foods and carried them to the table. Catherine deposited baskets of steaming bread; Stephanie grabbed his and Damon's arms, and dragged them to sit on either side of her; and Chrissy plopped down, her ponytail bobbing as she sipped freshly squeezed lemonade.

"So, what is all this urgency, Jean-Paul?" dark-haired Stephanie asked, eyes twinkling.

Jean-Paul clutched his bride's hand and grinned

like a cat that had just swallowed a canary. "Britta and I have an announcement." He turned to his wife. "Britta?"

Britta laughed. "Go ahead, you tell them, sweetheart."

Antwaun shifted uncomfortably. Not that he wasn't happy for Jean-Paul, but seeing his tough brother act so mushy was just plain weird.

His father, Pierre, tapped his wineglass. "Don't keep us in suspense, son. Spill it."

Jean-Paul grinned, then pressed his wife's hand to his chest. "Britta and I are expecting a baby."

Shouts erupted around the table. His mother dabbed tears from her eyes and jumped up to hug Britta and Jean-Paul. Catherine, little Chrissy and Stephanie joined the milieu of chattering excited voices.

Antwaun stood and pounded Jean-Paul on the back in congratulations. Damon's hand tightened around the wineglass in a white-knuckled grip. Then the glass shattered and red wine splattered all over the tablecloth, mingling with drops of blood spewing from Damon's palm.

DAMON BIT BACK A CURSE, and tried to mop up the spilled wine with his napkin.

"Damon, oh, my good gracious!" Chaos erupted, and Damon noticed the blood. His mother rushed to retrieve a towel, and Stephanie grabbed his hand and wrapped her napkin around the jagged cut.

"Are you all right, Damon?" she asked in a low voice.

Stephanie had always been the perceptive one. Sometimes he thought she sensed things, maybe possessed a touch of ESP. Feeling panic tease at his nerves, he masked his thoughts. He couldn't let anyone see inside his bleak, ugly mind.

Besides, this was his brother's moment. "I'm sorry, Jean-Paul. How clumsy of me. I didn't mean to spoil your announcement."

His oldest brother's eyes registered concern, but he shook off the apology and curved his arm around Britta's shoulders. "No problem, bro. Are you all right?"

Damon and Antwaun exchanged a glance, silently agreeing not to broach the latest challenge facing Antwaun. Hopefully the DNA would prove that the severed hand hadn't belonged to Kendra Yates and clear Antwaun of any suspicion.

But if the hand wasn't hers, then whose was it? Had another serial killer surfaced—one who enjoyed hacking off women's body parts and leaving them scattered all over the bayou?

"Do you need stitches?" his father asked.

Damon shook his head. "No, I'll just clean it up. Please continue the celebration."

His mother trailed him to the kitchen, removed the first-aid kit and played nursemaid as if he were five years old again and had just had a bicycle accident.

"What's troubling you, son?" Daniella asked.

He rinsed the droplets of blood down the drain, wishing he could rid his mind of the tormenting memories that dogged him daily. "Nothing, *Maman*, it was just a stupid accident."

She pierced him with a disbelieving frown. "There's more, Damon. I'm your *maman*, you cannot lie to me."

A family portrait in oils that hung on the opposite kitchen wall mocked him. God, he had to lie to her. If she knew the truth about the things he'd done, who he had been in the service, she wouldn't look at him with love in her eyes. No, she'd be sickened and appalled.

Guilt clouded his vision, making the veins in his head pulse with tension. "This is Jean-Paul and Britta's night, *Maman*. I want them to enjoy it." He brushed a kiss on her chubby cheek. "And you, too. You're about to be a *grand-mère* again."

His mother's face beamed with excitement. "I know, is it not wonderful? I can not wait to have another *bébé* in the house." She tweaked his cheek. "Maybe we'll have a little boy this time, another man to carry on the Dubois name."

Damon's throat thickened as he imagined the

scene. His formidable older brother with an infant in his arms. Jean-Paul was a hero. He deserved a family. A son.

But marriage and kids were not in the picture for *him.*

A man who had destroyed a family, the way he had, had no right to one of his own.

DESPAIR AND FEAR TINGED the frail sound of an infant's cry as it reverberated through the air like the strings of a harp that needed careful tuning.

Crystal jerked awake, her head swimming with confusion. A child…where? Had she dreamed the baby's cry or had it been real? Or had it been a memory?

Disoriented momentarily, she searched the dim light of her room for the doctor or the nurse. No. Maybe Lex had come to visit again.

But all was silent. She was alone.

The low sob echoed through the thin walls again as if the wind had captured the ghostly cry, beckoning her to listen. Reminding her that she wasn't alone in her pain and suffering.

Stiff from sleep, she stretched her limbs to force the circulation back around, an exercise she did routinely after her long hours in bed, then pushed her feet to the floor and into her slippers. She grabbed her thin cotton robe with one hand and shrugged it on, the other hand self-consciously touching the bandages on her face. At first she hadn't ventured outside the room, but lately, as she'd begun to heal and regain her strength, she'd taken daily walks.

The rehab facility was situated on acres of private property by the river, surrounded by the backwoods, offering privacy and seclusion for its inhabitants. During the day, other patients strolled the gardens or rested in their wheelchairs in the shade of gigantic live oaks. Some gathered to play cards in the solarium or watch television together in the common game room, but she had yet to join the social scene. Although others suffered injuries, scars, some disfigurements, hers had been one of the most severe cases the hospital had seen, or so she'd heard, and she hated the gossip and stares that accompanied her outings.

Padding slowly, she opened the door and peered into the hallway. Shadows flickered across the corridor. The dim light from the nurses' desk down the hall was just enough to allow her to see without being so stark it hurt her eyes or highlighted her own morbid appearance should another patient pass by. Blessedly, though, she was alone.

The cry jarred the air again, a low sob, then another. Realizing the sound originated from the room next to hers, she tiptoed toward the closed doorway.

Inhaling a deep breath and hoping her mummified

face wouldn't frighten the neighboring patient, she gently pushed on the door. She would just check and see if the person was all right.

Inside, a small night-light in the shape of a duck sent sparkles of faint yellow light across the white sheets and shadow-filled room. The bed seemed to swallow the tiny figure who lay curled into a ball, facing the window. Dark brown curls cascaded down the child's back, her little body jerking up and down with her cries.

Tears sprang to Crystal's eyes, but she blinked them away and slowly tiptoed into the room. The little girl turned toward her and lifted her face slightly, her arms in a death grip around a big brown teddy bear. She looked so lost and alone that Crystal's heart clenched.

"Hi, honey," she said softly. "My name is… Crystal."

The child's eyes widened momentarily, and Crystal wondered if she'd made a mistake in visiting, if her bandaged face terrified the toddler even more. Then she realized the little girl was Hispanic, and wondered if she spoke English, so she introduced herself in Spanish.

A second later, she realized she'd just learned something about herself. She was fluent in the language.

"Are you a ghost?" the little girl asked.

Crystal laughed softly, then they chatted for several minutes. The child's name was Maria, and she'd lost her mother in a car accident the day before. Maria's nana was supposed to come and get her the next day.

The self-pity Crystal had wallowed in for the last few months dissipated as compassion for the toddler mushroomed inside her. She sat down beside the girl, then read and sang to her until Maria finally fell asleep.

As Crystal made her way back to her own room, questions taunted her. Where had she learned to speak Spanish? Maybe she'd worked with children. Could she possibly have a child of her own?

IN THE DEN, Mr. Dubois sipped his coffee. "Damon, you will be at the upcoming Memorial Day celebration, won't you?"

Damon poured himself a cup of his parents' choice rich chicory blend. "I don't know."

The last thing he wanted was a commendation for honor and bravery now.

Laughter erupted in the background, drawing him back to the moment just as the doorbell rang. His sisters and mother were discussing baby names, debating over French versus American. Jean-Paul argued that they had to focus on boys' names since the firstborn would certainly be a son.

The doorbell dinged again, and Damon frowned

into his coffee, then gestured to his father that he would answer it.

Who the hell was stopping by on a Friday night unannounced? Not that he should be surprised that his parents would have company. They'd made a wealth of contacts and friends through their restaurant. And they had donated both time and money to so many charities following the hurricane that they were practically local celebrities.

Leaving his coffee cup on the table, he rammed a hand through his hair, then answered the door, hoping it was some salesman he could vent his anger on.

Instead, Lieutenant Phelps of the NOPD stood on the stoop.

A pair of silver-gray eyes wrought with turmoil met Damon's.

Not a good sign.

Lieutenant Phelps nodded. "Special Agent Dubois."

A formal greeting. Also not good.

"Lieutenant? What's going on?"

The man's eyes shifted over Damon's shoulder where Antwaun stood in the shadows of the entryway's arched doorway that led to the hall.

"We're here on official business," Lieutenant Phelps stated. "I need to speak to Antwaun."

Antwaun made a grunting sound in the background and Damon silently cursed.

"Guys, why don't we discuss this tomorrow?" Damon suggested. "It's Friday night, and we're having a family gathering." As if a Friday night had ever dissuaded him from following a lead or pursuing a case.

Behind Phelps, Antwaun's partner, George Smith, shifted nervously, avoiding eye contact with everyone.

"Sorry, guys. But you were both at the crime scene. We've ID'd the woman and have evidence that has to be answered for." The lieutenant's ruddy complexion colored with distress. "Antwaun, we need you to come with us for questioning."

CHAPTER THREE

ANTWAUN SCOWLED. "Are you arresting me?"

Phelps frowned. "Do we need to?"

Damon stepped up to run interference. "Lieutenant…we'll meet you at the station." He turned to his parents and tried to quiet his mother's shocked cry that seemed to still reverberate in the room. Injecting a calmness to his voice that he'd learned from his military training, he said, "*Maman,* Papa, don't worry. We'll clear this up and be back later tonight."

"Antwaun…what's going on?" Daniella screeched.

"Son." Pierre pressed a hand to Antwaun's shoulder. "Whatever you need…you can count on us."

Antwaun's eyes turned a tortured black. "I'll straighten it out," he muttered. "It's just a misunderstanding."

Jean-Paul appeared, a frown marring his forehead. "What in the hell is this?" He glared at the lieutenant. "This is inexcusable. If there was a problem, why didn't you phone me first instead of barging in on our family? We would have met you at the station."

The lieutenant's steady gaze flashed across the family, then settled on Jean-Paul. "The press knows about the partial body. We had to do this by the book or they'd slaughter us for protecting one of our own."

"You should protect your own," Damon muttered. So why weren't they? Damon wondered. Had Antwaun made an enemy on the force, someone who wanted to see him in trouble?

Lieutenant Phelps narrowed his eyes at Antwaun.

"I'm sorry, Jean-Paul," Antwaun said in a gravelly voice. "Please go back and finish your celebration. I'll have this issue resolved in no time."

"What does he need protecting from?" Jean-Paul snapped. The lieutenant opened his mouth to speak, but Jean-Paul cut him off. "Never mind. We'll settle this at the precinct."

The family had gathered in the hall to see what was happening, a mass of anger and bewilderment charging the air.

"We'll need your gun," Lieutenant Phelps ordered.

Antwaun glared at him, but Jean-Paul calmly retrieved the weapon from the locked cabinet. Damon's heart bled for his brother. He had never quite understood Antwaun and his temper, but he was blood kin, and he loved him just the same. Nothing would be more humiliating than being treated like a criminal in front of your family.

He should know—he feared it on a daily basis.

Still, as quiet murmurs of disbelief and support rumbled through the room from various family members, his gut tightened with worry.

"Damon, Jean-Paul," Stephanie said in a muffled voice. "What's happening?"

"We found a woman's body, that is, part of one, today in the bayou." Damon turned to his family while the officers escorted Antwaun to the squad car. "It may be someone Antwaun knows. I'm sure we can clear this up. But I need to go."

His mother pressed a hand to his back. "Yes, Damon, please go. Help your brother."

Jean-Paul touched Britta's cheek. "Sweetheart—"

"Shh. Go, Jean-Paul. Your *maman* is right. Take care of Antwaun."

His father pasted on a confident face as he curved an arm around Daniella, though anxiety lined his mouth. Catherine and Stephanie, encircled their parents like protective watchdogs. Their father had been injured during the last big hurricane, and they all worried about his health now, especially his heart.

His sisters agreed to stay with their parents while Damon and Jean-Paul rushed out. As soon as they climbed in the sedan, Jean-Paul barked, "How bad is it, Damon?"

Damon clenched his jaw. "I don't know. Like I said earlier, we found part of a body. A woman's hand." He explained about the ring and Antwaun's connection to Kendra Yates, and they both speculated over how the police had identified her so quickly.

Jean-Paul muttered something about Antwaun always finding trouble, then turned to stare out the window, and Damon stepped on the gas, his anxiety rising with every passing second. He wanted to hear exactly what Antwaun had to say.

His brother had lied to him before. Antwaun knew more than he'd admitted about this woman, Kendra. And Damon intended to find out what Antwaun was keeping from him and why the police, his own fellow officers, suspected he might be a murderer.

A PRESS MOB AWAITED ANTWAUN at the police station, turning his steel nerves to mush. How the hell had they identified this victim and discovered his involvement with her so quickly? Cameras flashed, reporters shoved microphones toward his face, firing questions at him that blurred in a giant fog.

"Officer Dubois, were you the last person to see Kendra Yates alive?"

"Is it true that she was mauled by the gators, that only her hand was found?"

"Do you know who left her to the gators?"

"Is there another serial killer in New Orleans?"

"Did you kill her, Officer Dubois?"

Antwaun barely resisted shooting daggers at the reporters with his eyes and clamped his mouth shut, knowing anything he said might be misconstrued. Why the fuck was the press so interested in this story? Who had leaked the details of the crime scene to them?

His throat clogged with emotions at the realization that Kendra was dead. *Mon coeur* he had called her. She'd asked about the French Cajun term and he'd taken her hand and placed it over his chest. "My heart," he'd said, letting her know it belonged to her.

She had been so young, so pretty, her body lithe and elegant like a dancer's. Her hands had been like magic, those slender fingers always gliding over him, so titillating and ready to please. And that tongue—she was sharp witted and quick with words, yet in bed she'd used that mile-long tongue to bathe him in ecstasy. Hell, she'd been a pussycat, who'd lapped him up like a bowl of cream. No wonder he'd fallen for her.

His partner ushered him to the side door while the lieutenant fended off questions with a statement about releasing information as soon as it became available.

Jean-Paul and Damon arrived and wove through the crowd. One of the reporters snagged Jean-Paul by the shirtsleeve, forcing him to stop. Jean-Paul curled his hand into a fist, and Antwaun waited with bated breath, half hoping his older brother would lose his cool just once and pound the guy's mouth shut.

"Detective Dubois?" the catty reporter snarled at Jean-Paul. "We know how the cops think. They protect their own. How can the public get justice in this case?"

Jean-Paul stabbed him with a knifelike glare, but kept his fist clenched by his side. "We are here to see that justice is served."

"How is that possible? Antwaun Dubois is not only surrounded by his friendly police force, but you and your brother, a federal agent, are here to defend him."

In a barely controlled move, Jean-Paul jerked the man by the tie, knotting it into his fist until the pissant coughed to get air. "My brother is here to help his fellow officers find this woman's murderer. Now, get out of the way."

Antwaun's emotions boomeranged between gratitude to have his brothers on his side, and humiliation that they had to be. His partner pushed him inside the door, and Antwaun glared at a couple of rookies who watched him with lecherous expressions as if they were ready to string him up and hang him.

Clenching his jaw, he braced himself to face being seated on the other side of the table in the interrogation room. He knew how the cops would play him; he'd acted the role of bad cop a hundred times himself, although truth be told, he didn't have to *act*.

At the same time, his mind spun with questions, theories, and...lies.

Had he been the last person to see Kendra alive?

"All right, Dubois." Lieutenant Phelps spread photos of the decimated hand across the scarred wooden table. "Do you recognize this woman?"

Antwaun forced himself to remain calm. He hadn't yet requested legal representation, but he would if needed. For now, he schooled his reactions. He didn't want to antagonize his superior, and calling in his union rep or a lawyer would do that. So would being a smart-ass. He'd had that lesson pounded into him in the military more times than he could count.

"It's a hand, Lieutenant. A very decomposed one at that," he said quietly. "I can't say with any certainty that I know who it belonged to, not without forensic reports." He paused, leaned back in his chair. Knew his brothers were watching from the other side of the two-way glass. If ever he'd wanted to impress them by being cool and professional, it was now.

But sweat rolled down his back, soaking his shirt and making it stick to the cheap vinyl chair. A droplet tickled his scalp, slowly making its way down his crown. The next thing he knew it would be trickling down into his eye. He'd wipe it, the cops would see that he was nervous, then they'd pounce like vultures hunting prey. Even aware of the goddamn drill, he still couldn't stop the flow of nervous energy seeping through his veins.

"Who do you think this woman is? And do you have proof?" Antwaun asked.

"We checked fingerprints. Her name is Kendra Yates," Lieutenant Phelps said with no inflection in his voice. "We also know that you and she dated. That the ring on the finger of the woman's hand we found was bought by you."

Antwaun schooled his reaction. They'd done their homework, and very quickly. "So. I haven't seen her in months."

"You were working undercover at the time?"

He nodded. "I thought she might have a connection to Karl Swafford."

"And what had you discovered about him?"

This was all in his report, but again, he wrestled his anger under control. He had to go through the motions. "Since Katrina, Karl Swafford has spent millions of dollars rebuilding the casinos. He was being investigated for possible connections to the mob, embezzlement, money laundering and murder."

"You suspected Miss Yates was involved with him?"

"Yes."

"What made you suspect they had a relationship?"

Antwaun hesitated. Kendra had no idea how he'd first seen her. What he'd thought. "I was doing surveillance on Swafford. I saw her in bed with the man." In fact, he'd watched her perform a very seductive strip show for the bastard. Had seen her give Swafford a blow job that had made Antwaun want her mouth wrapped around him. Then he'd watched Swafford run his fingers over her naked body, throw her down on the bed and bang her with such force that Antwaun had nearly ground his molars down to nubs with envy…and disgust.

When Swafford had crawled off her, he'd noticed the tears in Kendra's eyes. He'd never quite understood them, but that one glimpse of her vulnerability had twisted at heartstrings he hadn't even known he possessed.

But he was all about the job, and like a good cop, he'd cozied up to her to use her.

Then he'd been the recipient of that mouth, and he'd fallen in love.

No, lust. He might have mistaken the two a couple of times, but never again.

"You began seeing Miss Yates, hoping she'd squeal on Swafford?"

He nodded. He'd thought he could seduce her into talking. "But it didn't pan out. Turns out she was just a dancer who hooked up with him one night."

The lieutenant exchanged a querulous look with the female cop, and Antwaun knew he was cooked. Trouble was, he wasn't sure how. What did they have on him? On Kendra?

Sure, maybe he'd been an idiot. Gotten tangled up with a suspect. A woman who had slept with a man he'd been investigating for illegal activities.

And when she'd gone missing, he'd been curious, even suspicious at first. But reporting her missing would have blown his cover. And he'd wanted to put the guy away. Especially if he'd killed Kendra...

"Then what happened?" the lieutenant ordered in a brittle tone.

Antwaun chewed the inside of his cheek, then explained his reasoning. "She admitted that Swafford didn't want to end things with her." A river of tears had fallen afterward that had wrenched his heart. She'd claimed he'd blackmailed her into sex, trapped her into being with him, and that she wanted out. Shaking with rage toward Swafford, and tenderness toward her, Antwaun had drawn her into his arms. He'd have promised her anything to alleviate her pain and stop her cries. "Then she disappeared. I figured she'd left town to escape the bastard."

"You reported her missing?"

Antwaun shifted. "Not exactly. I couldn't let anyone know our connection. I asked around, but didn't find anything."

"You know I want to believe you." The lieutenant tilted his head sideways, his deep-set gray eyes narrowed to slits. "Kendra Yates didn't connect with Swafford by accident."

Antwaun frowned. The ax was about to drop.

"Neither did she meet you by coincidence either."

Anger burned a path down his belly as reality interceded. "She made me for a cop?"

The lieutenant offered a mirthless laugh. "Dammit, Antwaun. She didn't just make you for a cop. She was a reporter working undercover. She came onto *you* for information."

Antwaun gritted his teeth. "The *jolie fille* was a *reporter?*"

"Yes, the pretty lady was a reporter." The lieutenant leaned forward, accusations brimming in his condemning eyes. "And guess what her story was about?"

Antwaun shrugged, but his mind was spinning. Now he understood why the press had pounced so quickly. "Swafford's casinos, I suppose. It was common knowledge that he donated millions of dollars to rebuild them. She probably figured the same as we did, that he was crooked." He moved to the edge of his seat. "Don't you see? He probably found out who she was and killed her."

Lieutenant Phelps grunted. "What do you know about Swafford's operations?"

That he was linked to illegal activities. "I hadn't found anything definitive yet. The man is a master at hiding his actions and his money." He cleared his throat. "Then he disappeared. I figured it was to cover his ass, that he'd eventually resurface again."

"You didn't think that he might be dead?"

"Sure, the thought occurred to me. In fact, I was looking into the angle that one of his minions might have gotten selfish, wanted a bigger piece of the Swafford pie and offed him."

Another possibility needled him. The fact that Swafford and Kendra might have run off together. That still could have happened, then the man discovered who she was and killed her. Swafford could have also faked his death and disappeared so he wouldn't get caught. "Did Kendra have proof of his corruption?"

The lieutenant watched him with hooded eyes. "Not that we know of. But she had a theory."

Antwaun ground his teeth, tiring of the game. "Which was?"

One black eyebrow rose a fraction. "You don't know?"

Antwaun rolled his fingers into fists to rein in the anger churning in his gut. He'd been interrogated in the military behind enemy lines before and had handled it with aplomb. He had to get through this the same way. "No."

The lieutenant's eyes stabbed through him like lasers trying to cut out the truth he thought hidden behind Antwaun's steel mask. "Kendra Yates was not only investigating Swafford, but also dirty cops."

In spite of his control, the air whooshed from his chest in a painful rush. Fuck.

Their rendezvous took on an entirely new light. The seduction. The mind-blowing sex. The pillow talk.

Hell, he had thought he was in control, but he was a fool. She'd been using him all along, hadn't fallen for him at all. Had she believed that he was on Swafford's payroll? That he worked for the mob? That he might have killed Swafford? That he was dirty?

His gaze swung back to his superior as he mentally replayed their conversations. Kendra must have had notes on him. Notes that pertained to her story. Notes on things he'd said that might have been misinterpreted.

Holy hell.

They obviously thought he'd killed her because of something in her notes. Something that made it look as if he were on the take.

ESMERALDA PORTER, aka the Cat Lady, felt the tremble of the earth and the stench of death in the air. The whisper of danger rustled in the air as the winds rattled dry leaves from the weeping willow trees and sent them raining down onto the parched earth. In another place, it would have been a musical sound, but here the eerie, grating threads sounded like the devil's voice, announcing his presence.

She searched the backwoods from her porch. The rumors of the devil in the bayou taunted her—

legends of faceless monsters that roamed the land. Some wore smiles to masquerade their evil souls. Damned into the darkness, kissed by the devil's breath, they licked quietly at the blood on their fingertips as they ate away at the vestiges of man's humanity. Those had clawed their way through the dirt and debris of their own graves to rise again as if the devil had pushed them upward through the ground with spiny fingers. They preyed on the weak, leaving tattered bodies and hearts in their vicious wake like the swamp gators after a nightly feeding, jagged teeth crunching on bone.

Evil cannot be destroyed. Its black unbending heart beats on, old with rage, its tendrils of anger as choking as the twisted hands of lust that consumes man's soul.

But the battle wasn't over. She summoned the magic to help fight off the evil. After all, she was a *traiteur,* a healer, a soldier for good, though not a warrior herself.

Satan must have found a victim. A new soul to possess and carry out his vile will. Another source to spread pain and anger. She smelled his victory, a coppery scent like blood.

Her black cat, Midnight, slithered onto the stone hearth and yowled to the heavens, and her tabby, Persimmon, bellowed in a long-winded refrain of terror.

"Come here, *'tite chatte,*" she murmured, scooping up the little cat in her lap. The wind chimes hanging from the porch of her wood-frame house trembled, though, tinkling and clattering so hard one of the glass angels shattered.

She pulled her black shawl around her shoulders, urging her arthritic body and mental will not to fail her. Though she'd been blind for years now, she saw things through the darkness. Living in a world without sight had honed her other senses, especially her sense of smell.

She knew each feline by its odor, as well as the unique tone of its meow, the texture as she ran a fingertip across its nose. Gorgon, an orange-striped male, climbed on top of the organ and peered out the window as if planting himself as guard against the danger waiting in the bayou.

A danger that marched closer with every passing minute.

She mentally flipped through the recipes from her book of spells, searching for one to fend off the bad coming. Not that she had power, for the magic lay in the cats.

Once upon a time, she had been a nonbeliever. But her life had taken a drastic turn into misery, and she had learned to listen to the spirits.

Her dead husband spoke to her sometimes, crying out his rage at being taken so early. Yet his demise had come from his own wrongdoings. And he had taken more secrets to his grave. Secrets that might have offered comfort and closure to some while tormenting others with the twisted viciousness of his crimes.

His transgressions were plenty. Not only to her but to humanity. And he was burning in eternity for them now.

She'd feared her grandson had fallen to the same demon. And now in death, he lingered, caught between realms. Begging for a chance to redeem his soul and go to heaven.

Titan, a fat gray cat who'd come to her during the latest storm of violence in the bayou, pawed the floor and snarled. Suddenly the earth trembled again, more violently this time, and the scent of graveyard dust filled her nostrils.

The cats slithered from their posts, tails swishing, ears perked, listening as they formed a circle. In unison, they began to scratch at the wooden floor, hissing to the heavens as they united to protect her.

But another woman needed protecting. Lex had told her so. The image of a mangled face and body materialized in her blind mind. The woman was nearby. In danger.

Someone had tried to kill her before. They'd stolen her life already. Her memory. Her face.

And they would try to finish her off if someone didn't save her....

CHAPTER FOUR

CRYSTAL HAD CONTEMPLATED her loss of memory and her past so many times that she thought she was going crazy. Dr. Pace had informed her that since she had suffered a head trauma, the past might be erased permanently. The emotional trauma compounded the problem.

But after sitting with the child tonight, Crystal felt amazingly calmer. A sense of accomplishment washed over her, offering hope that she might return to a normal life someday, a welcome reprieve from the endless hours of dwelling on her own misfortune and the mystery of her missing life. Another memory had also begun to surface—one of her surrounded by small children. Feeding them. Singing to them. Helping them.

Back in her room, she flipped on the television set. It was time she connected with the real world again. And maybe she'd find a posting from someone in search of her…

She listened to the news coverage about the war

in Iraq and the upcoming local Memorial Day celebrations. Then a special report flashed on the screen and caused her to sit upright.

"Earlier today, police discovered the partial body of a local reporter named Kendra Yates. Her severed hand was found in the bayou but so far, the remainder of the woman's body has not been uncovered."

Crystal's heart raced. Kendra Yates... Why did that name seem familiar?

The reporter continued, "Sources tell us that Miss Yates was investigating the New Orleans Police Department on charges of corruption, and that tonight Officer Antwaun Dubois was brought in for questioning. An arrest is imminent in the alleged homicide."

Crystal frowned as the camera panned a dark wooded area where they had obviously found the woman's severed hand, then moved back to the steps of the precinct where a mob had gathered and the police were escorting a man inside. For a second, her heart sputtered as if she recognized him. Several reporters yelled questions and accusations at Antwaun Dubois, then a reporter pushed a mike toward another tall, dark-haired man who resembled him. "Detective Dubois, can you tell us more about the investigation?"

Detective Dubois glared at the reporter. "Antwaun Dubois is innocent. The NOPD is doing everything in their power to expedite this investigation and will bring Miss Yates's killer to justice."

Another reporter cornered a third man, this one even taller and more intimidating. Crystal's pulse jumped in her throat. He seemed familiar as well....

"Special Agent Dubois, were your brother and Miss Yates personally involved?"

"Was he on the take?" another reporter shouted.

"As Detective Dubois said, my brother is innocent," Special Agent Dubois stated. "Now, please move out of the way so we can do our jobs and find the real killer."

Crystal stared at the men as they rushed into the precinct. Something about Antwaun Dubois and the last man, Special Agent Dubois, triggered a memory. And the agent—his voice, she'd heard it before, she knew it, but she couldn't place it....

In fact, she was almost certain that she'd met both Antwaun and the agent.

But how would she know a cop or a federal agent?

DR. REGINALD PACE COULD HARDLY stand the anticipation of knowing that he would unveil Crystal's new face in the morning. He had sketched versions of each step in the rebuilding process on a specially designed medical computer program to craft her transition. She was going to be beautiful.

He wanted to show her off to the world. Let them

know that he was the first in his state to perform such an intricate surgery and that he was a genius in his field.

The only problem was that he couldn't reveal his work yet.

Because he hadn't exactly followed the book on this one.

He wiped at a drop of perspiration trickling from his scalp into his hair. Didn't matter. Crystal was his now. He had made her.

He had stood by her side when others had been repulsed. He'd soothed her in the darkest of hours and held her hand to his chest just to let her know that a breathing, living man cared for her.

Soon he would tell her that he loved her as well.

Then she would return the sentiment, and they would make love and all would be right with the world. When he'd won her completely over as his wife, then she'd sign the papers stating that she'd agreed to the face transplant, and that he was the man who had given her back her life.

Then he would be famous.

He tapped a series of keys that brought up the image of what his Crystal would look like when he finally unveiled her face, and blood surged through his cock. Exhilarated, he unzipped his pants, freed himself and slid his hand around his length. Soon he would give her the present of his seed. Then they could breed more Paces who would lend their genius to the world.

For now, he'd content himself with the image of her face as he gave himself release. But even as he did, he closed his eyes and envisioned himself pouring his come into her mouth.

In the images, he reveled in the blissful smile on her exquisite new face. And he silently thanked the dead woman for her part in it all.

DAMON CURSED. They were officially arresting Antwaun. Arguing that they had no body didn't help. The lieutenant must have evidence he wasn't sharing.

Even with Damon being a federal agent and Jean-Paul a detective with the NOPD, they had to push to see their brother.

Lieutenant Phelps was worried about how a private meeting would look to Internal Affairs. The mayor had called, the chief of police, even the governor of the state, ordering that justice be served for the vicious way in which the young woman had died. A screwup with the brothers, and the Dubois men would be pulled off the case.

And neither Damon nor Jean-Paul trusted their brother's destiny to the fates.

Or the local police, who might have a crooked cop in their midst.

Had Kendra Yates discovered a cop on the take?

Was her work related to her death, or had she been murdered by some kind of deranged sicko like the Swamp Devil?

Who had Antwaun pissed off so badly they'd frame him for murder?

Jean-Paul had phoned Jason Dryer, an attorney, who joined him and Damon in the small room. Dryer grilled Antwaun for the truth, while Damon and Jean-Paul watched silently.

"All right, Antwaun." Damon braced his legs apart, then leaned over with his elbows on them, hands clasped. "Come on, tell us what you've been leaving out."

Antwaun's cobalt eyes turned a smoky-gray as he ran a hand through his overly long hair. Damon zeroed in on the scars on his hand. He tried to remember where his brother had gotten the jagged marks but couldn't place the cause. Not that he knew each incident in his brother's life. Both of them had been in the military, had been to hell and back.

"I've told you everything. If I'd known Kendra was a fucking reporter, I sure as hell wouldn't have gotten involved with her."

Damon hissed. The lieutenant didn't want the FBI involved, but with Swafford's connection to Kendra, they already were. "I'll talk to her boss tomorrow and get a warrant for her files."

"Someone I know is setting me up," Antwaun

growled. "You have to get me released so I can track them down."

The last thing they needed was to have Antwaun on the streets, out of control, exacting his own brand of justice—revenge.

"I'll see what I can do," Dryer said. "But you know it will be morning before I can get a judge and bail hearing set."

Antwaun nodded.

"Do you have any idea who would frame you?" Damon asked.

Antwaun frowned. "I can think of a few names."

"Make a list," Jean-Paul said. "We'll check out the names for you."

"What was your cover with Swafford?" Damon asked.

Antwaun spoke in a low, gravelly tone. "I played the drug trafficking angle to get in with his organization."

"Do you think Swafford discovered her identity and killed her?" Damon asked.

Antwaun shrugged. "It's possible. When they both disappeared last year, I thought she might have run off with him. I went to her apartment and searched for clues as to where she might have gone but came up empty."

"What about her computer?"

"It wasn't there. But hell, I didn't think she had one. I thought she was a dancer."

"She might have left willingly with him at first," Damon said. "He could have found out her identity afterwards and killed her."

Antwaun scrubbed his hand over the dark stubble on his jaw. "Swafford wouldn't have done the deed himself. He has hired minions."

Another reason for the feds to be on the case. "We'll check into Swafford's organization. I'll need everything you have on him."

Antwaun nodded. "And don't forget my buddies on the force."

Damon grimaced. Antwaun didn't make buddies.

If there was corruption in the department, who knew how deep it went, or how far it reached. And Swafford was a slick businessman who said all the right things in public, a smarmy bastard the locals and feds had both been watching for months. A man some citizens protected because he'd helped the economy.

A man who'd disappeared without a trace.

But his money might be dirty, might be part of a money-laundering scheme. Men like Swafford thrived on power and would go to any lengths to protect themselves and their investments.

But if he and his men had killed Kendra Yates, why feed her to the gators?

To destroy evidence?

Another possibility reared its head. What if she was still alive?

They could have cut off her hand just to frame Antwaun.

"You know Swafford's body hasn't been discovered," Antwaun said.

"You're thinking that he isn't dead?"

"Maybe. What if he disappeared or faked his death, either because of Kendra's murder, or because he thought she planned to expose him? He could have cut off her hand to make it look like she was murdered, and to set me up and get me out of the way."

"We'll look into that angle," Damon agreed. "He has accounts set up all over the world. Hidden money, of course."

Antwaun looked grim. "With finances like that, he can disappear and never be found."

And a dirty cop could help him obtain a new identity and cement Antwaun's conviction.

The realization triggered memories of Damon's own past. The depths of deception by the government. The resources available to people to help them disappear and create new lives.

The same resources criminals utilized as well.

Damon's blood pounded in his ears as his adrenaline kicked in. He'd used those resources before himself....

Dammit, he couldn't let his little brother go to jail for a crime he hadn't committed.

No, if anyone deserved to be in prison for murder, it was *him*.

THERE WERE SOME PEOPLE so cold, so ruthless, so calculating that they craved the kill. Savored the pain they inflicted. Tasted the blood of their victims and drank it down like fine wine.

They were born to kill.

He knew their kind. He was one of them.

As he had thought Damon Dubois had been at one time. But Damon had betrayed him.

Just like the others.

The Dubois family—they had to pay.

He had found the perfect way.

The woman, Kendra Yates, had served his purpose well. He studied the dark lock of hair he had kept from her. His trophy, the police would call it.

He rubbed its fine silky texture between his fingers and recalled the way he'd wrapped it around his hands just before he'd pressed the blade of the knife to her pale throat. She hadn't understood that she was a sacrificial lamb for his cause.

A chuckle rumbled from deep in his chest. The file she had on Antwaun would be like a torpedo rocking the bastard's world. He would choose the exact moment that information would be revealed.

Making Antwaun suffer by being arrested for Kendra's murder was the perfect way to torture the man before he exposed him for what he really was.

The son of a murderer.

The brother of one as well.

Yes, he held the knowledge to tear the Dubois family apart once and for all. And he would enjoy every moment of their suffering until they begged for his forgiveness.

Just as Kendra had begged for her life.

The shock on her face when he'd made the first slice had been sweet. She had known her time was up. That she wouldn't die quickly or easily.

That he intended to carve her up in little pieces for his own pleasure.

He slid into the dark haunting shadows of the bayou, inhaling the musky scent of the swamp, the coppery scent of fresh blood from a dead animal, the pungent odor of the devil's breath heating the mossy banks and whispering through the tupelo trees.

The dense overgrown foliage hid his form as he slithered through the cypress trees toward his lair. Blood splattered the floor and walls of the dilapidated cabin, the smell of ripening flesh mingling with the loamy scent of the earth. The sound of Kendra's terrified screams still echoed in his ears, as shrill and chilling as the alligator's attack cry just before he bit into his victim.

He stepped into the cabin, his nose burning from the acrid odors of waste and rotting flesh.

Aah, sweet heaven.

Antwaun and Damon Dubois had both been shocked by the woman's severed hand.

Laughter bubbled in his throat. He couldn't wait to see their reactions when they found the rest of her.

CHAPTER FIVE

CRYSTAL TWISTED THE BEDSHEETS in her fists, the sound of a chilling cry ringing in her ears. Her own scream of terror boomeranged back, having fallen into deaf air, reminding her that she was alone.

Dying. No, alive. Barely. But forced to live in pain.

Because of the car explosion. The fire that licked and ate at her face and body.

She could almost feel the scalpel slicing through her frail skin. Cutting away dead flesh. Peeling away the brittle ashes and papery fabric of her face until her hand touched shattered bone.

She stared into the mirror, praying, hoping the nightmare would end. But horror seized her at the reflection that faced her. *Gory* and *inhuman* were the only two words to describe her. A hideous, faceless monster sentenced to live in the shadows.

A scream tore from her throat as the outer skin of her new forehead begin to peel away. One by one like the layers of an onion, the layers slid down her cheek, cracking and breaking into a thousand black pieces that scattered over the white bedsheet like charred ashes of a fire. The muscle of the right side of her face drooped, causing her lip to sag downward, and the bones in her face shifted, cracked and turned jagged, splinters of bone jutting out as if toothpicks had been jammed into her cheeks. Her right eye settled over the place where her cheekbone lay, while the left one inched upward, the eye milky-white.

Nausea gripped her stomach as her eye sockets curled, and her eyelids fell away. Her eyebrows disappeared into the folds of dead skin on the bed, and she felt her lips swelling, then bursting open. Blood dripped down her chin and trickled into a red river, the scarlet droplets splashing against her scarred breastbone.

No…

Her sob wrenched the air, and she balled her hand into a fist and slammed it into the mirror. Glass shattered and slivers pelted her, yet she hit the glass again and again. Blood cascaded down her wrist and fingers, and she picked up a fragment of jagged glass and held it to her wrist. Slice the main artery and she could end the pain and suffering. Never have to face the monster again.

It was so tempting.

She lifted the shard, jammed the point to the curve of her wrist, but suddenly a scream ripped through the air.

No… Don't die. Please don't die.

She whipped her head around. Was someone there? Calling to her? Someone who wanted her to live? Someone who cared…

Maybe a family, a man, husband, lover, child who wanted her.

And more children…the ones who needed her.

SHE JERKED AWAKE, HER breathing heavy and labored, her body sweating as she twisted and clenched the sheets. Memories of the nightmare and the past few months crashed like a tidal wave through her mind. The agony of the burn marks that had scalded the layers of skin and turned her face into a monster. The baths she'd been forced to endure had helped, but even then, mind-numbing pain had thrummed through her every cell. Endless surgeries and bandages to repair her disfigurement had added to the agony.

And now…

She lifted her hand to the bandages and felt them still covering her face.

"It's all right, Crystal."

Lex. His low voice soothed her in the darkness.

He pressed his scaly hand over hers, then brought their joined hands down to his chest. She felt the strong beating of his heart, and knew he'd heard her cries from his room.

Or had he already slipped in to watch her sleep like a ghost in the night, as he did sometimes?

At first that realization had frightened her. But he'd assured her he'd only come to protect her while she slept. To chase away the demons taunting her.

And she'd felt a small measure of relief that she hadn't been totally alone.

"You're nervous about having your bandages removed tomorrow?" he asked quietly.

She nodded as a tear escaped and shimmied down her cheek to dampen her bandage. "What if…"

"Shh, go back to sleep now." He stroked her hand with his thumb, gentle, comforting. "I will care for you and watch over you no matter how you look."

Blessed words to hear. Yet she didn't want to have to remain in the shadows. Or frighten the children who needed her.

That voice that had called her back from the nightmare echoed in her head. The sense that there was someone out there who loved her, who wanted her to fight for her survival, a reason why her sanity had kept her alive all these months. She wouldn't give up that hope now.

She closed her eyes, and tried to doze back to sleep. Tomorrow her face would be unveiled.

She prayed she would recognize the image in the mirror, that it wouldn't resemble the creature she'd seen in her dreams.

Damon steered the federal-issued sedan down the drive to his parents' house and parked. Both he and Jean-Paul took a long breath, then climbed out. Damon felt as if he were facing the firing squad, and he imagined Jean-Paul felt the same way.

A blustery wind rattled the leaves on the trees, making the spidery Spanish moss shiver, creating snakelike shadows along the ground. Dry grass crunched beneath his feet, the sound like brittle shells breaking in the quiet. The scent of the swamp grew bolder, more pungent, mingling with the hint of impending rain.

He pushed open the front door and paused as the ominous feeling of doom pervading his family home settled over him. It was almost as if someone had died.

As Damon expected, his entire family, except for his niece, was waiting up, all collected in the den, holding hands, comforting one another, praying and telling themselves that the evening had been a nightmare that would soon fade.

Jean-Paul assured them that Antwaun was all right, although his father insisted they be brutally honest and share the details of the charges and the investigation.

Damon relayed the facts that he knew so far. His mother's face paled, and she turned to stare at the family photos on the hearth as if the mere act could draw their family back together.

Stephanie stood beside her, rubbing slow circles on their mother's back to soothe her, while their father paced to the window and looked out into the dark sky. Storm clouds hung heavy and low with the certainty of bad weather. Thunder rumbled and shook the trees outside. More dry leaves scattered across the edges of the swamp. The woods beyond looked murky and ominous, filled with night crawlers and secrets of the bayou. Maybe another swamp devil lurked nearby.

The family drew together for a prayer, then parted, each hugging and promising to call soon.

After everyone left, Damon joined his parents in the kitchen and sipped a cup of coffee, waiting to see if they fell apart, but they insisted he leave and get some rest.

He promised them he'd be there for Antwaun's bail hearing and let himself out.

As he climbed inside the sedan, he automatically reached for his cell phone to call his partner from the bureau, but he'd left it inside the house. Going back he found it on the sofa, but his parents' voices echoed from the kitchen and caught his attention.

"Maybe we should tell them," Daniella screeched.

"Shh, no," his father said. "We promised each other a long time ago that we'd keep things to ourselves, and we have to stick to that vow."

"But, Pierre, what if we failed?" his mother cried.

"What if Antwaun really did hurt that woman? We know his history…"

"Shh, don't say that," his father said quietly. "Our Antwaun is not a killer. We raised him the same as we did the other boys. Jean-Paul and Damon will prove his innocence. We have to trust them, and pray."

"I hope you're right," his mother murmured. "Because if our secret comes out, it will only make Antwaun look guilty."

Damon's chest tightened. As he barged into the kitchen, he wondered what his parents could possibly know about Antwaun that would damn him to his fellow officers….

MORNING SUNLIGHT SHOT THROUGH the dark clouds and streamed through the blinds, sending slivers of light across the hospital room. Crystal blinked, searching the corners for Lex, eyes still sensitive and adjusting to bright lights.

But Lex was gone, the room empty.

She was alone again. She understood his need to stay in the darkness. She'd been hiding for months as well.

Would she be able to show her face after today?

Footsteps sounded in the hallway outside, and the door squeaked open. She braced herself for the doctor, forcing a smile past her stiff lips although she had no idea if he could see it with the bandages covering her face.

"Good morning, Crystal," Dr. Pace said.

She greeted him, but her voice quivered, giving away her nervous energy.

The nurse behind him offered her a warm but sympathetic smile, then took her vitals. "It's always scary when the bandages come off," she said softly. "But don't worry. Dr. Pace is the best."

Dr. Pace assembled supplies on the tray beside her, then motioned for her to lean back. "Just relax, Crystal. This part is painless."

She sucked in a sharp breath as he snipped at the bandages, then began to slowly peel them away. The nurse bustled out the door, leaving her alone with the doctor.

Another layer fell away, and she inhaled sharply. Cool air brushed bare skin, the whisper of hope causing goose bumps to cascade up her arms.

His lab coat glided against her elbow as he bent over her. She opened her eyes and stared into his. The gray orbs probed her face as his fingers gently assessed each area, from her eyelids to her nose and her cheeks to her chin.

Her throat clogged with emotions. "Well?"

"It looks good so far. There aren't any signs that you're rejecting the new skin. Of course, you still need to continue the antirejection meds."

She nodded. "Can I see now?"

He gave her a grave expression, one she remembered too well from the unsuccessful skin grafts.

"What's wrong?"

He released a long sigh. "You're going to look beautiful," he said in a husky voice. "Right now you still have a lot of redness, some slight swelling and bruising. I want you to get the full picture when you finally look in the mirror."

She didn't believe him. Had to touch her face herself, feel the scars, see if the skin was smooth. She lifted a hand to check, but Dr. Pace caught her.

"It would be better if you don't touch your face yet. Any germs could cause an infection."

Tears of fear choked her throat as she knotted her hands in her lap. "What aren't you telling me?"

He folded his arms. "We might need to make a few adjustments. But, like I said, things are progressing." He patted her arm. "Trust me, Crystal. When you see yourself, I want you to love your new face. Just be patient. I'll tell you when the time is right."

Unwanted tears filled her eyes, but she nodded. Compassion underscored his tone as he sat on the edge of the bed, pulled her into his arms and hugged her.

"Shh, don't cry. I promised you that I would make you beautiful again and that's what I'm doing. Just trust me, hold on a little longer."

She nodded against him, although inside she died a little, and the hope she'd felt dissipated. Something was wrong. Something he wasn't telling her.

She needed more surgeries. More skin grafts. More months of healing.

She was still a monster.

As much as she wanted to leave this place, what kind of life could she have if she couldn't stand to look at herself in the mirror?

DR. PACE SMILED TO HIMSELF as he left Crystal's room. Pride mushroomed inside him regarding the beautiful woman he had created.

She was exquisite now. Her bone structure, strong and restored, lifted her cheekbones to a model's perfection. Tissues had repaired and skin almost healed from the face transplant.

Yet he wasn't ready to tell her.

No, she might not be able to accept where the new skin that covered her face had come from.

She looked so much like the dead woman that it sent a chill up his neck.

A seed of guilt gnawed at him for his deception, but he cast it aside. He needed to keep her dependent on him a little longer.

Soon she would realize that she couldn't leave, either. That she needed him in every way. Then she would be his forever.

And none of the lies would matter.

But if she thought she was healed before he could completely win her, she might ask to be dismissed from the hospital.

And it was too soon for her to leave him.

If people recognized her, it would cause problems for him. And danger for her.

CHAPTER SIX

THE NEXT MORNING, DAMON was still stewing over the conversation with his parents while he drove to the courthouse for Antwaun's hearing.

Dammit. It wasn't as if *he* didn't have secrets from them. But he'd kept them to protect them. And some of them he'd been sworn to by the government, by his job, his duty. Others' lives might be endangered if he broke his vows.

This situation, their silence, was different. This had to do with his own damn brother.

Although they claimed they were protecting him. But, if he knew the secret, he might be able to better help Antwaun…. Had something happened to his brother in the military?

A half hour later, he, Jean-Paul, Antwaun's lawyer, Dryer, the D.A. and judge convened for the bond hearing. Antwaun shuffled in, handcuffed and shackled like a common criminal, his expression dark and hooded, his mouth set in a grim line. Damon knew it had been a rough night for his brother and tried to offer him a look of encouragement. But Antwaun's eyes seemed as empty this morning as if he'd already been tried and convicted.

The proceedings moved forward quickly. Antwaun pleaded not guilty. The D.A. muttered rhetoric about the blemishes on Antwaun's career, his ability to easily access phony ID and passports, his connection to the underbelly of crime in the city, then produced photos of Kendra Yates's mauled hand and emphasized the viciousness of the crime, using every punch he could think of in his request that Antwaun be remanded into custody until the grand jury reviewed the evidence. The police had searched Kendra Yates's apartment. The inside had been ransacked before they arrived, and blood had been smeared on the walls. They hadn't found a computer. The only fingerprints they'd discovered were Antwaun's.

Dryer argued the fact that only a hand was found, not a body, that all the evidence was circumstantial, and then cited Antwaun's work and the sacrifices he made daily for the city, his family background, and planting doubt about allowing the press to try the case instead of Antwaun receiving due process.

"The family has deep roots in the community, Your Honor, has donated time and money to rebuilding the city. Antwaun Dubois is not a flight risk. He is not wealthy, nor does he have a current passport. His parents are even willing to put up their home and business to cover the bail."

"Our resources show us that Mr. Dubois may not be wealthy, but that a sizable amount of money has recently been deposited in his account," the D.A. argued. "In fact, a deposit of one million dollars was placed into an offshore account for Mr. Dubois two days after Kendra Yates went missing."

Shock registered on Antwaun's face. He turned to his lawyer, leaned forward and hissed a denial. Dryer held up his hand in warning, then spoke. "Judge, Mr. Dubois has no idea where that money came from and denies receiving it."

But Damon studied the judge, read his body language, sensed that the D.A. had even more evidence that hadn't been shared with Antwaun's attorney. Evidence that threw a red flag up to the judge and went against Antwaun's favor.

Having picked up on the same vibe, Jean-Paul shot Damon an anxious glance.

Judge Mattehorn rolled his shoulders and pinned Antwaun in his seat with his gaze. "Due to the circumstances of the case, evidence before me, the recent change in Mr. Dubois's financial status, and the viciousness of the crime, along with the D.A.'s words, I'm denying bail. Antwaun Dubois, you will remain in custody until such time that the grand jury has reviewed and ruled whether or not to move forward with a trial."

Dryer cleared his throat. "Your Honor, we are seriously worried about Mr. Dubois's safety—"

Judge Mattehorn cut him off. "I will order administrative segregation until the next court appearance."

Judge Mattehorn pounded his gavel then stood, dismissing the proceedings and leaving Antwaun in shock. Even with administrative segregation, he faced the gruesome reality of spending more nights in jail, quartered near some of the very perps he had arrested.

The anger of injustice rolled through Damon. The judge's ruling only cemented in his mind the fact that Kendra Yates might have been right about a dirty cop on the force. Someone who could have accessed Antwaun's accounts and planted money to make it appear as if he'd accepted a bribe.

Or maybe someone who also had a judge in his pocket....

ALL NIGHT, CRYSTAL HAD struggled with nightmares about her face. She spent the morning with Maria, reading to her until her nana arrived.

Finally, she crawled back into bed and fell asleep, but images of another life taunted her. A beautiful family. A mother who loved her and was worried sick about her. A man who'd cared for her. No, she'd been wrong. He was bad. He didn't love her. She was surrounded by small children, yet they were starving. They needed her.

She jerked awake, bathed in sweat. Dark storm clouds obliterated the sunlight outside and cast a threatening, dreary gray hue on the room that mirrored her mood.

"Crystal, you had a bad dream again."

Lex. His husky voice reverberated through the shadows.

"Yes," she whispered, reaching for his hand. The scaly skin should have made her withdraw, but she barely noticed. Oddly though, his hand felt colder. Almost icy to the touch. And he didn't seem to react to her face at all. Maybe she wasn't so hideous...

"I dreamt I had a child somewhere." Her voice caught. "A baby crying for me."

He squeezed her hand, brushed her hair from her cheek. "You will find your way, my sweetness."

Tears clogged her throat. "But I've been gone for months. What if I have a child and he or she has forgotten me?" Panic seized her chest and turned her voice into a whimper.

"You will find your answers," Lex said calmly.

"Dr. Pace says I need to heal more. I hear what he's not telling me—I need more surgery. This latest treatment didn't work."

"Do not believe everything he tells you." Lex's

brittle tone sent goose bumps down her spine. Footsteps sounded outside the door, then suddenly a cold wind blew through the room, rattling the windowpanes. "He has his own agenda."

"What do you mean?" He had been everything to her these last few months: doctor, friend, savior.

"Don't trust anyone, Crystal. Even Dr. Pace."

Crystal shivered and turned to face Lex, but he was gone, and, once again, the room was empty.

THE REST OF THE AFTERNOON was a virtual nightmare. Damon and Jean-Paul met briefly with Antwaun and Dryer, but Antwaun was so volatile that they spent their short time together attempting to calm him. Jean-Paul gave him a good dressing-down about behaving inside, keeping a low profile and putting his ear to the wall. Sometimes, insiders talked, and Antwaun might possibly learn something helpful from one of the inmates.

Such as who had set him up. Which cops the prisoners liked to work with.

Antwaun finally agreed, and adopted his game face. The Chameleon—if there was one thing he knew how to do, it was to play a part. Lie.

Surely he wasn't lying to them about his innocence.

Jean-Paul went to the station to look into the offshore account and see if he could find out who had planted the bribe money, while Damon drove to his parents' to give them the bad news.

His heart wrenched at the pain on their faces. Even as he assured them he and Jean-Paul would clear Antwaun, the anguish of his family made him feel raw inside. Antwaun was innocent.

But *he* was not. If they knew what he had done, about the E-team and the missions they'd pulled off, about the woman who'd gotten caught in the middle and lost her life, it would kill them.

So many secrets… Tell and you die.

He wasn't worried about dying himself, but he knew repercussions would spread to his family. Not just the pain of the truth about his last mission—their lives would also be endangered.

When he left, he drove straight to Kendra Yates's apartment to meet Jean-Paul's partner, Detective Carson Graves. Kendra lived in a modest older unit on the fringes of Bourbon Street. The place had already been thoroughly searched and, as the police had reported, they found no computer or files. Damn. He wanted her research on the dirty cops. The furniture was a hodgepodge of antiques and crafty items that she had obviously picked up in the market. A few photos adorned the built-in bookshelf; one of her receiving some kind of journalism award drew Damon's eye. He stared at the face in the photo, trying to reconcile the beautiful brunette with a heart-shaped face and deep-set eyes with the mutilated hand they had found, and his stomach revolted.

"I can see why Antwaun was enthralled," Jean-Paul commented.

Damon nodded. He took a newspaper photo from the desk to have a reference when he asked around. Carson searched her bedroom, and Jean-Paul the den, finding a book planner the police and the people who'd ransacked the place had missed.

"There are a couple of names of contacts in here that I want to check out," Jean-Paul said. "They may be informants, may have talked to her before she disappeared."

"The police confiscated a toothbrush and hairbrush for DNA," Damon said. "Jean-Paul, can you access the results of the trace evidence the police found?"

Jean-Paul agreed and Damon thumbed through past issues of the papers stacked in the corner, searching for Kendra's byline, hoping to find another story she'd written that might have landed her in trouble. But nothing jumped out at him. "I'm going to the newspaper office and pushing the publisher to tell us what he knows."

They agreed to check in and left Carson to finish searching her apartment.

At the newspaper office where Kendra Yates had worked, Damon asked to speak with the head of the paper. Warren Allan, a middle-aged man with a bad comb-over, yellowed teeth from smoking and a jacket two sizes too small, gestured toward an orange vinyl chair. His desk overflowed with newspapers, clippings of various articles, bulging file folders, coffee cups, chewing-gum wrappers and an ashtray that looked as if it hadn't been emptied in days.

"I've been expecting you, Special Agent Dubois." A small smile stretched his thick lips into a rubbery line. "In fact, I expected an entire fort of you by now."

Damon narrowed his eyes to slits. "Then I'll cut to the chase, Mr. Allan. My brother is innocent. Someone is setting him up and I'm going to find out who it is."

Allan's chair squeaked as he leaned back and steepled his hands. "Are you sure about that? Maybe you don't know your brother as well as you thought."

"And you don't know him at all." Damon gritted his teeth. "Tell me what Kendra Yates had on Karl Swafford, and any tips she had on the possibility of corruption in the NOPD."

"You really think I'm going to divulge that information?" His cheeks swelled with his chuckle. "I'm sitting on the hottest story to hit New Orleans since the Swamp Devil murders last Mardi Gras. And the murdered victim happened to be one of my own reporters." He leaned forward, a menacing glint to his eyes. "I want the bastard who killed her to pay."

"So do I," Damon stated matter-of-factly. "And I can assure you that your cooperation will help us find the person responsible for her death."

A long, tension-filled pause stretched between the two men.

"Just give me something," Damon finally conceded. "Some hint as to where she was on the investigation. And I'll be certain that you get the exclusive on anything I find out, when the time is right, of course."

Allan hesitated, then nodded. He didn't believe that Kendra had run off with Swafford and thought the man had faked his own death and might have killed her. "She traced him to a plastic surgeon who works for the government."

Damon's blood heated. "His name?"

"Dr. Reginald Pace."

Damon gripped the edge of the chair with white knuckles. Reginald Pace…had assisted the E-team in secretive projects. He'd been known to alter appearances for the witness protection program. And he would also do the same for any criminal for the right price.

Unfortunately, extracting information from him was going to be nearly impossible.

LEX VAN WORMER RUBBED A HAND across his scaly skin, watching the dry particles float to the floor like dust. His skin grew drier, flakier every day as if death was slowly rusting away his flesh, tearing it from his brittle bones with jagged fingers. His body felt cold, too, chilled to the bone, as if ice had settled into his veins, or perhaps his blood had ceased to flow and had turned to stone. Sometimes darkness robbed him of precious seconds, minutes, hours, and the time he was able to drag himself from the depths grew shorter and less frequent as each day passed.

Only the thought of seeing Crystal spurred him to fight his way through the muck of quicksand trying to consume him.

He had waited all his life to find a woman like her. A woman to love. A woman who needed him. A woman to guide him into redemption.

For the devil had owned his soul most of his life.

Like an off-key song you couldn't get out of your mind, his father's vile descriptions of the devil's wrath burned in his head. He would pay for his transgressions. Burn for his sins. Spend eternity being punished.

Despair made his chest ache, and he dropped to his knees beside the bed, lowered his head against the mattress and prayed to the heavens to help him last another day. To help him find his way into the light. To allow him to atone for his sins by watching over Crystal.

For she was in grave danger.

Dr. Pace pretended to care, but Lex knew his lies. Lex had seen the man's other side. He, too, had been possessed by the devil.

CHAPTER SEVEN

IT TOOK DAMON ANOTHER week to get in touch with Dr. Pace, a week of anxious hell for Antwaun and the family.

"Dr. Pace, thank you for agreeing to see me on such short notice." Damon settled into the leather wing chair across the plastic surgeon's desk. Although Pace consulted and sometimes took on patients not associated with government projects, many were of a confidential nature. He also worked with universities on the latest research techniques involving plastic surgery and had assisted in cutting-edge work with facial reconstruction on severely injured patients, including infants with birth defects.

"Yes, well, we do have a history, Special Agent Dubois." Pace stared at him over his reading glasses. "So, to what do I owe this visit? Your team have another problem you want me to take care of?"

Damon swallowed at the reminder of his secret military missions. The E-team, the Erasers, had been a special-ops elite squad, carefully chosen for their individual skills. Damon, a tactical leader as well as an explosives expert; Max Levine, helicopter pilot and computer genius; Calvin Norris, sniper and search-and-rescue leader; and Lex Van Wormer, security specialist.

If there was any problem the government wanted taken care of, sanctioned or not, the E-team was called in to erase it. No one was to know of their existence. Even Pace didn't know the details of their work. And no member would ever tell.

Tell and you die.

"I'm with the bureau now," Damon responded.

Pace nodded, a small grin splitting his face. "Yes, that's right. FBI."

Damon almost laughed. Pace didn't believe him. The team was tight-knit and was virtually impossible to escape. But when he'd left, the three guys on the original E-team had formed a private business after they'd left the military, conducting government missions as well as taking on private cases. Max had said some of the new members were even needlessly violent, and had asked about his defection

Damon had opted out and left, although the others hadn't liked it one damn bit.

"I need to know any information you may have on a man named Karl Swafford." Damon watched Pace for signs of recognition. But not so much as a blink of an eye or a twitch. Of course, the man was

trained in scrutinizing body gestures and hiding them
as well.

"I've heard of him, as most of the people in New
Orleans have."

Damon grunted. "I have reason to believe that he
faked his death and disappeared. And that you
helped him."

Pace's eyebrow arched upward. "And where did
you get this information?"

"Let's just say that the death of a certain reporter
brought it to light."

"You mean Kendra Yates, the woman your brother
is accused of murdering."

"Antwaun is innocent," Damon said. "And I need
your help, Reginald. If Swafford is alive, he may
have killed Miss Yates. I also think he has someone
on the inside who helped frame my brother for her
death."

"Interesting theory. I wish I could help you, but I
can't."

"Did Kendra Yates question you about Swafford?"

"No. And I did not perform plastic surgery on him
either."

Damon silently cursed, then withdrew the photo
of Kendra and placed it on the desk. "Look at this
carefully, Reginald. Are you sure this woman didn't
approach you? She might have worn a disguise."

Dr. Pace made a token show of examining the photo, then exhaled and leaned back nonchalantly. "No, I've never seen her before in my life."

Damon understood the reason for Dr. Pace's secrecy. His silence protected not only himself, but the members of the E-team, government VIPs, witnesses in the WITSEC program and current patients. Hell, his secrecy had kept Damon alive.

But the tiny tremor in the doctor's eyelid gave him away this time. He had seen Kendra Yates, but he didn't want to admit to it.

Possibilities floated through Damon's head. What if Kendra had threatened to write about Dr. Pace in the paper?

Perhaps he'd panicked and killed her. Or he might have reported her snooping to the military or another fed who'd decided she needed to be diposed of.

His gut tightened. What if the insider who'd killed her and set up Antwaun wasn't with the local police department but was one of his coworkers at the agency?

CRYSTAL FELT AS IF she were crawling out of her skin. She had to get out of the room.

The sidewalk was dimly lit, the woods creating shadowy nooks that offered privacy. Surely the garden would be empty, and she wouldn't have to worry about being seen or the pitying gossip.

She dressed in a cotton warm-up suit and slippers, then padded down the hall and out the door. Unable to stop herself, she glanced in the window, searching for her reflection, but the frosted glass only allowed for small patches of her features to come through. The swelling had gone down. She couldn't tell much, but she thought she looked almost normal.

And why hadn't Dr. Pace allowed her to see herself? Was the image distorted?

A slight breeze ruffled the leaves of the tupelo trees and colorful pansies danced in the flower boxes flanking the brick walkway that wove through the garden. This slice of heaven was her reprieve. She hugged her arms around her waist as she examined each section of flowers, sniffed the delicate petals of the lilies, inhaled the scent of magnolias and honeysuckle, and finally stopped to admire the roses. Thankfully all her senses were freed for such enjoyments, unlike after the accident when the only thing she could smell was the strong odor of antiseptic and charred flesh.

Suddenly a shiver rippled through her, and she glanced toward the dark woods beyond, knowing dangers lurked there, hidden and waiting to pounce. Gators floated just beneath the murky Mississippi, their yellowed eyes piercing the darkness, teeth gnashing and sharpening as they waited to strike. Snakes slithered through the mossy banks and water, curling in the trees, silent vipers that could kill a person with a single bite. And the legends of other monsters, half human, half beast—like the Swamp Devil who'd combed the murk—haunted her with what-ifs.

What if she left here and one of those monsters came after her?

Sometimes she ached to leave, while other times she feared she wouldn't be safe if she did. In her nightmares, her accident hadn't been an accident at all. Someone had tried to kill her, had caused her disfigurement intentionally when they'd tried to take her life.

She spun around, feeling a bit agoraphobic, anxious to retreat inside to the safety of her hospital room, when she spotted a man exiting the back sliding glass doors of the solarium. He looked huge in the shadows of the door frame, stood well over six feet with muscled broad shoulders, thick dark hair clipped neatly on his high forehead, and he wore a dark suit and tie. He glanced around the property, his stance rigid and determined, then he seemed to zero in on her. Suddenly he moved toward her, his body controlled, yet he reminded her of a black panther stalking his prey.

She froze, frantically searching for some place to run, to hide, but he saw her and was coming closer, and there was no way to elude him. Again, that tingling of recognition rippled through her, as if they'd met.

He had an odd expression on his face, as if he knew her, too.

DAMON STARED AT THE WOMAN walking alone in the garden, the blood pumping through his veins. She resembled the woman in the photo he'd just shown Pace.

A faint streak of moonlight illuminated her through the weeping willows, making her look like a *petite fleur* in the night. Except this *fleur* had her arms wrapped around herself in a defensive gesture that reeked of pain and fear.

The moment she saw him, she stiffened and began to tremble.

Wavy brown hair fell across her shoulders, slight hints of red and gold shimmering in the moonlight as if it had been finger-painted in. She was small, probably around five-four, slender but with just enough curves to make a man groan. She backed away, butting into the brick wall as he approached. Dressed in a pale blue summer jogging suit, she shouldn't have looked sexy, but his libido woke up and screamed. Touching her would be pure heaven to his tortured soul.

He hesitated, had to regroup. He was here on business, to save his brother, not react like a teenager in lust toward a *jolie fille*.

Her fragile stance alerted him to the fact that she was quite afraid of him. "I'm not going to hurt you," he said in a deep, throaty voice. "I'd just like to talk."

Her breathing quivered, rattling in the tension-laden quiet. In the distance, cicadas sang and frogs croaked, other night sounds of the bayou whistling in the wind.

"You're the agent from the news report?"

He nodded and removed his badge and ID to show her. So she'd seen the report about Antwaun's arrest and hadn't come forward. "Special Agent Damon Dubois."

"The brother of the man who was arrested?"

He flinched, and her eyes widened. Then she finally lifted her face, and his heart thumped wildly, adrenaline racing through his blood. *Bon Dieu!*

She was Kendra Yates—the woman he was inquiring about. The one whose mutilated hand he had seen with his own eyes. The fingerprint must have been wrong—or had the cops faked them?

Could it be possible that she was Kendra Yates? And if so, why was she hiding out here while his brother took the fall for her murder?

CRYSTAL CLUTCHED the brick wall, a mixture of fear and excitement racing through her. Her first response was wariness that this man might find her hideous in appearance. Now that she could see his face, she realized just how masculine and sexy he was. God, she'd been shut away so long that she'd forgotten what sexy looked like.

It looked like this man. Dark-haired, tall with broad shoulders, a square jaw, eyes brown as dark chocolate, and prominent cheekbones that sculpted a strong face. An intensity radiated off him that screamed of raw, primal male. He was not only a cop, but the hard commanding air in his expression made her think he'd been military as well.

Dr. Pace had told her he'd alerted the police and FBI to find her identity—was that the reason this federal agent was here now?

Nerves triggered butterflies to dance in her stomach. He didn't look as if he wanted to help her. Rather, anger radiated from his stark features.

What if he knew her identity, and she was some kind of criminal? She'd had nightmares about her past that seemed so real she sensed that something bad had happened, that she had been running from someone when she'd had the accident…

"If you saw the report about my brother's arrest, then why haven't you come forward?" Special Agent Dubois said.

She frowned. "I…don't understand. Why would I?"

His eyes narrowed. "Don't lie to me. You're Kendra Yates, the woman Antwaun is accused of murdering. You seduced my brother, and now you're hiding out here while he's sitting in a jail cell."

Fear tightened her throat. "I don't know what you're talking about. Kendra Yates... She's the woman that was killed. I saw the report."

"What happened, Kendra?" he asked harshly. "Did you get too close to Swafford, and he threatened you, so you decided to disappear? Or was it the dirty cop you were on to? Did he scare you enough to make you seek out Pace for a new identity?"

She shook her head. "I really don't know what you're talking about. Tell me why you think I'm this reporter."

He jerked a newspaper clipping from his pocket, unfolded it and shoved it toward her.

She glanced down at the picture, studying the face of the woman. It was the same woman they'd shown on the news report. She had seemed familiar....

Could she really be this woman Kendra? And if so, what had happened to her?

He gripped her arms, and she stiffened, suddenly terrified by the fury in his eyes. "Tell me the truth, Kendra. You may be a pretty woman and you fooled my brother, but I know you had your own agenda."

"I...am telling you the truth," she said, trying to jerk away. "I don't remember what happened to me. I had an accident months ago, wound up here. I was severely burned, had several surgeries..."

A perplexed look tightened Agent Dubois's features. "You had an accident?"

"Yes. My car exploded and caught fire." Her hand automatically went to her face, felt the sensitive new skin, and she angled her head downward. "That's why I…had plastic surgery. Why I'm scarred."

His grip on her arms loosened. His breath rattled out as if he was weighing her statement, trying to decide whether or not to believe her.

"You have amnesia?" he asked.

She nodded, rubbing at her arms where he'd clenched them. An odd expression—regret maybe—inched onto his face. "Dr. Pace performed your surgery?"

"Yes. He says I need more, but I'm better now."

His frown deepened, calling attention to the dark shadows beneath his eyes. He looked troubled, upset, as if he hadn't slept in days. "Let's talk to Dr. Pace together."

She hesitated, didn't know whether to trust him or not. The article said that Kendra Yates had been investigating dirty cops. What if this man or his brother was corrupt? What if Antwaun Dubois had been the man in her nightmare, the one who'd tried to hurt her?

DAMON SCRUTINIZED the *petite fleur*'s facial expressions and body language for any clue that she was lying. Any clue that she indeed knew her real name and had framed his brother for murder.

But if she'd been seasoned to go into WITSEC or to change identities for another reason, whoever had trained her had done so well.

She really did appear to be suffering from amnesia, to be completely stunned and shocked at his statements. That didn't mean that she hadn't faked her death, though, and wasn't here to disappear beneath a transformed appearance. Maybe because she was terrified of Swafford's men or the cop or federal agent she had discovered was crooked.

And if this woman was Kendra Yates, whose hand had they found in the bayou?

Another possibility teased his mind—what if she wasn't really Kendra Yates, but someone who resembled her? Maybe a relative, a sister? Or someone who'd had plastic surgery to look like her?

But why would a person want to have plastic surgery to look like Kendra?

She pulled back from him. "Dr. Pace said he sent my DNA away to be analyzed and have the authorities look for a match." Her voice quivered with nerves. "Is that how you found me?"

"No." But he'd check and see if Pace really had sent her DNA to the cops. If so, why wouldn't the results have come up when Kendra Yates had been reported missing?

Unless Pace had never reported her appearance at the hospital...

But why wouldn't he?

CRYSTAL FELT COMPLETELY spooked by the agent's scrutiny. He thought she was lying about the amnesia. She wished to goodness she *did* know her identity, wished she *could* remember what had happened to her before the accident. Her head ached from struggling to make sense of what he'd told her.

The mention of the articles teased her memory, but a curtain fell and the black abyss in her mind swirled deeper and darker, an empty hole of nothing. Thunder grumbled behind her, shaking the trees, and a streak of lightning zigzagged across the gray sky. The storm brewing outside mirrored the one rumbling in her mind.

"All right, let's go." She moved past Damon, aware of his hulking size towering over her, of his deadly gaze on her back, of the slight brush of his hand on her waist as he opened the door for her.

Hope and dread knotted her stomach. She'd wanted answers for months.

Yet she was terrified of what she might find.

CHAPTER EIGHT

DR. PACE'S COMPLEXION paled when Crystal walked into his office alongside Agent Dubois.

"Reginald?" Agent Dubois said tersely.

Crystal's head jerked sideways as she realized that the men knew each other personally.

"Special Agent Dubois, I thought you'd left."

"I was on my way out when I noticed one of your patients." He gestured toward her. "She strikes an amazing resemblance to Kendra Yates."

Dr. Pace twisted his mouth into a grimace. "Is that so?"

Agent Dubois grunted. "Don't tell me that you didn't see it when I showed you her photo. Why did you lie to me?"

Dr. Pace shrugged, but Crystal saw him take a step back, one hand clutching the desk as if he needed to steady himself. "Actually, they look more alike now, I suppose, than they did before the surgery, so I didn't really see the point."

"Maybe you should explain yourself," Agent

Dubois said, his voice hardening to a menacing tone. "Though I understand the confidential nature of your work, you know that you can trust me. I need the truth."

"The truth is that she was a Jane Doe burn victim, the result of a nasty explosion and fire. You know I'm bound by doctor-patient confidentiality."

Crystal thought she detected a slight flicker of emotion in the agent's face at the mention of the accident, but he quickly recovered.

"Please, Dr. Pace," Crystal pleaded. "I want to find out who I am."

He gave her an odd look, caring, concerned, but also worried. "All right. But I won't divulge anything you don't want me to about your medical condition."

"If it helps uncover my identity, it's all right. Maybe Agent Dubois can help."

"Very well then." His mouth formed a flat line. "Crystal…Jane Doe was transported here from the local hospital a year ago."

"Really?"

"Yes," Pace continued. "Her condition was critical. She sustained massive injuries to her chest and abdomen, and her face was essentially…destroyed."

Detective Dubois folded his arms. "I want to see documentation of the date she was admitted. Pictures of before and after."

Dr. Pace glanced at Crystal for approval.

Crystal felt exposed and vulnerable. "It's true…my face was ruined. Dr. Pace saved my life and performed several surgeries over the past few months."

"And you have reports to prove when she arrived and the details of her condition?" Agent Dubois asked.

"Of course."

Suspicion flared in the agent's eyes. "You can fake those if needed."

"You don't trust me, Dubois?" Dr. Pace asked with a raised brow.

"My brother has been arrested for murdering Kendra Yates," Agent Dubois snapped. "If this woman is Kendra, if she's alive, I can clear him."

Crystal sucked in a much-needed breath. "I need answers, Dr. Pace. Show him the photos." Crystal swallowed back emotions as Dr. Pace removed a form detailing her admission, another one with various notations about her condition, photos of her face and body following the accident, then some of her bandaged after a series of surgeries. She barely looked human.

"Am I Kendra Yates?" she asked the doctor.

"I honestly don't know your real name. I told you that I never received anything back from the police so I assumed they didn't find you in the system."

"And you did file a report with the police when she was admitted?" Agent Dubois asked.

Dr. Pace nodded.

"When was that?"

Dr. Pace consulted the file. "June 1."

"Why was she brought here, instead of a regular hospital?"

"She was taken to the hospital but we transferred her here because she needed long-term care, and because of my expertise."

Agent Dubois unpocketed his cell phone, clicked a few numbers, identified himself, then asked the party on the line to verify the information the plastic surgeon had just given him. A minute later, he ended the call, then snapped the phone shut. "There is no record that you ever contacted the police regarding this woman."

Dr. Pace looked appalled. "Then someone on your side made a mistake." He gestured toward the file. "My records prove I did."

"And you didn't falsify those files?"

"What possible reason would I have to do so?" Dr. Pace glared at the agent.

Crystal cringed. She'd never seen the doctor so angry. And what reason would he have? He'd been nothing but kind to her, patient, comforting. `

"I don't know," Agent Dubois said. "But I know you're lying now." He waved a hand toward Crystal. "She said you told her she needed more surgery."

A hint of guilt flickered in the doctor's eyes.

She pressed a hand to her cheek. Felt for any imperfection, a drooping cheek or eye, grooves of scar tissue, but her face felt smooth. Normal for the first time in ages.

"Let me see for myself," she said.

Dr. Pace's nostrils flared. "I only meant that we'd have to wait for some of the redness to fade. Make sure the skin wasn't rejected."

She nodded, but trembled as he removed a hand mirror from his credenza. His pleading look as he handed it to her confused her even more. "I was only trying to take care of you, Crystal. Everything I've done, I've done to help you. To protect you."

The doctor sounded so sincere, yet fear laced his voice as if he'd gotten caught doing something wrong. She didn't understand him, or why she suddenly felt drawn to the agent, as if *he* were the one protecting her. Something about him just seemed so familiar. His voice, it was husky, low, dangerous, but sexy. She'd heard it somewhere before.

But if she was Kendra, she'd known his brother, not him....

She lifted the mirror slowly; her breath locked in her chest as she studied the face in the reflection. Slim, oval, a small nose, high cheekbones, dark eyebrows arched above pale green eyes. Other than a slight swelling around her eyes and some redness along her chin and her temples, the face was healed.

Not only healed, but attractive.

Relief brought a wave of tears to her eyes. She was no longer a monster.

Then why hadn't Dr. Pace wanted her to see herself? He'd performed miracles.

A chill suddenly coursed through her as questions bombarded her. Questions about herself, about the doctor. If he'd lied to her and told her she needed more surgery, maybe he had lied about filing the report to the police. But why would he do such a thing? Did he know her identity and have some reason to keep it from her?

Another shiver rippled through her, and she had the uncanny realization that this face wasn't hers.

It belonged to that stranger, to Kendra Yates.

DAMON HADN'T QUITE EXPECTED Reginald Pace to cooperate fully, but he hadn't been prepared for the number of questions interrogating him raised. Crystal—Kendra?—appeared genuinely confused as well.

At least if those photos of her were actually of her. The woman in the pictures had been scarred severely, was unrecognizable. She must have suffered terribly. Been in pain for months. The injuries she'd sustained during her accident along with heavy medication she must have been under could have caused her amnesia.

The mention of fire caused a wave of nausea to

flow through him. Memories of that last mission, of the explosion, the fire scorching his skin as he'd run through the flames to try and save the woman. Her screams as the heat and flames consumed her...

Crystal dropped into the chair, a long sigh escaping her, dragging him back to the moment.

Pace was an expert in manipulating evidence, so Damon didn't take anything at face value. If Kendra Yates had come here investigating Pace, and he or someone Pace knew had killed her, why perform plastic surgery to make another patient look like her? Kendra's killer wouldn't want to draw attention to the fact that she had been here, or that she might be alive. And if Kendra Yates had come to fake her death and disappear with a new identity, why hadn't she?

Unless she had been so severely injured she'd needed time to heal first...

None of it made sense.

"Crystal," he said, using the name she'd referred to herself as. "We confiscated a brush and toothbrush from Kendra's apartment. I'd like to take your DNA, fingerprints to compare, see if we can determine your real identity." He watched her carefully for any sign that she intended to run. But she seemed vulnerable, even frightened. She *wanted* help....

Obviously, if she didn't remember and had been in trouble or running from something or *someone,*

then maybe she feared the cops, or was afraid someone was still after her. And she was probably right.
If Swafford or the real corrupt cop knew she was on
to him, he'd want her dead.

"All right," she said, although her voice
trembled. "In fact, I think I'd like to go with you
when you leave."

Damon glanced at Pace. "Is she strong enough to
be dismissed?"

The plastic surgeon shifted, and Damon noted the
subtle play of fear and anxiety on his face. He'd
known Reginald Pace for five years and had never
seen him react emotionally.

An underlying air of panic radiated from him that
suggested something else was going on here. Something more sinister.

"No. Absolutely not."

"Please, Dr. Pace," Crystal said. "You've given me
a new face now, helped me heal. I feel healthier. I
need to do this, to find out who I am. I think I do have
a connection to this woman Kendra."

"But, Crystal." He gripped her wrist so tightly
that Crystal winced. "I'm not sure you're strong
enough. You need rest, need to be careful. Too much
sun exposure, too much stress might cause adverse
reactions."

"I'll check back in, continue the antirejection
medications."

A vein throbbed in his forehead. "No, I won't release you. Not yet."

"You lied to me," Crystal said. "You made me think I was still scarred and ugly. Why would you do that?"

"You need me," he said in a harsh, almost desperate tone. "You've made it this far only because of me. You can't leave me now."

Damon squared his shoulders. Pace's behavior was odd, almost possessive. Was he in love with Crystal?

Or was Pace afraid of what she might find out about him if she left?

"No, I have to do this," she said as if she, too, picked up on Pace's strange behavior and found it threatening. "But I want to say goodbye to Lex before I go."

"Lex?" Pace's brow drew into a scowl.

"Yes, Lex Van Wormer," Crystal said.

Damon tensed. Lex Van Wormer—he had been part of the secret elite squad that Damon had joined in the military. Lex had been injured and had taken a medical discharge. Damon knew he'd been admitted here for treatment, but Damon's neighbor, Lex's *grand-mère* Esmeralda, had said Lex had died.

How did Crystal know him? Had he told her about the E-team?

Pace frowned. "You must be confused, Crystal. Lex was a patient here last year, but he passed away months ago."

Crystal swayed and Damon watched as Dr. Pace knelt to rub her back.

"No," Crystal whispered. "I saw him, I spoke to him, I held his hand just last night." She turned a shocked look toward Pace. "He told me stories about the military. And he played blues tunes on his harmonica at night."

Pace went to his file cabinet, removed a folder, then consulted it. "Lex Van Wormer had an incurable disease caused by exposure to an unknown chemical when he was in the service. He—"

"I know that," Crystal screeched. "He had scales on his arms, dry patches, the skin fell away. He used an antibiotic cream." She brought her fingers to her nose. "I can still smell it, or at least I could in the room."

"Crystal," Pace said as if he were speaking to a child, "Lex Van Wormer died just shortly after you were brought in."

Damon studied the interplay with renewed skepticism.

What in the hell was going on?

Was Pace lying about Van Wormer? Was he really dead? And if so, how could this woman have seen him? Was she mentally unstable?

AN HOUR LATER, Reginald Pace poured himself a stiff Dewars on ice and tossed it down. One more, then he threw the glass against the wall and watched it shatter.

Goddamn it. Why the fuck did Dubois have to be the agent on the case?

Because his brother was framed for the murder…

And they had set up Antwaun.

But Reginald hadn't expected Damon to track Kendra here.

Reginald picked up the phone and frantically punched in numbers. The man who'd brought Kendra Yates to him would be pissed to know Dubois was snooping about.

The phone rang three times, then the man's hoarse voice reverberated over the line. "What the hell are you doing calling me?"

"We have trouble. Damon Dubois just left my office. He met our patient and is asking questions."

A chuckle rumbled from the other end. "So, Dubois figured out that Kendra Yates was on to you. Big deal. We knew he'd get that far."

"You don't understand," Reginald said, his heart beating like a racehorse. "The surgery… It didn't turn out exactly as I'd expected."

"What do you mean?"

"When I removed the bandages, the woman looks remarkably like Miss Yates."

"But *you said* after the surgery she *wouldn't* look like Kendra."

"It's not supposed to work that way, but this woman had such similar bone structure that she is almost a dead ringer for Yates. I planned to perform another surgery to make minor changes and alleviate the problem, but Dubois showed up tonight and recognized her from a press photo."

The man cursed, then sighed audibly. "It doesn't matter. Dubois and his brother are both going to pay in the end. And if the woman is a casualty, so be it."

Normally Reginald would agree. Shit happened. Some patients died, some lived. All in a day's work.

Some even had to be sacrificed for the greater good. For research. And this woman…in the scheme of things, she didn't matter, which was the very reason he had been able to use her to begin with. No one had asked about her, knew she was missing, because she had no ties.

Not anymore.

Of course, if she found out the truth, the things he knew about her, the things he'd kept from her, the leeway he'd given himself in her transformation, she'd hate him.

Worse, he was playing a dangerous game by informing this man of the problem.

His friend had no idea about the real identity of

the woman with the new face or how she had come to Reginald. If he did...

If he did, he'd kill her.

All the more reason that Reginald had to help him eliminate Dubois and his brother.

He hung up, desperate to convince Crystal that she couldn't leave him. Her livelihood, her future depended on him.

But when he looked in her room, he found it empty. Frantic, he combed the entire hospital, searched all the patients' rooms, then the gardens.

But she was gone.

At least she hadn't left with Dubois, because after her Van Wormer comment, the agent thought she was crazy.

YES, THE DUBOIS BROTHERS had to die. But not yet.

First they had to suffer. Sweat. Feel the slow torture of death on its way.

He knew exactly how to hurt them.

Antwaun Dubois's fate would be the big finale. The shock would rock the entire Dubois family and tear them apart forever.

And Damon...sweet Beelzebub. Damon was the ultimate foreplay in his game of revenge. He was going to squirm and agonize over every moment.

He brought the sharp blade of the knife up to the light, examined the dried blood still clinging to the edges, and grinned. Then he closed his eyes, remembering how delicious it had been to mutilate the woman's body.

Touching the blade to her flesh had given him a hard-on. At first he'd watched her eyes bulge and widen in horror as he'd dug the tip just deep enough into her pale throat to cause pain. Withdrawing it, he'd nearly orgasmed as he'd softly tapped a path along her naked body from her chin to her sex, where he'd planned to gut her.

She'd whimpered and begged, pleaded and offered to do anything he wanted.

He'd smiled as he'd driven the knife deep inside and experienced the bliss of satisfaction that only spilled lifeblood could offer.

A laugh errupted from deep within him, rumbling through the blood-soaked cabin and out into the bayou. Outside a water moccasin slithered through the murky surface of the water and the gators waited for their next meal. An offering he would likely give them.

But not tonight. He'd have to find another to feed them.

He needed this one to torture the enemy.

He grabbed his camera and photographed every inch of the woman's tattered body. Spread her on the floor as the first mutilator had done, careful to tie her legs apart and take the angle shots that would showcase his carvings. The intricate web of cuts on her throat, her breasts, her belly. The completeness of his act when he'd forced the knife up inside her.

He wondered how long it would take for the Dubois men to put the pieces of her back together. And to connect the gruesome scene with the first mutilator.

Only then would they truly understand that they were responsible for her death. That they had brought all this pain upon themselves.

And if they didn't stop him, there would be others.

CHAPTER NINE

CRYSTAL'S HEAD REELED with confusion as she settled into the car beside Special Agent Dubois. His face registered surprise to see her in the seat.

"What are you doing?"

"You said you'd help me find out who I am."

"That's true. But are you sure you want to leave?"

"Yes." Dr. Pace had frightened her. And she needed answers. She'd been hiding long enough.

If she was Kendra Yates, she'd apparently been working on stories that might have put her in danger. She'd be safer with an FBI agent than on her own, wouldn't she?

He started the engine and drove the sedan down the long winding drive through the secluded woods. Her stomach clenched as the building disappeared from sight. It had been her home for months. Had offered her safety and security.

But tonight she'd felt it had become a prison.

Lex. She shivered and wrapped her arms around herself, then glanced at the agent through the darkness. He'd followed her into her room where she'd hoped Lex would be waiting, but the room had been empty. Dr. Pace had tried to explain that the medication and anesthesia could have confused her. But she'd seen the concern in his eyes. She'd torn down the hall, searching each room on her floor but they had all been empty as well. There hadn't been a harmonica either...

Agent Dubois had said nothing. He'd simply stared at her as if he wondered about her sanity.

She was beginning to wonder about it, too.

And that was the very reason she'd sneaked out to his car. She'd been in that hospital so long she feared she was losing her mind. Maybe getting out, meeting others would trigger some memory of her past.

She was stronger now physically. And mentally...she was determined to find out who she was and what had happened to her.

"Are you all right?" Agent Dubois cut his dark gaze toward her. A streak of moonlight seeped through the storm clouds and settled on his chiseled face, making him seem wolfish, and her like a schoolgirl.

"I think so."

"Did you know this man Lex Van Wormer before you were hospitalized?"

She frowned and picked at the edge of the seat

belt, searching her blank mind. "No. At least not that I remember."

"But he came to visit you in your room?"

"Yes. But only at night." She licked her dry lips. "I assumed he didn't like to be seen in the light because of his condition. I...understood why he felt the need to remain in the shadows."

He veered onto the main highway. "You never visited his room or saw him outside?"

"No." She chewed her bottom lip, wondering what he was getting at. "I was too weak at first, and avoided leaving my room. The other patients, when there were others, whispered about me. They thought I was a monster."

His square jaw tightened, and he reached out to slide his hand over hers. "You're not a monster, Crystal. You're a *petite fleur, jolie fille.*"

"What does that mean?"

"A little flower, a pretty woman."

Warmth spread through her at his tone and compliment. It had been so long since she'd been away from the hospital, or with anyone other than Dr. Pace, the occasional nurse, and...Lex.

But Dr. Pace insisted Lex was dead.

Had she really been talking to a ghost all these months? Had she been hallucinating from the medication? Or was he lying to her to make her think she was crazy?

DAMON'S HAND TINGLED AS he closed it over the woman's. A surge of sexual heat shot through his body unlike anything he'd experienced in a long time. He felt an instant connection with Crystal/Kendra—whatever the hell her name was—a connection that tempted him to believe her.

But he had no idea if she was lying to him, or if she was the woman his brother was accused of murdering. The woman his brother had slept with and fallen for…

A woman Damon could absolutely not get involved with.

He jerked his hand away, but his fingers fell cold suddenly.

Dammit, even if she wasn't Kendra Yates, she looked a helluva lot like her, so much so that it was disturbing. And who knew what he would discover about her past? She might be a criminal. Or insane, for all he knew.

But she also might be in trouble and needed him.

His thoughts turned to the E-team. If she'd met Lex, perhaps he'd divulged secrets about his past and their missions before his demise.

Meaning she could expose them. If Cal or Max knew, they'd want to silence her.

He had to find out how much she knew. It was the only way to protect the E-team.

Being attracted to her would only interfere with work.

His cell phone rang, saving him from explaining the thoughts boomeranging in his head. He checked the number and answered.

"Damon. Jean-Paul." Short, clipped, to the point. "No leads yet on who wired that money transfer into the phony account for Antwaun, but I'm working on it. Anything on your end?"

"I tracked down Dr. Pace. And…you won't believe what I found." He explained about his conversation with the plastic surgeon, and the woman in the seat beside him, well aware she watched him warily. Had she felt the heat, the lust that had shot through his body?

Did she know he'd been part of the E-team, and a friend of Lex's? That they would kill her if she tried to expose them?

"Damon—"

"Sorry. Anyway, Pace claims he sent her DNA for testing, but I called the agency and there was no record of it. She's coming with me so we can run her DNA and fingerprints and find out her identity."

"Do you think she's Kendra Yates?" Jean-Paul asked.

"I don't know. She certainly looks like her, but she has amnesia. And I'm not sure the timing is right." He hesitated. "Check and see if Miss Yates had any siblings. Maybe a sister who resembled her, or a twin."

"I'm on it."

A long pause. "How are *Maman* and Papa holding up?"

Jean-Paul's long sigh said it all. "As well as can be expected. The press mobbed them at the restaurant today. I talked to Steph and she's going to stay with them for a few days until the worst dies down."

"Dammit. This scandal could destroy their new business."

"I know. All the more reason for us to work quickly."

"I'll get the DNA and fingerprints sent out tonight. Then I'm going straight to the jail to see if she recognizes Antwaun or vice versa." If she was Kendra Yates, which he hoped to hell she was, they could clear his brother and get him out of jail. Then Antwaun could figure out what had happened to her, and whether or not the two of them had any kind of relationship to pursue, or if she'd only been using his brother for information on the police force.

And if she wasn't Kendra…

He'd figure out why she looked like her. If she was related or if Pace had some reason to recreate Kendra Yates's face on another woman. Something nagged at the back of his mind, something about Pace's work, but he couldn't quite pinpoint it.

"I'm still digging into the police-corruption angle," Jean-Paul said. "If this woman is Kendra Yates and a dirty cop thinks she's on to him, he may come after her."

Damon grimaced, his brother's conclusions mirroring his own. He wanted answers, but the thought of using Crystal gnawed at his conscience. He agreed to keep Jean-Paul posted, hung up, and glanced at Crystal. She looked pale, exhausted, frightened. He wanted to soothe her again, reach out, touch her and promise her that she wasn't alone, that he would protect her.

But how could he when he didn't know the truth about her?

Dammit. He dared not get close to her.

Wanting to help her was one thing, but wanting her on a physical level was impossible.

After all, he just might have to use her as bait to catch a killer….

AS THEY DROVE, Crystal clung to the hope that Agent Dubois could help her, yet the heat emanating from him when he'd touched her rattled her. She'd felt an immediate thrill that had aroused her senses in a way that she hadn't thought about during her hospitalization.

Of course, the past few months she'd been consumed with struggling to survive. She had hoped to look human, but to be…*beautiful,* as Damon Dubois had called her, was a miracle.

But tension radiated from the agent in waves, reminding her that he suspected she was Kendra, that she held the key to his brother's release from jail. That the homicide investigation was his *only* interest in her.

What if he was right? Would she remember Antwaun Dubois? Had she really been a reporter?

And what if she wasn't Kendra Yates? Then she'd be back to square one—a woman with no name, no past, no knowledge of her former life. A woman no one cared enough about to look for…

A woman who resembled a dead reporter. A reporter someone may have tried to murder.

A shudder coursed through her at the thought. What had happened to Kendra Yates? What if she *was* Kendra and Antwaun Dubois had tried to kill her? Maybe Damon Dubois was walking her into some kind of trap?

The terror that had overwhelmed her during her nightmares about the accident haunted her. She'd seen the flames, a man's dead body… But who was he? And what had happened?

In spite of the stifling summer heat, she huddled within herself, feeling cold and alone. Could she really trust Agent Dubois?

She'd sensed the anger in him when she'd seen

that television interview, and when he'd first laid eyes on her. He'd staunchly defended his brother.

The men *were* brothers. Antwaun's guilt or innocence might not matter. Agent Dubois might defend him anyway. And this supposed attraction between them might be one-sided. Maybe he thought that if he pretended to care, even seduced her, she'd help him.

She massaged her temple where a headache pulsed, already feeling the weight of fatigue on her muscles.

"Are you all right?"

The agent's husky voice sent another frisson of alarm and…sexual energy flowing through her. "Yes."

"If you're not feeling well, I'll take you somewhere to rest and we can meet my brother later."

She turned to study him in the dim light of the car. His masculine scent, big body, even his low breathing filled the confines with an intensity that bordered on frightening. Yet tenderness also underscored the dark hooded look in his eyes as he made the offer.

"I thought you wanted this meeting immediately, Agent Dubois," she said, confused.

"I do, but you look exhausted. And please call me Damon."

Calling him by his first name seemed somehow too intimate. He scrubbed a hand over his cheek, the rasp of his five o'clock shadow echoing between them, and making her even more aware of his potency.

"No, let's get the meeting over with," she said, determined to follow through with any lead on her identity.

His eyes darkened. "Are you sure?"

His concern touched her. Surely if he meant her harm or was leading her into a trap, he wouldn't offer to let her rest.

"Yes, I want to do this," she said, lifting her chin and struggling for courage. "If I'm Kendra Yates, then I can help your brother. And I'll know something about myself. If I'm not, I won't be any worse off than I've been the past few months."

He nodded and focused on the road. She tried to relax. But by the time they reached the jail, her head throbbed full force, and nerves gripped her shoulders so tightly she ached all over.

Agent Dubois led her into the police station, through security and into a holding room to talk to his brother. In spite of her fears, Crystal was impressed with Damon's quiet commanding authority and the respect he garnered from the other officers. Still, she sensed animosity between a few of them as the other officers passed through the department, as if they understood his personal agenda and perhaps believed his brother was guilty of the charges.

Their whispers and shocked expressions reminded her that her new face looked like the woman they had charged Antwaun Dubois of murdering.

As soon as they stepped inside the room, Antwaun entered, handcuffed and shackled. At first glance, the brothers resembled one another, and a frisson of attraction lit her insides. Antwaun's hair was wavier, and instead of dark brown eyes, his were an odd silver cobalt-blue. They settled on her, steely with rage.

He looked every bit like a killer.

She sucked in a deep breath, and searched for recognition, for some memory to surface, even a fleeting one that might alert her to the fact that she had known him. For a brief second, she felt it. Then the strong sense that he hated her for what she'd put him through overwhelmed her, and she moved closer to Damon.

"Kendra?" Antwaun stalked toward her, his eyes scrutinizing her every feature as if he were looking at a ghost.

She shook her head. "I'm sorry…I…don't remember you."

Agent Dubois cleared his throat. "Antwaun, I found this woman at a rehab hospital." He explained how she'd wound up at Dr. Pace's, about her amnesia and the plastic surgery. "According to Dr. Pace, she's been hospitalized for the past several months."

"Why are you doing this to me, Kendra?" Antwaun

asked, his gaze still glued to her. "The last time I saw you, we talked about having a life together. Were you just using me?"

She backed away, his anger palpable. "I…I'm sorry. I don't remember that at all."

Antwaun jerked his gaze toward his brother as if he thought she was lying.

"She's agreed to be fingerprinted and have her DNA tested," Agent Dubois said. "We'll find out the truth, Antwaun."

Crystal bit down on her lip. As much as she wanted to know her identity and had half hoped she was this reporter, she sensed she wouldn't have gotten involved with Agent Dubois's brother. He was certainly handsome, but regarding him she felt more fear than chemistry.

"Jean-Paul's checking into Kendra's family," Damon told Antwaun. "Soon we'll know if Kendra has a sister, cousin, someone who looks like her."

Antwaun turned those glacier eyes on her. "You're lying, trying to run away and get a new identity—and trying to leave me framed for being corrupt when I'm not. Turn over your notes, Kendra, whatever you had. Let me look at them, for God's sake."

A dizzy spell assaulted Crystal, and she clutched the chair. Then anger suddenly rallied inside her. She hadn't asked for any of this, at least not that she recalled. "Look, I wish I remembered you and what happened. Like I told your brother, I woke up several months ago in a hospital with burns and injuries all over my body." She pushed up the sleeves of her shirt to reveal scars. "I almost died, and have undergone one surgery after another." She wanted to hit him and lash out. "I'm not pretending to have amnesia. I'd give anything to have my life back."

An odd look muddied Damon's eyes. "The injuries and plastic surgery are for real," Damon said. "I saw photos, Antwaun. She's telling the truth."

Antwaun folded his big arms. "That doesn't mean she didn't use me. Maybe Swafford or the real dirty cop she was investigating discovered she was on to him, and he caused her so-called accident. Maybe she tried to disappear, and somehow faked the dead woman's fingerprints in the system so everyone would think she'd died."

Crystal swallowed hard, terror seizing her. "If that's true, then I'm still in danger."

"She's right," Damon said. "And if that's the case, helping her remember is our best bet to clear you, Antwaun, and find the person setting you up."

Antwaun glared at her, but nodded, although his mouth tightened as the guard approached. Damon assured his brother that he would get to the bottom of the matter, then escorted her to another office and collected her DNA. After that, she endured his taking her fingerprints, all the time feeling as if she were a criminal, not a medical victim.

Damon placed a hand at her waist to steady her as he walked her to his car. "I'm sorry my brother was so brusque, Crystal. But he's having a rough time."

She nodded, although she was trembling. "He thinks this is easy on me? I've lived in the darkness for months," she said in a tired voice. "I need some answers."

They paused at the door, and he looked at her as if he wanted to reach out and soothe her, assuage her fears. But if she was Kendra, she had been his brother's lover.

"Even if finding them might turn up something you don't want to hear?"

She nodded again, although her mind raced with questions and uncertainty.

Maybe no one was looking for her because she was a bad person. Maybe her nightmares had been real, and someone had tried to kill her. The same person who'd framed Antwaun.

If so, that cop might come after her again. She scanned the dark exterior of the police station, her skin crawling.

As CRYSTAL CLIMBED into the car, Damon checked his phone for messages and saw that the governor had called, wanting info about the case. He'd also left a reminder about the hero's welcome during the Memorial Day parade.

Damon didn't intend to go but would tell the governor later. Make up an excuse. The parade was for heroes, and he wasn't one.

Beside him, Crystal massaged her temples.

He was contemplating where to take her for the night to ensure her safety when his cell phone trilled. Jean-Paul again. "Yeah?"

"How did it go with Antwaun?"

"Not well," Damon said. "What did you find out, Jean-Paul?"

"Kendra Yates's father died when she was twelve, but her mother is still alive. She was an only child, though. No sister. No long-lost twin."

Jean-Paul's phone beeped in that he had another call, and he put Damon on hold. Damon glanced at Crystal again. She'd leaned her head back against the seat and closed her eyes. After the ordeal of her surgeries, she obviously needed rest.

Jean-Paul clicked back on the line. "Shit, you're not going to believe this, but the lieutenant just called. Locals found a woman's body out in the bayou. At least pieces of one. It's been mutilated."

"They know who she is?" Damon asked, although a bad feeling clawed at him.

"No, but she's missing a hand."

"Where?"

Jean-Paul gave the GPS coordinates and Damon cranked the engine and sped from the parking lot. They might just have found the rest of Kendra Yates's body. Or at least the body of the woman they'd first thought to be her.

So whom was the woman sitting next to him?

What was her connection to a severed hand in the bayou?

CHAPTER TEN

CRYSTAL HATED FEELING WEAK, but fatigue weighed her down. She refused to go back to Dr. Pace and that hospital, but she did need to find a bed soon.

The grim look Damon gave her made her nerves ping with anxiety. Something was very, very wrong.

"What was that call about?" she asked.

"My other brother, Jean-Paul. He's a detective with the NOPD. The police found a body. It belongs to the woman with the missing hand."

Bile rose to her throat. This was the woman they'd thought to be Kendra?

He cleared his throat. "I need to go to the crime scene ASAP."

"All right."

He veered around the street corner, tires squealing as he increased his speed. "I'm going to drop you at a safe place to rest for the night first."

"If it's out of your way, you don't have to do that. I could wait in the car."

He shook his head. "No, it might take hours to

process the scene." He shot her a worried glance. "You obviously need some sleep."

Relief surged through her, and she sagged against the door.

She couldn't think anymore tonight.

She closed her eyes and must have dozed off because the next time she opened them, they were parking in front of a gray Victorian house complete with turrets, a wraparound porch and a white picket fence. The house looked spooky set against the inky sky and the swampland. A black cat lay curled beneath a swing on the front porch and two others flanked each side of the doorway like watchdogs.

She couldn't imagine this house belonging to the tough detective.

"I thought you were taking me to a hotel," she said.

"You said you knew Lex. This place… It belongs to his *grand-mère*. It's also close to my house if you need me." He hesitated, switched off the engine. "I don't want you to be alone, not after just leaving the hospital."

His concern warmed her heart, and chopped away at the distrust she'd felt earlier. If Damon wanted to harm her, he'd had plenty of opportunity.

"But it's late. I hate to disturb Lex's grandmother."

A smile tugged at Agent Dubois's face. His first ever, as far as she knew. "Esmeralda is a late-night person," he said. "She's a little eccentric, but her doors are always open." He reached out and rubbed his thumb along her cheek. "You'll be safe here."

Her throat convulsed. "How much danger do you think I'm in, Agent Dubois?"

"I don't know. And I asked you to call me Damon." His smile faded, making her wish for its return. She wanted to see more of that side of him, rather than the cold, hard man he presented on the surface. "You don't remember your accident or your past. And you look almost identical to a woman who disappeared a while ago, a woman we think may have been murdered. A woman who might have been connected to you in some way."

"I…I have wondered if my accident was really an accident," she admitted. "I've had nightmares where I feel like someone was after me."

He nodded, that dark intensity back in his eyes. "When we learn your name, I'll help you find out the rest."

"Thank you, Damon. I know you're hoping I can help clear your brother."

"I am," he admitted, a muscle ticking in his jaw. "But I'll help you even if you can't."

He meant it, too. She heard the conviction in his statement and knew this man was one she could rely on. Trust.

A second later, self-doubt filled her.

She sensed she'd trusted another man before and had been wrong. So wrong that something bad had happened because of her misjudgment.

ESMERALDA KNEW THE WOMAN was coming before she showed up at the door with Damon Dubois. Lex had told her.

Poor Lex. He had held on long enough to try and save the woman. But Lex needed to move on. Still, he clung to the world in between life and death, good and evil, heaven and hell.

For protection, she'd sprinkled salt around the edges of the house outside, on the doorstep and inside the room in the adjoining cottage where the woman would sleep. And she had primed the cats and summoned their magic. She might be ninety-one now and blind as a bat, but she could see the danger coming, and she would use her insight and the powers of her feline friends to protect Lex's friend.

After all, if Lex saved her, she would, in return, become his savior.

The knock sounded at the same time the teakettle whistled, so she turned off the stove, tugged her black shawl around her neck and hobbled to the door.

In spite of the sultry heat rolling off the swamp land behind her, a bitter chill filled the room as if the angel of death waltzed around the woman, begging her for one last dance.

An evil force had risen from the bowels of the backwater to try and take her before God had called. But she was somehow sure that the woman's journey was not meant to end yet.

"Esmeralda, can we come in?"

She smiled at the handsome federal agent who had once been Lex's friend. "Certainly. I've been expecting you."

The pretty woman hesitated at the doorway as if wondering how Esmerelda had known—Damon Dubois hadn't bothered to phone.

"Esmeralda has a way of seeing things," Agent Dubois said in a husky voice.

The old woman swept her hand to the side to gesture them inside, and the tabby Persimmon brushed her legs in acknowledgment. Gorgon, the striped male, purred his delight, and Titan, her fat gray friend, swished his tail at her feet.

When Damon had seated himself and the woman on the antique sofa, he introduced Lex's friend. "Her name... Well, we're uncertain about her identity, but for now we're calling her Crystal."

"Hello, Esmeralda," Crystal said in a low voice. "I'm sorry for disturbing you so late at night. But Damon told me that Lex is your grandson. He was so kind to me in the hospital."

"You do not disturb me, child. I am here for you now, just as Lex would want." A grin tugged at her mouth as Crystal whispered a soothing word to Midnight.

"So you like cats," Esmeralda said.

Crystal laughed softly. "Yes. You have quite a collection."

"The kids around here call me the Cat Lady." Yet some of the kids feared her and her magic. "The felines are my friends, my protectors, all that I need."

"This black one is watching me as if he's human."

Esmeralda cackled with laughter as she shuffled to the stove in the adjoining kitchen. Crystal must be a supersensitive, with how Midnight was watching her and her ability to see Lex.

Esmerelda settled the teakettle and three cups on a tray along with sugar and cream and carried it to the coffee table. There she poured each of them a cup of the chamomile tea, sat back and sipped hers while the agent explained Crystal's predicament.

"She needs a safe place to rest for the night," he said. "And I have to go. A woman has been murdered, her body found in the bayou. The crime-scene unit and police are already there."

Esmeralda nodded, reached to the couch's armrest and pressed a hand over his. "Crystal will be fine here."

His clothes rustled as he turned toward Crystal. "I need to go. I'll come back tomorrow and check on you."

"Thank you for…everything, Damon," Crystal said.

Agent Dubois stood, removed a cell phone from his pocket, then handed it to Crystal. "Take my phone and call me if you need anything. I've already programmed my number in. Now get some rest and I'll be back in the morning."

Esmeralda walked him to the door and lowered her voice to a near whisper in his ear. "There is an evil force at work in the bayou, a depravity of such kind as we haven't seen the depths of before."

"I have a feeling you're right." Agent Dubois leaned closer. "We found a woman's severed hand in the swamp, and tonight police found the rest of her body, mutilated."

Esmeralda frowned at the fact that the devil had won.

"Esmeralda, I don't know who Crystal is, but she said something that disturbed me at the hospital. She claimed Lex had visited her, that he was at the hospital the same time she was." He paused, studied Esmeralda's craggy face. "But I thought you told me that Lex died, and Dr. Pace said the same thing. Is he still alive?"

Esmeralda's thin lips straightened into a tight line. "No, he's not of this earth. I stood by his grave myself."

"I'm sorry, Esmeralda. Lex was…a good man."

Not always, she wanted to say, but refrained.

This man and Lex shared some of the same regrets. They had teamed together in their own way to fight for justice, yet they'd created pain in their wake. Agent Dubois already carried the weight of the world upon his shoulders. She'd felt the burden of his sadness and guilt in his aura the first time they'd met. He was responsible to the point of denying his own needs.

Crystal held the key to releasing him and Lex both from their hell. Only the devil would try to destroy her and the agent before peace could be found.

Esmerelda wished she could assure him that his anguish and suffering would soon end, but that was not the case. Not yet.

ONCE, IN KUWAIT, Damon had been shot and almost died. He remembered lying in the insufferable heat of the desert, closing his eyes and hallucinating that he had a woman who loved him waiting at home. For days, he'd held on to life through that fantasy, telling himself he had to live so he could have one more night in her bed. One more night to feel her lush naked body wrapped up with his, his hard cock thrusting inside her, her whispering his name in the throes of passion.

He had felt dread for the last few months, had moved through each day like a zombie, with no *joie de vivre,* joy of life, tortured by the screams of another woman he had caused to die.

So, Damon's blood ran hot when Crystal appeared at the door and touched his arm. The trust he saw reflected in her luminous eyes nearly made his knees buckle. He didn't deserve for her to look at him as if he were some kind of hero, and he felt humbled by it.

Touching this woman, being with her, made him want to live. As if she'd read his mind or shared his ridiculous fantasy, she stood on tiptoe, brushed her fingers along his jaw then pressed her lips to his. The tentative kiss was so tender and sweet that his heart pounded with the need to deepen it.

Then something much more primal and elemental passed between them, and his body surged with desire. Damn.

But he felt the chill of the other woman's dying breath on his neck, and he pulled away.

"I'm sorry," she whispered, flushing as if she thought he hadn't wanted it. The trouble was he wanted it too damn badly. In fact, he wanted her lips on him everywhere.

But he had a case to solve and she was part of it.

Besides, if she was Kendra, his brother had been in love with her….

And she had deceived him.

He cleared his throat of emotions, wishing he

could clear his mind of the memories of that woman's death. "Like I said, call if you need me."

Struggling against temptation, he spun on his heel and ducked out the door, well aware that even being blind, somehow Esmeralda had seen the kiss. He was playing with fire.

Worry nagged at Damon as he left Crystal and drove toward the bayou and the body. He forced himself to forget that kiss and to analyze the situation. Crystal was exhausted, confused, frightened. She probably should have stayed at the hospital, but he didn't trust Pace worth a damn. The fact that she claimed she'd talked to Lex disturbed him even more. Pace had said she'd suffered a head injury, and she'd no doubt been heavily medicated for months. She must have heard Lex's name and hallucinated a visitor, or confused him with someone else. There was no other explanation.

Lex Van Wormer was dead. Another casualty of the war.

Another reminder of the E-team and the reason Damon didn't deserve a life himself.

Yet, the image of Crystal's face flashed in his mind and hunger heated his bloodstream again. Then another, an image of her naked beneath him, filled his head, and a savage need spread through him. He could almost feel her soft fingertips gliding over his skin, the gentle pressure of her succulent lips molding to his, her mouth opening to invite him inside, legs spread wide, taking him into her body with the same carnal lust that throbbed in his veins.

He cursed and accelerated.

Those damn fantasies only proved he was an evil son of a bitch who had lost his honor a long time ago.

She was a goddamn victim of some horrible accident, a woman who needed to know her name and the reason she'd spent long painful months rehabilitating, while all he could think about was how much he wanted her in his bed.

Beat the hell out of thinking about the grisly night ahead.

Sweat rolled down the side of his face. He cranked his window down and breathed in the fresh air and smell of the bayou. By the time he reached the crime scene, law-enforcement vehicles littered the road, along with the coroner's car, and a news van—dammit.

How had the press found out about the body so quickly?

He parked, scanned the area, noting the cabin in the beam of his headlights. Switching off the lights, he climbed out, and threaded his way through the woods to the cabin. Crime-scene tape roped off the area surrounding the sagging wooden structure, taking him back to the Swamp Devil murders. Two officers walked the border, fending off the press to keep them from contaminating the scene and snagging pictures of the inside of the cabin and the body.

Damon plowed through them. Outside the shanty, crime techs already worked taking photos, searching for forensics. Lieutenant Phelps and Jean-Paul stood on the porch, both wearing grim expressions. Damon checked in with the officer in charge, accepted plastic gloves and baggies for his shoes, then climbed the steps.

"What do we have here, gentlemen?" he asked, glancing first at Jean-Paul, then the lieutenant.

"Some sick pervert's idea of fun," Lieutenant Phelps muttered.

"It's the worst I've ever seen," Jean-Paul said, one hand actually shaking as he lifted it to shove his hair off his forehead. "He mutilated her to pieces, Damon. I mean...there's not much left."

Damon braced himself, but he had to see the crime scene for himself. The odor was hideous, a mixture of the swampland, dried blood, human waste and rotting flesh. Bugs had already begun to eat at the tissue that remained.

But it wasn't the sight of the cuts and wounds on the woman's mangled body that made him gag.

She had been literally stripped of the outer layer of her skin—essentially the woman had no face.

CHAPTER ELEVEN

CRYSTAL PRESSED A FINGER to her lips, the heat of Agent Dubois's lips still imprinted on her mouth. She didn't know what had possessed her to kiss him— she'd only meant to kiss his cheek in thanks. But once she'd felt his face with her fingertips, the desire to be closer had overpowered her.

"You have a connection with this man," Esmeralda said.

Crystal spun around, shocked at the woman's comment. Esmeralda was blind—she couldn't have seen the kiss. "I hope he can help me learn who I am."

Esmeralda's gnarled fingers worried the cross at her neck. "I hope you are ready for the knowledge, my dear."

"Why do you say that?"

"Sometimes our mind has a way of protecting us from pain." Esmeralda's eyes expressed compassion and sympathy. "Traumatic events can rob one's soul. You'll remember when you're ready to handle the truth."

"I guess you're right," Crystal said softly. "But I am feeling stronger every day."

"Agent Dubois," Esmeralda said, "he is a good man."

The image of the agent's stark features rose in Crystal's mind. He was intense, brooding, mysterious and almost sullen. Yet pain echoed in his voice and the quiet control he emanated. "Yes, I think you're right," she finally said.

The woman continued to stroke the gold cross. "He needs you, too. Remember that."

Crystal frowned. Maybe the older woman was a little addled. "What do you mean? How could he need me?" Then it hit her. "To solve the case?"

Esmeralda bent to pet a huge tabby cat. "No, to heal his heart. But this connection you have—there is trouble and pain that goes with it."

Crystal clenched her hands together. Now the woman was frightening her.

"I'm sorry, I don't mean to scare you, dear." Esmeralda patted Crystal's hand. "You are strong, you have burdens to bear, but follow your heart and you will survive."

Leaving off on that odd comment, she poured milk into bowls and dished a portion of food for each of the cats on saucers lined up beside the kitchen sink. The black cat Midnight swished his tail against her legs, and studied her as if he was in tune with her every move. There was something eerie about the woman and this gigantic old house. It was as isolated as the rehab center, so far away from civilization that if Crystal needed to escape it seemed there would be no place to go except into the swamp where the night crawlers and gators waited to pounce.

But Damon trusted Esmeralda, and she was Lex's grandmother. And besides, Damon had told her his house was nearby. How close?

Her head swam, the headache she'd had earlier returning full force. She was exhausted. Thoughts of that dead woman's mutilated body made her wonder if she might be next. After all, she looked like the reporter—what if the killer had confused the two of them?

"I appreciate you letting me stay here, Esmeralda," Crystal said, snapping out of her fear. "I can't tell you how much your grandson has meant to me since my hosipitalization." Emotions choked her. She hadn't imagined him; he'd been very real. "I don't think I would have survived if he hadn't visited me."

A sense of peace washed over Esmeralda's face. "Yes, he cares for you, dear."

"Then he was really at the hospital. And you've talked to him…so Dr. Pace was lying. Lex is not dead."

The old woman rubbed her fingers over the cross

around her neck. "He has passed, Crystal. But still, he is with you and with me now. Though we must let him go soon."

Sadness nearly robbed Crystal of her voice. Lex had been her only friend, her lifeline during the past few horrific months....

"You need to lie down, dear. The cottage is already prepared. You'll have privacy and the rest you need."

Crystal cradled the older woman's hands in her own. "Thank you for your kindness. If I can ever do anything to help you, please let me know."

Esmeralda reached out bony arms and pulled her into an embrace. Tears welled in Crystal's eyes. She didn't know if she had family or not, but if she did, she hoped they were as kind and loving as this lady. "You already have, dear."

Crystal had no idea what she meant, and Esmeralda didn't elaborate. She simply picked Midnight up in her arms and led the way through a small portico, out the kitchen to an adjoining carriage house. Wind chimes danced outside, and as they entered the cottage, Crystal noticed glass angels hanging in the doorways, as if to guard the spaces. Silver crosses created an artful arrangement above the sofa, and crystals dangled from the mirror on the entry wall.

"There are fresh linens in the bathroom, an extra

blanket in the chest at the foot of the bed, and a night-light in the bathroom." Esmeralda's wrinkled face creased as she smiled. "If you need anything, all you have to do is tell Midnight, and he'll get me."

Crystal frowned at this last bit. But she didn't want to hurt the old woman's feelings or insult her by asking, not after Esmeralda had been so kind, so she promised she would, then locked the door with her departure. Yawning, she stripped to her underwear and fell into the antique four-poster bed. Lace curtains draped the bed as if to offer privacy, and a slight breeze blew through the opened windows. The smell of jasmine and lavender scented the air, and the faint sound of the river lapping up against the embankment soothed her nerves.

Tomorrow she needed to get some clothes. And maybe soon Agent Dubois—Damon—would know her identity, and if she had any family looking for her.

If she'd been involved with his brother…well, she'd deal with that, and any stories she might have been investigating.

Although the idea of her investigating stories, cops, felt strange.

Somewhere in the distance, the sound of a harmonica wailed out a sad blues tune. She closed her eyes and felt Lex nearby, could have sworn she smelled the scent of his antibiotic cream, heard the whisper of his voice. She said a silent prayer that he was at peace.

But when she finally slept, more nightmares invaded her rest. Some man was after her, chasing her with a knife. Catching her in the bayou, he was going to cut off her hands. Blood spurted from her wrist as he made the first slice....

She jerked awake, and thought she heard someone breathing in the silence. The uncanny sensation of being watched sent a chill through her.

For whatever reason, she wasn't safe. Even here where Damon had promised her she would be.

DAMON'S STOMACH PROTESTED the gruesome sight of the woman's mutilated body. It appeared that the killer had literally carved her slowly with small knife wounds, then watched her bleed for a while, then grown more aggressive and violent and progressed in his torture.

Why?

Had he been trying to extract information from the woman, or had he simply enjoyed inflicting pain?

Whoever the perpetrator was, he had to be a sociopath. Any person with a conscience could not have destroyed another human's body so completely.

His brother had not done this. Even if he had had opportunity, which he could not since he was in jail...

Still, there were inconsistencies with the body, rigor and blood suggesting she might have been dead longer than a day or two, that she *might* have been kept on ice…

Which could put her death back on his brother.

Antwaun might have a temper, but he wasn't sadistic. He certainly didn't have it within him to be this brutal to a woman. None of the Dubois men did.

As if to mock his thoughts, the image of the woman being engulfed in flames rose to haunt him. He had caused horrific pain to her—he had caused the explosion that took her, but, God help him, he hadn't meant to. She was never supposed to have been there.

Not that it made any difference. She'd died at his hands, and her screams echoed forever in his head, drilling home the fact that he had once been an assassin. A paid killer.

The fact that he'd killed the enemy didn't matter.

"Cause of death," the medical examiner said as he wiped his forehead with his arm. "Officially a homicide. It appears that the victim bled out, but I'll know more after the autopsy."

"What can you tell us from the stab wounds?" Jean-Paul asked.

The doctor pointed to her chest. "The chest wound was pre-mortem, although some of the other slashes look post… He obviously enjoyed watching her bleed." He pointed to the wall that was smeared in dried blood. "Looks like the sick bastard played in it."

Perspiration trickled down Damon's neck and into his shirt. The heat was stifling, making the stench of the bayou and remains of the body insufferable.

"There has to be some DNA or forensic evidence left by him in this mess," Jean-Paul said grimly.

Lieutenant Phelps leaned against the doorjamb and wheezed as if desperate for fresh air. Sweat stains marked his white shirt, and he looked as if he might get sick any minute. "If there is, our CSI team will find it. And we don't need you here, Agent Dubois."

Damon frowned. "Actually, I'm officially on the case because of our interest in Swafford." He pointed to the body. "We need to ID her. And we have to keep the press from posting a photo of this scene, or her, or the town will panic again."

"We can't cover it up," the lieutenant said. "Thanks to your brother, IA is all over everybody in the department."

Jean-Paul glared at his superior. "This is not Antwaun's fault. If there is a cop on the take, it isn't him. And you'd better be looking at your men and figuring out who it is."

Damon heard the threat in his oldest brother's voice but also saw the determination and condemnation in Phelps's eyes. He'd already tried and convicted Antwaun.

"I don't understand how anyone can be so depraved," Jean-Paul said as the lieutenant walked outside. "If this is one of my guys, I want to see him pay."

Damon moved closer, forced himself to study the carvings the killer had made. But his focus drifted to her face. The missing outer layer of skin. The bones and tissue were exposed. Somehow the cutting seemed different.

Smith, Antwaun's partner, had been first on the scene and was examining the body. Damon made a mental note to tell Jean-Paul to find out more about the officer. What if he was the dirty cop who'd set up Antwaun? Damon narrowed his eyes and squatted down, examining the viciousness of the other knife marks. They were jagged, angry, uncontrolled, with no definite pattern.

The area around her face however looked as if it had been cut by a skilled professional. Even the cuts around her hairline were drawn carefully, done so in a nice neat line, almost as if a surgeon had drawn an oval around her face to keep the skin intact.

He rocked back on his heels, his mind spinning with questions. Memories bombarded him—of being in Pace's office, seeing the sketches he drew on dummies before facial reconstruction surgeries, how he drew off the areas where he intended to work. Then Pace talking about current research he was working on. Cutting-edge techniques that other doctors were also exploring, but that were controversial and dangerous. The press hinting about a new discovery to be unveiled soon.

The procedure—face transplants.

Damon had seen a special news report on the possibilities a few weeks ago, and had thought of Pace and his cutting-edge work. Pace had been researching the procedure for years.

His jaw tightened as he realized that Crystal might have been a recipient of one herself. That the reason she resembled Kendra Yates might not be because she was the woman, but because she had received her face.

And if Pace had given it to her, then he had to know something about Kendra Yates's murder.

ANTWAUN STARED at his brothers in the prison visiting room, his body humming with angry tension. It was barely dawn, although he hadn't been sleeping when they'd arrived. After the way they'd described the woman's body—Kendra's body, most likely—he didn't know if he'd ever sleep again.

To think that the woman he'd been involved with had died such a horrible death choked the breath from his lungs. He braced one hand on the cell bars and inhaled, battling nausea. What if somehow he was responsible? Maybe someone had a grudge against him and had killed Kendra to get revenge on him.

"I'm sorry, Antwaun," Damon said. "But we wanted you to hear this from us, not see it in the paper tomorrow or hear it from one of the guards or another cop."

"You really think it's Kendra?"

Jean-Paul shrugged. "We can't be sure until we get the results of the DNA, but preliminary blood tests are a match."

"Then who the hell is the woman you brought here earlier?" Antwaun asked.

"I don't know yet, but we'll find out," Damon said. "I'm waiting on DNA and blood tests now."

"Did you check out my list of enemies?" Antwaun asked.

Jean-Paul nodded. "Carson has been checking out the list you gave me, but so far we haven't turned up anything."

"Are you sure you can trust him?" Antwaun asked.

"Like a brother."

Damon gritted his teeth. "Do you think Swafford's men are capable of this kind of murder?"

Antwaun retraced the last few months' investigation in his mind. "So far, they've been into money laundering big-time, but not murder. Although he has some thugs on his payroll, their style would be a bullet in the head execution style, not this type of violence."

"I'd say it was personal, a crime of passion," Damon said. "But this crime was colder. It was almost overkill. The guy wanted to make a statement."

"It's not a cop's style either," Jean-Paul interjected. "Cops would be more likely to use a gun as well."

Damon shoved his hair back from his forehead. "The crime scene reads like a sociopath," he surmised. "The brutality, viciousness, the mutilations… This guy enjoyed inflicting pain. He probably hates women. Maybe Kendra—or whoever this woman was—was someone he was stalking. Or she could have been an innocent victim. But definitely not his first kill."

"So you don't think the murder is related to Swafford, or Kendra's story on dirty cops at all?" Antwaun asked.

"It's too early to tell," Damon said. "But we have to look at every angle. By the way, Antwaun, how well do you know your partner?"

Antwaun shrugged. "Not well. He just joined the squad."

Jean-Paul clinched his teeth. "I'll look into him."

Damon turned to Jean-Paul. "I haven't seen a case with an MO like this, but we'll need to search the databases again."

"I'll get on it," Jean-Paul agreed.

"Damon?" Antwaun growled. "You know something. I can see it in your eyes."

Damon's mouth twisted in disgust. "The mutilated woman we found in the bayou—the sick bastard removed the top layer of her face."

Antwaun rolled back on his heels. "What?"

"I think this plastic surgeon, Dr. Pace, may be involved. He works for the government, helps witnesses and others who need to disappear get a new life. Sometimes a new face. He's also been researching cutting-edge techniques with burn patients that involve complete face transplants from cadavers."

He paused and Antwaun tried to follow his train of thought. "You think Pace had something to do with Kendra's disappearance or her death?"

"Maybe." Damon grunted. "If the dead woman is Kendra, maybe Pace removed her skin and transplanted it onto the woman I brought here last night. That's why this other woman resembles Kendra."

Antwaun's stomach knotted. "Then Pace must know what happened to Kendra and who killed her."

Damon motioned for the guard to open the door. "I'm on my way to talk to him now."

THE SUNRISE IN THE BAYOU streaked the gray sky with purple and dark red lines. Crystal carried a cup of coffee onto Esmeralda's front porch and settled into the wicker rocking chair with the morning paper. She'd hated to ask Esmeralda, but she'd wondered why a blind woman received the paper at all. But Esmeralda had laughed good-naturedly, then admitted that she had a friend who came and read to her. The odd twitch in her smile made Crystal wonder if the elderly lady had a boyfriend.

Then again, when Crystal had first walked into the kitchen of the main house this morning, Esmeralda had been mumbling out loud, talking to someone named Cooter.

Oddly though, no one had been in the room.

When Crystal had questioned her, Esmeralda had professed that she was talking to her long-dead brother. In fact, she'd acted as if the interaction was perfectly normal. Then she'd pointed to two pennies lying on the table and commented on the scent of Old Spice in the room, insisting both were evidence that had alerted her to his presence before she'd even heard his voice.

Was the old woman batty, or did she really think she could talk to ghosts?

Then again, Esmeralda had said that Lex was dead, just as Dr. Pace had, and she'd sworn she had seen him. Maybe in Crystal's near-death state, *she* had been able to channel into the realm of death....

Midnight suddenly arched his back and hissed, his

green eyes staring at the woods beyond. She stroked his back to calm him, but he remained coiled with tension.

A shadow fell across the sun as Crystal picked up the morning newspaper and read the headlines.

Woman's Body Found Mutilated in the Bayou.

She shivered and zoned in on the gruesome image of two rescue workers carrying a body bag through a section of dark, isolated swampland. Another photo showed Agent Damon Dubois and his brother, Detective Jean-Paul Dubois, on the porch of a rotting shanty, their heads lowered in concentration, scowls on both their faces. Dragging her eyes away, she read on.

Do we have another sadistic serial killer stalking the city of New Orleans?

Or is this woman Kendra Yates, the woman allegedly murdered by Officer Antwaun Dubois?

Are the two connected?

Sources at the scene admit that the woman was mutilated, her body unrecognizable. The coroner confirmed they needed DNA evidence to identify the victim, and Lieutenant Phelps of the NOPD assured us that every possible resource would be utilized to find the killer and bring justice to the woman and her family.

Special FBI Agent Damon Dubois, a decorated marine who served in Iraq, and Detective
Jean-Paul Dubois of the NOPD, who received
an honorary commendation from the state for
his heroism during Hurricane Katrina, are
ironically both brothers of the accused suspect
Officer Antwaun Dubois. Both refused comment, although staunchly defended their brother at his hearing.

If you have any clues or evidence that would
aid the police in solving this crime, please
contact the NOPD immediately.

Crystal searched the rest of the paper to see if
there was any mention of her being Kendra Yates or
a missing woman, but found nothing.

The photo of the body bag caught her eye again,
and she remembered the picture Damon had shown
her of Kendra Yates, and the story about her journalism career. She felt drawn to the woman somehow,
and wanted to know what had happened to her.
Maybe because she resembled her...

She glanced back at Damon Dubois's photo and
that connection to him she'd sensed earlier returned
stronger than ever. He'd said he would help her, and
he was obviously a man who kept his word, a man
of honor.

But she'd been wrong before....

She wished he were here now, though. Somehow just being close to him gave her comfort. And that husky deep voice of his—she had heard it before. Maybe if she spent more time with him, she would remember why.

Midnight suddenly lurched up and hissed again, arching his back as he stared into the woods beyond. Two other cats, a fat gray one and a striped orange one, rose and paced the front porch like panthers, as if they sensed something dangerous lurking in the shadows of the swamp. Leaves rustled and a twig snapped. A gator screeched in the distance.

Crystal tensed as the cats formed a close circle around her. A fierce cackle erupted in the tense silence that sounded half human, half animal and then a shadow moved beneath a copse of trees....

Esmeralda suddenly rushed through the front door, wielding a shotgun. The screen door slapped against the doorjamb just as the old woman blasted a shot at the shadow.

"Call Agent Dubois!" Esmeralda shouted.

As Crystal ran in for the phone, the old woman fired another shot into the woods while the cats hissed and scratched the wooden slats of the porch. Midnight dove from the railing and darted into the woods in chase.

CHAPTER TWELVE

DAMON'S HEART RACED ninety miles a minute as he careened around the curve and veered into the long driveway that led to Esmeralda's place. Damn! Someone had been in the woods watching Crystal. Someone who must have followed them there. Either that or Pace had told someone Crystal had left and had guessed she was with Damon.

He would kill the goddamn doctor if anything happened to Crystal.

Refusing to analyze the reason for his fury over a woman he'd just met, he swerved sideways to avoid a cat darting across the road. When he jumped out, he had his gun aimed and ready.

He scanned the outside of the house, the perimeter of the lot, then the trees skimming the edge of the backwoods that surrounded the property.

"He's gone, Agent Dubois."

Esmeralda's low but confident voice echoed from the front porch.

His gaze still tracked the shadows in the backwoods. He spotted a gator sliding up onto the bank in search of sunshine. A frog croaked nearby. Leaves rustled and a bird cawed shrilly. "How do you know?"

"I know," she said simply.

Lex had once told him that his grandmother had a second sight, that she delved in magic, but Damon didn't believe in that nonsense. Especially magic.

"I scared him away with my rifle," Esmeralda said. "The cats did the rest."

Damon made a grunting sound and turned to see Crystal watching him. She looked soft and beautiful in the dim early morning light, her dark hair floating around her shoulders like a waterfall. Was she his brother's lover? If not, who in the hell was she? "Are you all right?" he asked.

She nodded. "I don't understand why anyone would want to hurt me."

Neither did he, yet, but he would figure out the reason and protect her. "I can't leave you here now," he said. "It's too dangerous for you and Esmeralda."

"I'm not afraid." Esmeralda squared her bony shoulders.

Crystal slid an arm around the older woman's waist. "I appreciate that, but I could never forgive myself if something happened to you. This is my problem, my battle, not yours."

Damon kept one eye on the woods, searching the

shadows as he moved up the steps and took Crystal's hand. "You're not alone now, *chère*. We'll find the answers and the person after you."

CRYSTAL HAD BEEN A BUNDLE of nerves ever since she'd seen the figure lurking in the woods.

No, even before that when she'd read the newspaper article about the woman's murder. The sense of loss and grief intensified with each passing moment.

Esmeralda invited them both in for coffee, and Damon claimed a seat on the couch, accepting the mug and a tray of homemade apple bread and poppy-seed muffins. Crystal tried to nibble on a muffin, but could barely choke it down. "I saw the paper," she said. "What more do you know, Damon?"

He frowned and sipped the coffee. "We're working on an ID now."

"Do you have any clue as to who killed her?"

"Not yet." He paused, spread his knees and leaned his elbows on them. "It appears she was stabbed and bled to death, maybe a few weeks ago."

Crystal swallowed although dry bread crumbs stuck in her throat. "The paper said she was mutilated."

"Damn press," he muttered.

Crystal glanced at Esmeralda and realized the agent was leaving something out. "Tell me what's going on. I feel like I might have known this woman. I realize that sounds crazy, but maybe we'd met."

He hesitated. "I have a theory, but we need to talk to Dr. Pace again. I was on my way there when you called."

Crystal wiped her hands on a napkin. "Does that theory have to do with me?"

He gave her an odd look. "Maybe. I can't say yet."

"Then let's go."

"Are you sure you're up for it?" Damon asked.

"Yes. I can't move on with my life until I know the truth. All of it."

Esmeralda rose on wobbly legs, her back bowed as she cradled Crystal's hands in her own. "Remember what I said. Be strong, dear. This was meant to be."

"What was meant to be?" Crystal whispered, confused.

"You'll understand," was all Esmeralda said.

The tension was palpable as Crystal and the agent drove to the rehab hospital. Entering the gated compound this time gave her an eerie, almost claustrophobic feeling, as if she wanted to crawl out of her skin. Memories of the long agonizing months of surgeries and painful rehab taunted her. Her desperation to know her name and what had happened to her. Her growing dependence on the doctor's visits. On Lex's.

She wound her fingers together as they took the sterile corridor past the solarium to Dr. Pace's office. The place seemed empty, tomb-like. No patients were sitting in the garden area or game room.

Dr. Pace's eyes lit up when he saw her, and she had an uncanny sense that he was more than glad to see her. Maybe relieved?

Could he have known that someone was after her?

Menace filled Damon's narrowed eyes. "I want the truth, Pace. From beginning to end."

The plastic surgeon shifted nervously. "I don't know what you're talking about."

"Listen to me," Damon growled. "We found a dead woman in the bayou. A woman who had been stabbed so many times you couldn't see a section of skin that hadn't been pierced. We believe she's Kendra Yates, although forensics is trying to verify that now, and the coroner is checking dental records."

Pace visibly paled. "She had multiple stab wounds?"

"Yes, dammit. And not just multiple. This guy carved her up like a damn animal. He severed her hand and left it in the bayou for us to find as some kind of sick joke." Damon slammed his fist on Pace's desk, making his coffee cup rattle. "And she had her entire face removed, all the skin taken off completely."

Crystal's breath caught in her throat.

The Adam's apple bobbed in Pace's throat. "What makes you think I had something to do with her?"

"Because the facial skin was removed by someone who knew what he was doing. There was no violence about it, only carefully orchestrated surgical markings." He leaned closer, thrusting his face into Pace's. "And *you* were researching face transplant procedures."

Damon turned and gave Crystal a strange look, a mixture of regret and accusation. Crystal's stomach plummeted as she realized where he was headed. Denial rose in her throat.

Damon ignored her reaction and pressed on. "You took the skin off of the dead woman's face and transplanted it onto Crystal, didn't you?"

Pace's gaze flitted toward the door as if he wanted to run. "And what if I did? The skin came from a cadaver."

"Did you kill her to get her face?" Damon bellowed.

"No!" Pace screeched. "Don't be absurd. I'm a doctor, a healer, not a killer. She was already dead when I saw her."

"You can't just remove a face from a body. You knew her identity," Damon continued, "yet you didn't report her murder."

"That's not true." Pace wiped sweat from his forehead. "Crystal had been here for months, suffering, undergoing countless surgical procedures and skin grafts. Nothing was working." He turned and tried to reach for her, but Crystal backed away in horror. She was shaking all over now, nausea rising like a tidal wave inside her.

"Crystal, you were, had already rejected several skin grafts. In fact you were close to death from the last one. You'd not only rejected the tissue, but you had a terrible reaction. I was desperate, waiting on a donor. I had your information in the system looking for a match." He paced across the room, restless and fidgety. "When a Jane Doe, DOA, was brought in, I checked the tissue and she matched. I only had a short window of time to lift the skin and perform the surgery and didn't have time to ask questions, wait on the woman to be IDed and her family contacted."

"So you removed her skin without even trying to contact the family to get permission?" Agent Dubois snarled.

"I told you, there wasn't time—and *she was a Jane Doe*. Besides, Agent Dubois," Dr. Pace shouted as if legalities didn't matter when it came to science, "there was nothing else I could do for her." Pace's breathing had become erratic. "On the other hand, Crystal was on her death bed, so I took the opportunity." Again, he began to walk toward her, but she threw up a hand in warning.

She had to breathe deeply, felt as if she might pass out any minute.

"Who called you?" Damon asked.

"It was an anonymous tip."

"Who let you in to see the body?"

"I can't say."

Damon cursed. "If you saw her in the hospital, how the hell did she wind up in the bayou?"

"I don't know," the doctor cried.

"You're lying." Damon paced the room like a wild animal. He didn't believe the man, and Crystal didn't know what to think.

"No, it's true. When I finished, I left her body in the morgue," Pace said, although his voice warbled. "I assumed she would be buried as a Jane Doe."

"What about other doctors? Nurses? Can they verify your story?"

"No, it was late, everyone had gone for the night. I... You know how I work, Dubois. Information is dispensed on a need-to-know basis, and there was no need for me to know her identity or what happened to her later. I assumed she was a criminal or a witness who'd been killed. That they got rid of the body quietly." A vein throbbed in his forehead. "Obviously someone took her body though and dumped it in the bayou."

"At the very place she was murdered," Damon said. "Her dried blood was all over the shanty."

Crystal stared at the man in horror.

"When did you perform the transplant?" Damon asked.

Pace glanced at Crystal. "About three weeks ago."

Damon frowned. The timing might fit.

Pace raced to Crystal, grabbed her hands. "Don't look at me like I'm the bad guy, Crystal. I'm your friend, the man who saved your life, the man who sat by your side during your darkest hours, consoled you and promised to make you beautiful. And I did." His eyes flitted in different directions, wild with emotions. "I made you what you are, made you able to face the world, made you the perfect woman."

He sounded almost demented. "I appreciate everything you did for me, Reginald," Crystal said shakily. "But you lied to me, should have told me the truth. In fact, you kept me isolated here, and now I know the reason."

"But I love you," he said in a pleading tone. "You're my model, the example of how successful the face transplant can be. I want to show you off."

Crystal jerked her hands free. This man who she'd thought was her friend, who'd comforted her, who'd saved her life, had lied to her so many times.

She didn't trust him *now*.

SUSPICIONS CLOUDED Damon's mind. He didn't know whether to believe Pace or not. He'd been on the underside of similar clandestine missions and cases before, and it was possible Pace was telling the truth.

Then again, he was a consummate liar.

Just as Damon had been when he'd worked with the E-team.

So many secrets. Tell and you die.

Their other mantra—*Never leave a witness alive.*

If Kendra Yates had dug so deeply she'd discovered information on a government cover-up or a dirty cop, someone might have ordered her extermination.

One of his own from the E-team could have done the job.

But if so, why allow her body to resurface at all? And why the mutilation? The E-team wouldn't have used such obvious violence—not the team *he* knew. It didn't make sense....

"Why perform plastic surgery to make Crystal look like a murder victim?" Damon asked, struggling with the logic and details of Pace's story.

Pace inhaled sharply. "The transplant wasn't supposed to make the patient look like the donor. Using a cadaver requires only lifting the skin. The facial construction, bone and muscle structure, etcetera, is unique with each individual, meaning the skin molds to it to give a different appearance. But Crystal's bone structure was so similar..."

"That she resembles her," Agent Dubois finished.

He scrubbed a hand through his hair. "You do realize that if Kendra was murdered because of something she'd seen or knew, then Crystal may be in danger just because she looks like her."

Pace frowned. "I suppose that's a possibility."

Damon grilled him a few minutes longer but got nowhere. Finally, he turned to Crystal. She looked shell-shocked, as if she might be ill. He didn't blame her.

Not only was she a carbon copy of the murder victim, but the victim's killer might be after her.

Then again, he had no ID on Crystal yet, no way of knowing if she had her own enemies....

His contacts at the bureau or the E-team might know. But what if alerting them to the fact that she was still alive led the wrong people to her door?

Hell, he couldn't protect her if he didn't know what he was up against.

She was the first person in months, maybe years, to make him want to live, to continue fighting the evil.

He would give his life to protect her.

HE GRIPPED THE PHONE and listened to Pace rant with a smile on his face. The man was in a panic. He was also obsessed with getting the woman back and thought he was in love with her.

Laughter erupted from deep in his belly. Love?

What the hell was that? Emotion only interfered with business. Turned men sloppy. Caused them to make mistakes.

And he did not have room for mistakes in the game. Not when he was so close to exacting his revenge.

The Dubois family had to pay for his suffering.

They had robbed him of a life and given it to their own boys. At least that was what they called them.

He poured himself a stiff whiskey and studied the photos of each of the victims of the first mutilator, admiring the man's handiwork, noting the lack of control in his first carvings versus the total and absolute precision he had used on later victims. One by one he stabbed the pictures with his knife, then jammed a thumbtack into the center and pinned them to the wall beside his bed.

Defense wounds marked the first victim's hands—the hands that belonged to the mutilator's mother. He must have been a young teenager when he'd killed her.

The next two women's hands held similar wounds, yet by the third, he'd learned to tie the victim spread-eagle first. Though his thrusts had been sloppy and jagged in the beginning, the mutilator had eventually perfected his technique, learning to begin with small one-inch slashes that barely scored the woman's skin. Then, each cut had pierced deeper and deeper until he'd severed muscle and tendons. Finally he'd ripped into the internal organs. Blood, guts—the woman's insides had spilled out onto the floor, then the mutilator had spread his hands in the blood and smeared it on the walls, painting a mural with his destruction.

He went down the row, counting the victims until he came to the fifth woman. Pale white skin like milk. Honey-colored hair. Eyes the color of an angel's.

Yet the devil often danced in disguise, and so had this woman or else the mutilator wouldn't have killed her.

Ironic though. Before her death, she had given birth to the mutilator's son.

He licked his lips, picked up a photo of *his* first mutilation and grinned.

And he'd make sure the Duboises saw the fruits of his handiwork.

Laughing hysterically, he slid the photos into a manila envelope and carried them to his car. He'd drop them off now. They thought they'd been hurting before.

Now their suffering would truly begin.

Like father like son—yes, he would make Daddy proud.

CHAPTER THIRTEEN

CRYSTAL'S STOMACH ROILED as Agent Dubois escorted her to his sedan and they drove away from the rehab center. She clenched her purse, thinking about the antirejection meds the doctor had given her. Dr. Pace's admission about the face transplant replayed in her head as she tried to assimilate his story. He claimed he'd taken Kendra's face to save Crystal's life.

But who had killed the woman? Was he lying about not knowing?

How did she come to be at the center?

Damon steered the vehicle onto the highway then slid a hand over hers. His fingers felt warm to the touch, a lifeline she desperately needed right now.

"Are you all right?" he asked in a gruff voice.

Her chest heaved up and down as she tried to gather a breath. "I don't know."

"I'm sorry I had to do that to you," he said with a grimace. "When I saw the woman's mutilated body, especially her face, I started putting two and two together."

Her heart capitulated. "You thought I knew?"

His dark look skated over her, unreadable and pinning her to the seat. "I had to be sure."

Anger mingled with hurt and disbelief. "You thought I might have had something to do with Kendra's death? That I had her killed so I could trade my life for hers?"

"No, nothing like that," he said. "I just… I don't know what I thought. But I didn't want to tell you about the face transplant if it wasn't true."

A deadly quiet descended between them, fraught with the truth and the questions still plaguing her about her identity and how she'd gotten caught up in this bizarre situation. She lifted her free hand and touched her cheek, felt her body shudder, her skin tingle. Guilt engulfed her. Just thinking about her face coming from a cadaver repulsed her. And poor Kendra…

Agent Dubois's cell phone rang, and he flipped it open. "Special Agent Dubois."

His jaw tightened, and he suddenly sped up. "I'll meet you at the restaurant."

He flipped the phone closed with a curse.

"What's wrong?" Crystal asked.

"That was my father. The press are all over my parents' restaurant. And someone sent them disturbing photos. My mother opened them."

Crystal clutched the door handle as he flew

around a Toyota and accelerated, weaving in and out of traffic as they neared New Orleans. Although it was early afternoon, tourists crowded the streets for late lunches, celebrating the summer and upcoming Memorial Day weekend. Along with colorful flowers, flags adorned the streets, and small markers along the edges of the sidewalks boasted the names of fallen soldiers being honored with the holiday. Jazz and zydeco music floated from nearby cafés and restaurants, and Bourbon Street already held its share of partyers sipping beer, margaritas and cocktails. Local artisans sold their wares, a hodgepodge of various art forms, sketches of the city, Mardi Gras masks, voodoo dolls, beads, scenes of the French Quarter and gator souvenirs.

Agent Dubois parked, climbed out, came around to her side and opened the door.

The heat and stench of stale beer, cigarette smoke and sweat permeated the air as they wove through the crowded street. Damon was right about the press mob. Several reporters flanked the door of the café, driving any potential customers away with their questions, while a small group had gathered with signs condemning the Dubois's son as a murderer. Damon curved an arm around her waist and ushered her through the crowd, trying to avoid another reporter who pounced on him, shouting questions and accusations.

Damon muttered, "No comment," then pushed her inside the door.

Just then one of the reporters shouted, "She looks like Kendra Yates!"

The reporter snapped her photo, and Damon slammed the door. She leaned against the wall, breathing heavily, trying to compose herself. But a middle-aged man appeared, his dark thinning hair spiked, his forehead furrowed with worry. He embraced Damon.

"Thank you for coming so quickly, son."

Damon pulled back. "Is *Maman* okay?"

"Yes, I called Jean-Paul, too. The pictures… They're horrible, Damon. Your *maman* did not need to see this."

Damon gestured toward Crystal. "Papa, this is Crystal. She's the woman I told you about."

"*Oui,* hello." He wiped his hand on an apron, then extended it and shook her hand, his eyes narrowing as he studied her. "Sorry to meet you under these circumstances." He glanced back at his son as if confirming how much she resembled Kendra, but was polite enough to refrain from comment.

Then he led them through the café. Crystal couldn't help but admire the New Orleans artwork—charcoal sketches and watercolors of the market, Mardi Gras, the bayou, and a series of hand-painted masks. Above the hostesses' stand a mix of family

photos were displayed, several of Damon and his
brothers in military uniforms. A large bulletin board
also held signed photos of families who'd donated
toward a hurricane relief fund sponsored by the café.
Heavenly smells of Cajun dishes filled the air, along
with the scent of chicory coffee, beignets and rich,
dark chocolate.

But the atmosphere faded as Crystal spotted Damon's mother bent over the sleek oak bar crying as
she stared at photos of a woman lying on blood-
stained sheets.

At least Crystal thought they were of a woman.

She'd never seen anything so gruesome and vile.
Blood coated the body parts, flowed in a river around
the woman's chest, formed a puddle beneath her
head. The body had been cut so many times that
the flesh had literally been carved away, exposing
jagged, splintered bones and organs.

The early nausea she'd been battling rose to her
throat, then she spotted the number one printed at the
top of the photo and froze in renewed horror.

Number *one*—there would be more.

JUDGING FROM THE PHOTOGRAPH, Damon knew that
this victim was *not* the same one they had found in
the bayou—it was of another crime. From the setting, discoloration of the photo and the quality, the
picture had probably been taken years ago, which

meant the crime was an old one. Details of the cuts were different, too. Tentative slices marred the upper torso, and defense wounds scarred the victim's arms indicating she had not been tied down during the assault. She had fought back.

The recent victim hadn't had a chance to fight. She'd been tied spread-eagle. Although she had struggled against the bindings—rope burns on her ankles and wrists revealed how desperately she'd clawed to free herself.

The number one either meant she was a victim of the first mutilator or the first victim in a series of many.

Did they have a copycat serial killer on their hands now?

Damon swallowed back fury at the bastard's audacity in sending photos to his parents. His mother's face was streaked with tears and horror, while his father looked haggard, torn between comforting Daniella and controlling his own anger and disgust over the photos. Why had the killer sent these snapshots to his folks instead of to him or the press?

He wanted to torture the family....

Sick, sadistic bastard. His mother hadn't needed to witness this. And his father...Damon worried about his heart.

Jean-Paul suddenly burst into the restaurant and raced toward his parents. "Where are the pictures?"

Damon gestured toward the bar, and Jean-Paul noticed Crystal and paused as if he'd seen a ghost. "Damn, she does look like Kendra Yates."

Crystal bit down on her lip, and Damon reached for her, feeling protective and certain she was an innocent victim.

She sank onto a stool, and his mother roused from her shocked state, introduced herself, then offered everyone coffee or tea. Crystal asked for water, and his mother jumped into the task as if she needed something to do to distract her from the sight of those hideous pictures. Damon walked behind the bar and slid a comforting hand to his mother's back while Jean-Paul studied the pictures.

"*Maman,* I'm sorry you had to see those."

His mother's hand trembled as she tucked her curly dark hair into her bun. "*Oui.* What do you think it means, Damon? That the person who committed that murder is the same one who killed Kendra Yates?"

"I don't know. I'm going to search the system when we leave and find out where that photo was taken, where and when the murder occurred, and if the killer was ever caught." He handed Crystal the water, hating the pallor of her complexion, then paused, leaned against the counter and spoke to his mother again. "Depending on how old this case is, maybe the killer is someone Antwaun knew or crossed and they're setting him up. Although, that photo looks years old…"

He'd never seen his mother look so distressed. Although, *bon Dieu*, she'd just personally received photos of a brutal murder scene. Of course she'd be upset.

Another thought occurred to him, and he addressed both his parents. "*Maman*, Papa, do you remember anything about a similar case occurring here in New Orleans in the past?"

His father poured himself coffee, working his jaw from side to side, then moved closer to stand beside Damon's *maman*. "No, not that I recall."

"New Orleans has had many brutal crimes over the years," his mother said, her hand fluttering about her face nervously. "I can't even think straight right now."

Damon nodded, although his parents both seemed really off.

He grimaced, disgusted with himself. He'd been working cases and dealing with the dregs of society so long now that he was doubting his own family. For God's sake, they wanted to help free Antwaun more than anyone.

They would have absolutely no reason to lie.

As HARRY CONNICK JR.'S DEEP voice filled the room, Crystal watched the interplay between Agent Dubois and his family with envy. This family obviously cared a great deal for one another. Judging from the pictures on the wall, and the articles about each of the sons and the hurricane, they'd had troubles but managed to stick together. One article revealed that the Duboises' first business had been destroyed during the storms. Damon's oldest brother Jean-Paul had also been married previously and had lost his wife in the midst of Katrina. But apparently the family had somehow pulled together, rebuilt their home and business, and now, even in this terrible crisis, seemed to be working together, supporting one another.

A well of sadness threatened to engulf her. Did she not have any family herself? If so, why weren't they doing everything possible to find her?

Had she done something to make them not love her? Had nobody *ever* loved her?

Was that the reason she couldn't remember? Because she'd committed a horrible act, maybe caused someone's death, and she didn't want to face herself or them again?

"Crystal, we're going to the precinct now," Agent Dubois said. "I want to research this photograph."

"I'll meet you there," Jean-Paul said. "I phoned Stephanie and she's coming by to stay with *Maman* and Papa."

"I told Catherine to keep Chrissy away." Mrs.

Dubois gestured at the empty restaurant. "It looks like we're not going to have any business today anyway."

The men nodded grimly, and Crystal slid off the bar stool and stood beside Damon.

"I can take you to a hotel to rest," Damon offered.

"No, I'd like to go with you." She jutted up her chin, determination kicking in. "Somehow I'm involved in all this, and I need to know how."

His look of sympathy touched her but also hardened her. She was beginning to really like this man, to want to know him better. Someday, to have a relationship with him. But that was impossible until she learned her identity. For all she knew, she had a lover or a husband somewhere.

Her heart squeezed, and she could hardly breathe as her nightmarish images returned. An image of a man dying beside her, his cold eyes staring up at her. An explosion rocked the world around her, and flames suddenly engulfed his clothes. She'd screamed and then…the world had gone black.

Don't die, don't die….

Those two words again. That deep throaty voice pleading with her to live.

Had they been spoken by the man dying beside her? Someone else?

She gripped the edge of the bar, struggling to make the image/memory return, for more details or clues as to her name, the man's name, but the memory disappeared into the dark cavern of her mind as fast as it had come.

Only it left her more troubled than ever, with more questions. The man who'd died had been someone she'd cared for once.

And somehow his death had been her fault.

DAMON HAD COAXED CRYSTAL into sitting in Jean-Paul's office at the police department. Hoping the picture was from a prior case, he consulted the FBI databases for the photo's origin.

Jean-Paul hung up his phone and turned to Damon. "I have a lead on a teller that may have been involved in helping arrange that phony account in Antwaun's name. I'm going to talk to her now."

Damon nodded, although his attention was focused on the data spilling onto his screen. He'd checked for current cases with a similar MO across the States but had come up empty. Then he'd plugged in the photo his parents had received, and had hit pay dirt. "Look at this, Jean-Paul."

Jean-Paul stood and craned his neck to look over his brother's shoulder while Damon summarized the contents out loud.

"This crime goes back thirty years. A serial killer the police called the Mutilator killed twelve women in a year's time before he was caught. After interrogating the suspect, they learned the man's first kill had been his very own mother when he was thirteen years old."

Photos of each of the man's murder victims scrolled across the screen, each one more bloody and gory than the last, indicating the man's violent tendencies and bloodlust had escalated with each crime. A true sociopath—a man who loved to kill.

"His name is Frederick Fenton," Damon continued.

Jean-Paul muttered a curse. "Says here that he plead guilty. He's a lifer in the state pen in Angola now."

"He should have received the death penalty," Damon said.

"Yeah, but the deal saved him. In exchange for life, he told them where he'd left four bodies they hadn't found at the time of his arrest."

"I say we take a trip to Angola and visit Mr. Fenton tomorrow. Maybe he can tell us who's copying him now. And why they sent the picture to our parents."

Jean-Paul nodded. "Set it up. I'm going to go talk to this bank teller and see if she can fill us in on who's framing our little brother."

"Anything on Smith yet?" Damon asked.

Jean-Paul nodded. "He had some trouble at his former precinct. I'm still working on the details."

Damon sighed. Maybe Smith was the guy.

He glanced up to see Crystal studying the photographs. "My God, that man is sick." She placed a hand on Damon's shoulder, and regrets for the killer he had once been shot through him.

"I don't know how you do this job," she said softly.

Sometimes he didn't know either. But he'd vowed long ago to fight the bad guys and he had to keep at it.

The soft pressure of her hand against him made him hot. He wanted to turn and take her in his arms, shield her from seeing any more of the vile side that consumed his life.

But she needed more than that from him. She needed answers and so did he. The truth might be the only way to protect her. He'd promised to help her find out more about herself, so he entered the date Pace claimed he'd found her at the hospital and ran a check on automobile accidents that might match the one that had injured her.

She sat down beside him, her gaze intent on the screen, her hands knotted in her lap. Tension stretched between them as they waited for the information. Several reports of accidents during that week appeared, but none involved a woman being burned.

"I don't see anything," Crystal said in a strained voice.

"Maybe Pace had the dates wrong." He punched in dates ranging from three months prior to and after the time Pace had given him, and they scanned through each of them, but again no Jane Doe had been found or taken to a hospital as a result of a car explosion.

"Do you think that someone covered up my accident?" she asked.

Damon scrubbed a hand through his hair. "I don't know. It's possible."

"You said you'd worked with Dr. Pace before. That he performs facial reconstructions and helps witnesses and people in the WITSEC program obtain new identities. Do you think that's what happened to me?"

"I asked my partner at the bureau to check out that angle, but so far I haven't heard anything."

"Damon, I...had a flash of a memory," she said quietly.

He pivoted to study her. "What did you remember?"

She bit down on her lip as if afraid to tell him, then exhaled sharply. "I was looking at a car exploding, into the eyes of a dead man."

His heart rate picked up. He wished he could comfort her. "Crystal...it's all right."

She stood, shook her head savagely and turned away. "No, you don't understand. I...think it was my fault that the man was dead." Her voice warbled and when she spun back to face him, tears glittered in her eyes. "What if I killed him? What if I caused the accident and the fire? What if I don't remember because I'm a *murderer?*"

CRYSTAL WAS SHAKING all over. Ever since she'd had the brief flash of memory, her guilt had mounted inside. She knew she was responsible, that she had hurt someone she'd loved, that they were dead because of her.

"Crystal, shh." Damon gripped her arms. "You are not a murderer," he said, stroking her arms up and down. "Trust me, I've seen killers, I know how they think, how they act, how they behave. And I've been with you long enough to know that you have never and could never hurt anyone."

"But I *did,*" Crystal cried. "I saw this man's eyes looking at me with accusations as he died."

He traced a finger along her jaw, then pressed it over her lips. "You're remembering something completely out of context, maybe even jumbling different memories that may or may not be related."

A sob caught in her throat. "I'm scared, Damon."

He pulled her into his arms and held her. "I know, *chère,* but it's going to be all right. I promise."

She wanted to believe him, wanted him to keep holding her and comforting her, to make her believe that her nightmares weren't real.

"Trust me," he murmured as he stroked her hair from her cheek.

She lifted her hand to his face and pressed it to his jaw. "I do. I trust you. But what if I'm a killer, or I've done something horrible and I deserve to go to jail?"

"Then I wouldn't feel like this toward you," he said. "I wouldn't want you so damn much."

His admission sparked a fire in her belly and she clung to his arms. His brown eyes searched hers, filled with promises, but also with hints of the darkness and pain he'd seen in his job, the criminals he had dealt with. Like the one that had killed the woman whose face she now wore.

A shudder rippled through her, and he hugged her again, their bodies pressed tightly together, heat thrumming through hers, her heart racing.

Then he pulled away abruptly, breathing deeply as if he, too, had too keenly felt the burning need and wanted to act upon it.

She felt instantly bereft as he released her. He shut down his computer, packed it up with his phone, then turned back to her. "Come on, you've been through enough today. I'm taking you home."

"Home?" If only she knew where that was.

He nodded. "To my house. You'll be safe and can rest there."

She didn't want rest. And she didn't want safe if it meant he was pulling away from her again. She wanted all the things she couldn't have. More moments in his arms. Him kissing her and holding her all night.

Him naked and making love to her while he whispered her real, unknown name.

DAMON FELT OUT OF CONTROL. Never in his life had he been so driven to protect a woman, to soothe her pain and make love to her. Images of taking Crystal to his bed drove him to press the speed limit as he headed to his house. He imagined stripping off her clothes, unveiling the lush body he knew waited beneath.

In his mind, he felt her mouth beneath his lips, saw her nipples stiffening as he twisted them in his fingers, felt her foot glide up to tease his calf, felt the soft skin of her inner thigh as he parted her legs and slid his fingers into her wetness there, felt her body quiver as he thrust inside her and drove her mad with his cock.

Bon Dieu! What was wrong with him? He should be focusing on this case. Lust was making him insane.

So insane that he hadn't been paying attention, and a car suddenly darted from the side road, nearly blinding him with his lights. It roared toward him and slammed into the passenger side. Crystal screamed; his car skidded into a tailspin as a shot pierced his front window and cracked the glass.

CHAPTER FOURTEEN

ANOTHER SHOT HIT THE side of the car. Crystal screamed again, and Damon reached out to shield her, pushing her head to her knees. "Holy hell! Get down!"

Damon swerved and tires squealed as he spun the car around and headed away from the shooter, but the car raced up behind him, lights bright. Night had fallen and with it the shadows of the woods along the deserted road. He sped up, but the car rammed into him—metal skimmed along the guardrail, sending sparks flying. Damon grappled for control, but they were hit again and his sedan skidded toward the river.

"Hold on!" he yelled to Crystal.

Another shot pinged off the driver's side, and he fumbled for his gun, praying that he could hold the car on the road and fire in retaliation.

But the car rammed them again, he lost control and the sedan screeched and rolled. The air bags deployed, slamming him back into the seat and jerking his neck so hard he thought it had broken. He couldn't do anything, much less see if Crystal was all right.

Glass shattered; brakes squealed; metal screeched and buckled; and car parts splintered off, flying across the asphalt as they skated into the swampland. Mud and water gurgled and sucked at the car, pulling them under.

Damon dug his knife from his pocket, flipped it open and cut away the air bag. He unfastened his seat belt and ripped at the air bag blocking Crystal. "Crystal?"

Her eyes were closed, her mouth slack. He couldn't tell if she was breathing and terror streaked through him.

"Don't die on me, Crystal," he pleaded as he patted her cheek. "Please, dear God, don't die."

She moaned and slowly opened her eyes, although they appeared glassy and disoriented. "Crystal," he said gruffly. "Are you all right? Can you move your arms and legs?"

A whimper tore from her throat, but she nodded. "I think so."

Blood trickled down her arm, but he couldn't see the source. "We have to get out of here."

She nodded, then her eyes widened as a water moccasin slithered across the broken window.

"Damon! It's coming inside…"

"Be still and hold on." Rage swelled inside him

as he jiggled the seat belt, but the damn thing was stuck.

She struggled as well, her breathing ragged as the muddy Mississippi rose and churned around them. The snake slithered across the splintered front window, and she recoiled against Damon.

"Shh, we'll make it," he said softly as he began sawing away her seat belt.

"I h-hate snakes," she whispered. "Please, Damon…"

"I've got you."

With one deft movement, he flipped his wrist and sliced the snake in two, then threw it away from the car toward the embankment.

"Come on." He used the butt of his gun to push out the front glass pane, which barely clung to the frame. Muddy water and debris seeped in, rising fast. He crawled through it then turned and pulled Crystal through the opening. Shoving at a tree branch, he helped her slog through the murky knee-high grass, weeds and muck-filled water. Somewhere in the distance, a gator slid into the river with a splash; another snake hissed from a tree, his tongue darting in and out as he wound down the limbs overhanging their crossing. Bugs nipped at Damon's face and arms, and he refused to think about what was chewing at his legs beneath the water. Crystal trembled as he dragged

her up the embankment to the woods bordering
the highway. He searched the dark, but the car had
disappeared.

"Who ran us off the road?" Crystal said as she
sank onto the grass and began to frantically flail off
the grime, bugs and nasty leeches.

Damon kicked them off his boots with a curse.

"Damon?"

"I don't know," he growled, hating the tiny sound
of her voice. "But when I find him, I'm going to kill
the motherfucker with my bare hands."

THE NEXT HOUR RUSHED BY in a blur. Damon dragged
Crystal behind a cluster of trees to hide in case the
shooter returned. Amazingly, he'd kept his phone dry,
so he called his brother for help. Still furious, he
removed his handkerchief and wiped the blood dotting her arm where a shard of glass had pricked it, but
she insisted that she was fine and didn't need stitches.
She only wanted a shower and a safe place to hide.

It seemed she'd been hiding the last few months.
Hiding from others. From herself.

And now from a killer.

Was he after her because of her own past, or
because she had Kendra Yates's face? Or maybe the
shooter wanted to kill Damon to scare him off the investigation which might save his brother?

Damon kept a vigil watch in case the car that had

hit them returned, while Crystal huddled beside him, holding her breath each time a vehicle passed.

Finally a black sedan slowed and pulled to the side of the road, and Damon clutched her hand. "Come on, it's Jean-Paul."

She nodded and raced toward the vehicle, clinging to Damon. He ushered her inside the backseat, grabbed a blanket from his brother and wrapped it around her before climbing into the front with Jean-Paul.

Minutes later, two more police cars arrived, along with a crime scene unit and tow truck.

"What the hell happened?" Jean-Paul asked.

"Some son of a bitch shot at us and ran me off the road."

"Did you get a license? Make of the car? Anything?"

Damon shook his head, his face a mask of anger. "No, dammit, he came out of nowhere. Pushed us into the river, then left us for dead."

Jean-Paul glanced at Crystal over his shoulder. "Do you need a doctor?"

"No," she said. "Just a place to get cleaned up. And maybe some clothes."

"Damon?" Jean-Paul asked. "Are you all right, man?"

Emotion hardened Jean-Paul's voice, and her heart clenched. The brothers obviously loved one another dearly. She ached for that kind of love from family.

From anybody.

From Damon.

No, she couldn't allow herself to fantasize or dream about his love when she had no idea if she'd done something to bring this danger on him.

For all she knew, she might be the reason he'd almost been killed.

The realization sobered her and renewed her resolve to uncover her identity. If she were to blame, she'd pay the consequences. She wouldn't allow this strong, wonderful man or his family to be hurt because of her.

DAMON GLANCED BACK at Crystal to make sure she was okay, his heart clenching at the fear still darkening her pale green eyes. Anger at the person who'd nearly killed them surged through him again, and he balled his hands into knots.

"Stay here, Crystal. I have to talk to the police."

She nodded while he and Jean-Paul got out, then he explained to Jean-Paul's partner, Carson, and the other officers what had happened.

"I want the car impounded," Jean-Paul said. "And we need that bullet casing."

"I'll make sure it gets to forensics myself," Carson assured him.

For a moment, Damon wondered if he should trust Carson, but, remembering that his brother trusted him put him at ease.

The crime-scene unit began to photograph the highway, skid marks and place where Damon's vehicle had slid into the river, while the tow truck team hooked up equipment to extricate his car from the swamp.

Jean-Paul conferred with his partner again, then offered to drive Damon and Crystal home. Crystal remained quiet, huddled inside the blanket as they drove along the deserted bayou road, and Damon kept scanning the highway in the wild hope he'd see the shooter return.

"I questioned that teller, Damon," Jean-Paul said. "She didn't want to talk, but I pushed her, and she admitted that she'd set up the phony account with Antwaun's name on it. She claims she was being blackmailed."

"By who?" Damon asked.

"She doesn't know. Says she got an anonymous call saying her father was embezzling from his construction company and that the police were about to come down on him, but this guy could make it go away if she did him this one favor."

"Can you trace the person who called her?"

"I'm working on it now."

Damon brushed at wet leaves clinging to his shirt. "If you need help from my guys, just let me know."

"Thanks. Maybe forensics will turn up something," Jean-Paul said.

He wove down the long clamshelled drive to Damon's house and parked. "I'll ask Britta to put together some clothes and things for Crystal," Jean-Paul said.

"Thanks, man." Damon climbed out, then opened the door and extended his hand to help Crystal. She clutched the blanket around her shoulders and their gazes locked, a moment of tension traveling between them that nearly sucked the air from his lungs. His adrenaline was churning, making him want a physical release by pounding somebody.

The look she gave him screamed with the same need.

Jean-Paul cleared his throat. "I'll drop that bag off in the morning."

"Good." Damon jerked his gaze back to his brother to find a half smile splitting his face. What was he grinning about? Had he guessed Damon's thoughts?

Probably. Hell, he hadn't exactly been subtle.

"I'll have some new wheels sent over in the morning, too," Jean-Paul said.

That reminded Damon to ask him to get Crystal a new cell phone, too. Then, he hugged his brother and led Crystal into his house. Darkness bathed the interior, the night sounds of the swamp playing their symphony in the background accompanied by the soft lull of the Mississippi lapping against the bank. He left the curtains closed and simply flipped on a lamp as they entered the mudroom. He kicked off his boots, and she did the same with her sandals.

"I'll show you to the guest room so you can shower," he said, while his hands itched to touch her.

"Thank you, Damon."

He nodded, although she might not thank him if she knew the dangerous train of thought racing through his head. Still, while she showered, he'd be fantasizing about her naked body and washing her off himself.

CRYSTAL SENSED A DEEP anger radiating from Damon, but the strong chemistry between them overrode any questions in her mind. She wanted to be with him tonight, wanted him to hold her and kiss her and make her forget that a killer had just tried to take their lives.

He showed her up the spiral hardwood staircase to a guest room furnished with a Jenny Lind–style bed draped in an old-fashioned white chenille bedspread, it looked like something his mother must have given him. She wondered what his room was like and pictured it in masculine shades of deep reds and blues or greens. And the room would smell of him, all masculine energy and strength, power and control. Sex appeal and utter desire.

Her body quivered with need as she closed the bathroom door behind her and turned on the shower water.

Soft fluffy towels of yellow and green were

draped over pewter rods, and a plush white terry cloth bathrobe hung from a hook on the door. Probably also compliments of his mother or sisters.

Or maybe Damon had a lover or girlfriend?

The thought unsettled her more than she wanted to admit. Then again, if he did, he'd certainly made no mention or effort to call her.

No, the man was a loner. Obsessed with his job.

Which she had to remember. Once he helped her discover her identity, he'd leave her and go on with his life. And she'd be…where? Alone again?

Maybe in jail if the guilt weighing on her proved to be correct.

The hot water sluicing over her bare skin felt heavenly, and she closed her eyes, imagined Damon stepping inside, his strong, blunt fingers tracing a path of fire along her body where the hot water now pulsed. Her nipples beaded and a pool of moisture welled between her thighs. She almost gave into temptation, rolled her hips and let the water do the rest, but the satisfaction of an arousal being quenched so quickly was not what she wanted. It would make her feel even emptier.

She wanted Damon Dubois's hands and mouth on her. Wanted to feel him inside her making her whole again.

Tortured by the fantasies and driven by the need to see him again, she quickly scrubbed the grime from her body, banishing the memory of the bugs and leeches that had assaulted her earlier as the bubbles beaded on her skin. She shampooed her hair and conditioned it, wondering if Damon had chosen the sweet scent himself. Maybe with a woman in mind.

A thrill shot through her, and she rinsed off, dried her body and pulled on the robe. After towel-drying her hair, she left it loose around her shoulders, then found a pair of white bedroom slippers still inside a package beside the bed and put them on.

When she opened the door, the sultry sound of a saxophone echoed from below. The music was so beautiful that at first she thought it was a CD, but as she descended the stairs, she spotted Damon on the balcony through the French doors that stood open letting in the night air. Moonlight spilled across his handsome features, and his thick dark hair was still damp. So was his bare chest. Her mouth literally watered at the sight. Then her gaze dipped lower to the waistband of his jeans where they hung low on his lean hips, jeans that showcased muscular thighs and a washboard stomach that stirred heat in her belly.

But it was the hypnotic wail of the blues tune that he played with his own hands and lips that drew her, and made her heart clench. The song reeked of pain and loneliness, emotions she knew well.

Desperately wanting to touch him, wanting more, she slowly walked through the den. Noted the stack of jazz and blues albums he'd collected, the photos of famous New Orleans musicians, a photo of him and his brothers when they were teenagers playing in a band. Mesmerized by his hands and mouth on the instrument, she stepped outside, never taking her eyes off his fingers as he stroked the keys or his lips curled around the mouthpiece. Heat spread through her in an erotic wave of sensations. God help her, but she felt his music and pain deep in her soul. And she wanted those fingers and lips on her, bringing her pleasure just as she would do for him.

His head was thrown back, his eyes closed, his heart pouring into the music. Then he seemed to realize she was there and opened his eyes. The raw pain and need in his expression sent liquid fire sizzling through her veins.

"Damon…that was beautiful."

"Go to bed, Crystal."

His gruff voice reeked of hunger. A smile curved her mouth. She'd almost died tonight. She felt daring and risky and way more alive than she'd felt in months. And she wanted him. Everything he could give.

Even if it was only a kiss.

No, that wouldn't be enough. Not of this man.

DAMON PRAYED CRYSTAL WOULD follow his command because his willpower dwindled with every second she stared at him like that. But the look of desire in her eyes told him she was reckless and needy; he recognized the signs.

"I understand what you're feeling, Crystal," he said, wrapping his hands tighter around the saxophone to keep from grabbing her. "Danger heightens adrenalin. It's a rush that makes you want to do something wild."

He set the instrument down on the inside of the door, and turned away from her to stare at the woods, battling for restraint. "It's not me you want, but human contact. That's all."

"No." She shook her head. "It's you."

"My *chère*." His groan of denial filled the air.

"You want it, too," she whispered. Then she shocked him by moving up behind him, by sliding her arms around his waist, by leaning her face against his bare back and pressing kisses to his skin. He bit his tongue to stifle a moan of pleasure, willing himself to be strong.

"I can feel your hunger, Damon. Your body is hot beneath my hands," she said softly.

"That doesn't make it right." He cleared his throat, pointed to the shadows streaking the backwoods. "There are gators out there that would eat you alive, other monsters in the city that would, too. Both tried to kill us tonight."

"But we're safe now, and…I want to be in your arms."

He stiffened. Nothing about him taking her would be right. He was a federal agent working a case. She had amnesia, might have a husband or boyfriend looking for her, or even a child who needed her.

"It's my job to protect you, to help you find out who you are," he said roughly.

"I just want tonight," she said softly.

Bon Dieu, avoir pitié! She was offering him a way out. He was such a bastard he wanted to take her, but he couldn't.

She threaded her fingers through the back of his hair, moved around in front of him and kissed his neck. He had to think about Antwaun. "You look like the woman my brother is accused of murdering," he said, hating to hurt her, but determined to do the right thing. "The woman he was in love with."

She tensed, her breath bathing his bare chest, heating his skin. "But I'm not her," she whispered with a longing in her voice that echoed his own thoughts. "I know that. I…felt nothing when I saw your brother, not like I do when I'm with you."

Her sultry admission shredded his resolve, and he snapped.

In one fierce move, he jerked her in his arms, kissed her savagely, ran his hands through her hair, over her shoulders, down her back. His tongue coaxed her mouth open, teased her lips, danced inside, exploring the deep recesses of her mouth. She met his thrust with her own desire, running her hands over his back, moaning into him, then pressing her heat against his rock-hard erection.

Red-hot fire ripped through him, shot through his veins, made him inch his fingers back to cup her breasts in his hands. They felt heavy, and she groaned as if aching for him. Her hunger triggered his own lust, and he tore open the robe and licked his way from her chin down to the tight buds of her nipples, which stood pouty and swollen, begging for his taste.

He licked each one, flicked them with his tongue, caught one in his mouth and suckled it until her legs buckled, and she clutched his arms and groaned.

"I want you, Damon. I've never felt so hot and needy."

Neither had he. And it scared him to death.

But he'd been dead for months now. And she was life in his arms.

He sucked her other breast, traced his fingers down her belly to her mound. Toyed with the soft curls at the juncture of her thighs, parted her legs with his hand and thrust a finger inside her. She was wet, willing, moaning his name, pleading for him not to stop.

He plunged another finger deep inside her, then teased her nipples again, pumping his fingers in and out of her slick wet opening until she quivered, and he felt her body clench around him. She clung to him, crying his name, begging him for more, and he deepened the thrusts until she fell apart in his arms.

She kissed him frantically, pushed at his jeans to remove them. But a shrill sound cut through the night.

A gator's cry.

He paused, jerked his head around to listen and remembered where they were—standing outside in the open air of his backyard, exposed.

Dammit. What was he thinking? A shooter had tried to kill them today. He was a fool to leave them vulnerable like this.

The shrill sound cut through the silence again, mingling with her erratic breathing, and his own. This time it wasn't a gator but the damn phone.

He grabbed her and whisked her inside, his cop instincts kicking in. Then he slammed the door shut. She looked stunned, dazed, her face flushed, her hands still trying to tear at his jeans.

"Crystal, stop," he said huskily.

"No. I want you," she cried.

He clutched her hands, pressed them to his sides. His body ached for her, but his brain had awakened. "I have to answer the phone."

He reached up and kissed her on the mouth, then grabbed his cell phone off the desk where he'd also laid his weapon.

"Damon, it's Jean-Paul. I just talked to the coroner. They have an ID on the woman's body. It's Kendra Yates."

No big surprise, although it looked bad for Antwaun.

"Kendra's mother is back in town, finally. I say we talk to her in the morning, after we visit Fenton in jail," Jean-Paul said. "Maybe Kendra told her something."

"Right. Good idea." He glanced at the passionate woman beside him, the one he wanted in his bed. "Any word on Crystal's identity?"

"They're still working on it." Jean-Paul coughed into the phone. "I don't have to tell you to be careful with that one, man. You don't know who she is or what she's done in the past. So don't get in too deep with her."

Damon nodded, although he could taste her skin on his lips, smell her orgasm in the heat still radiating between them, and knew that his brother's warning was too late. He'd been in too deep since the moment he'd laid eyes on her.

HE HAD TO COVER HIS ASS. He'd learned from his connections that Kendra's mother was back in town. He had to question her. See if she and her daughter had shared a mother-daughter chat before her demise. Or if she'd sent her mom a package of some kind, anything.

The rules of the game—*never leave a witness behind.* Destroy anyone who got in the way. Cover your ass no matter who had to die.

Which meant Kendra Yates's mother was on her way bye-bye.

He'd sharpened the knife blade to perfection, examined the edges to make sure they were clean. Slipped on his gloves. The silly woman had no security system. A broken latch on the laundry-room window allowed him easy entry. And the house was situated on a backwoods lot a mile from nowhere. Only God and the gators to listen to her screams.

Laughter caught in his throat, but he tamped it down as he padded silently into her room. First, the kill.

Then he'd mutilate her and leave her for Dubois to see. To feel guilty about. He might even send a picture of her bloody body to his dear old dad. Let him see what he'd learned from him.

Wouldn't the bastard be proud?

Then he'd search the old broad's place and eliminate any evidence that might tie him to her daughter or to her.

Tomorrow when the police arrived to question her, they'd find her floating in a bloody river like the one poured from Kendra.

CHAPTER FIFTEEN

CRYSTAL STILL QUIVERED with need as Damon disconnected the phone call. She ached to finish what they'd begun, wanted to see him naked and feel his body gliding against hers, his rigid length inside her, see him lose control as he murmured her name.

But when he turned toward her, moonlight played off his chiseled face, and regret flickered in his eyes.

"Damon, please…" She reached for him, determined he see that she herself had no regrets. All she wanted tonight was to forget the danger and questions. Tomorrow would throw them back in her face.

"Crystal, it's late. You need to get some rest."

She clutched his arms, forced him to look at her. "Why don't we lie down together? Let me love you the way you did me."

His jaw snapped rigid, and he caught her hands in his and lifted them away from him. "I've already crossed the line. Taken advantage of you when I knew better."

"You didn't take advantage of me, Damon. I

wanted you and you wanted me. It's as simple as that."

"Nothing about our relationship is simple," he barked. "You don't even know your name. What if you're married, Crystal? What if you have a family somewhere, a husband who wants you back?"

"If I do, then why hasn't he come looking for me?" All the pent-up emotions and anger she'd felt the last few months thickened her voice.

"Maybe he thinks you left him for some reason, or that you're dead."

"That still doesn't explain why he wouldn't have filed a missing report on me." She curled her hands into fists, desperate for his touch again. "There is obviously no one," she whispered, finally admitting the truth to herself. "No one cares about me, Damon. That's why there's been no report, no search." She pressed her hand to her heart. "I feel it in here."

He stared at her long and hard, emotions warring in his eyes. Then a breath hissed between his teeth, and the cold, hard cop was back. "That was Jean-Paul. They have a positive ID on the mutilated woman. It *was* Kendra Yates."

Sadness swelled in her chest although she had no idea why she'd experience grief for a woman she hadn't known. Guilt was there, too, for benefiting from the death of another woman. Fear quickly followed.

"What about my ID?"

"Nothing yet, but maybe tomorrow." He moved to the French doors, locked them and pulled down the shades. "Jean-Paul and I plan to question Fenton, the first Mutilator, in jail in Angola tomorrow. And I'm going to see Kendra's mother."

"Her mother is here in New Orleans?"

Damon nodded. "Yes, she flew back after the police contacted her to inform her about the ID."

"I should go with you," she said, although anxiety knotted her shoulders. "If I did know Kendra, seeing her mother might help trigger my memory." *And I do have her daughter's face.*

But how would Kendra's mother react to the sight of her?

DAMON SPENT HALF THE NIGHT studying the files on the investigation and arrest of the Mutilator thirty years ago, researching the victims, looking for a pattern between the women he'd chosen to kill, delving into the man's past. Damon was desperate to find a material connection between the first killer and the man who'd murdered Kendra Yates. And *something* had to keep his mind off of wanting to climb into the bed with Crystal and sating himself with her lush body.

There didn't seem to be a solid pattern between the victims of the Mutilator. Fenton had first killed his mother, a savage murder that the social workers had justified as self-defense—apparently Fenton had suffered terrible abuse at her hands. As typical with other serial killers, he'd transferred his hatred of her to other members of her sex, had repeated patterns of abuse with women he'd dated as he'd aged. Eventually he'd turned murder into a game. Twelve victims in a one-year span. One woman a month.

Cold. Sadistic. The man had expressed no remorse during the trial. Some victims had been single, some married, although he'd supposedly met them all in bars—that was at least *some* connection.

Kendra Yates was a professional—she would not have fit the MO. Still, the man who'd killed her had chosen to imitate the Mutilator's crimes. Why? Did he know Fenton?

Damon searched for cell mates who had been housed with Fenton, but found none who had been recently released. According to his data, Fenton had no siblings or children either. Where the hell was the connection?

Exhausted, he finally forced himself to bed, but when he fell asleep, nightmares tormented him.

HE WAS OUTSIDE THE HOUSE where Diego Bolton was supposed to be hiding out. Max had landed the E-team chopper in a clearing less than a mile away. The men were in place to erase the terrorist as ordered.

Damon had scoped out the property and created a tactical plan. Lex froze the security long enough for the team to slip in and set the explosives in place. Black-faced and hiding in the shadows, they counted down the seconds until the bomb exploded.

Then the mission went awry.

Diego was supposed to be alone, but Max spotted a woman entering the house on the opposite side. Somehow she'd bypassed security, meaning she must've known the code. Probably one of Diego's lovers.

Still, killing an innocent woman was not on Damon's agenda.

As soon as Damon heard Max on the radio, he ordered the team to abort the plan. He jumped up to make sure the remote didn't go off, but Cal grabbed the device, and it clicked, setting the timer. Dammit. Damon looked through the binoculars but he'd lost the woman. Where was she? Had she gone out the back door?

They had only seconds before the house blew....

Damon ran toward the house. "I have to get the woman out," he insisted.

Max caught him at the door. "It's too late, man. You'll expose us all if you do that."

"I don't intend on killing an innocent woman," Damon argued.

Max jerked him back. "Don't fuck this up. Diego

is an assassin and a traitor, and she may be his accomplice. He's responsible for hundreds of lost lives. What's one more casualty of the war?"

"But what if she's innocent?" Damon hissed. Suddenly the bomb went off, knocking them both through the air. His head slammed against a tree in the woods with such force he blacked out for a second. Fire erupted instantly, the entire place going up in a blazing inferno.

Damon slowly came to. Blurry-eyed, he crawled forward, pushed himself up from his knees. Blood dripped down his face; he tasted it in his mouth. But he ran toward the house again, determined to rescue the woman.

Fire hissed and sprayed splintered wood all over the ground. The roof caved in, crashing with a thunderous roar. Flames ripped along the grass outside, swallowed the bushes surrounding the house, climbed upward, an orange-and-red dragon of a fireball coloring the dark sky. A shrill scream pierced the air.

The woman might still be alive.

Damon dodged patches of flames, falling debris, crackling wood and furniture that rained down. Smoke choked him, and he dragged out a handkerchief, covered his mouth and searched the burning rooms for the woman. Then Max rushed up beside him, cursing at him and trying to drag him out. Lex was there, too, yelling at them to all get out, that Diego was dead.

A falling beam struck Damon's neck and sent him to the floor. Heat singed his skin; smoke clogged his throat and eyes. He thought he spotted her. A female body curled on the floor. Wide, sightless eyes staring at him. Fire breathing down her hair. Then he spotted the baby rattle lying on the floor. She must have been holding it.

God, no, she had a baby. Or was she pregnant now?

He grabbed the plastic yellow rattle. "I have to get her!" he shouted.

"She's already dead!" Cal shouted.

"No, don't die," he yelled. "Please don't die."

Another beam crashed down, shooting flames at his feet and hands, falling into the woman, and he choked back a cry.

DAMON JERKED AWAKE, his heart racing, sweat pouring down his face. Or was it tears?

He felt smothered by the anguish filling his chest. He should have died that day, too. Sometimes he wished he had.

But Crystal's face flashed in his head. Crystal, the woman without a name. The woman he'd wanted to make love to. The woman who made him want to live again.

He rose, padded to the dresser and opened the drawer, then removed the baby rattle he'd found.

The one he hadn't been able to leave behind, or throw away.

Cal would have a fit if he knew Damon had kept it, that he'd broken another rule—*destroy any evidence that could connect you to the scene or victim.*

He'd kept this rattle to remind him of the woman's death. And that he didn't deserve to have a family himself.

CRYSTAL TWISTED HER FINGERS together, scanning the scenery as Damon drove the country road toward Kendra Yates's mother's house. She'd gone to bed aching for Damon and his comforting arms, and this morning, as she contemplated the woman's potential reactions to seeing her daughter's face on another, she needed him even more.

But he had withdrawn into a silent shell, thrown up walls to keep her from getting close again and held a white-knuckled grip on the steering wheel of the car Jean-Paul had dropped off. The morning had been awkward as they'd shared coffee and beignets, but she'd been grateful for the bag of clothes and toiletries Britta had collected.

Even wearing the simple cotton sleeveless tank, denim skirt and sandals in the air-conditioning, her skin felt clammy with the insufferable heat and nerves. She'd secured her hair off her neck into a ponytail, but perspiration made the unruly tendrils curl even more and cling to her neck. Damon flipped the radio to a local jazz station to fill the silence, but the blues song only let in thoughts of her troubles.

Damon veered down a graveled road past an old service station and several houses that had been nearly destroyed in the hurricane, reminding her of the lost lives and difficulties the survivors faced. She had no reason to indulge in a pity party. Soon she would have answers. Then she could move on.

If they discovered she was single and free, would Damon want to be part of her life? Was that the only thing holding him back? She sensed there was more. Something about the pain in the way he'd played that saxophone suggested that he didn't want a relationship at all. Just a night of raw primal sex…

Another memory tugged at her consciousness. A handsome man…a seduction. Lies. A man she trusted. A man who'd betrayed her. No, an involvement with this cop was impossible.

The car bumped over the potholes and uneven graveled patches, jerking her mind back to the immediate task facing her: meeting Kendra's mother.

Damon slowed the vehicle as they approached a battered two-story white Georgian home. The structure begged for paint just as the weed-filled, scraggly yard begged for landscaping. Kendra's mother had probably suffered hurricane damage and was still struggling to recover.

And now she'd lost her daughter....

Damon cut the engine then turned to Crystal, worry lining his handsome face. "This has to be difficult, maybe even unpleasant for you. Kendra's mother already endured a terrible shock, and she doesn't yet know about the transplant. Are you sure you want to meet her?"

Doubts suddenly assailed Crystal. "You think meeting me will make things worse for her?"

"I don't know. I... It's hard to say how she'll react."

Crystal stared up at the house, her heart full of trepidation. She didn't want to hurt this woman, but she'd like to repay Kendra by easing her mother's suffering, if possible. Somehow she felt close to Kendra, felt as if being here was right, that Kendra would have wanted her to meet her mother, to console her in her grief.

"I have to," she said softly. "Kendra wouldn't want her mother to be alone now."

He nodded, his frown softening slightly, resurrecting memories of the night before when just for a moment he'd let down his guard.

But as they walked up the drive to the front porch, Crystal's knees wobbled, and the hair on the back of her neck bristled. Something was wrong. She could feel it.

Damon rang the doorbell, and they waited, the

sultry air stirring scents of honeysuckle and the bayou around them. But no one answered.

A vulture circled the house above the chimney, sending an eerie feeling through her skin. Heat pounded her back, bringing with it another odor she couldn't define. Something rancid. Damon punched the bell again, but the house remained silent. He reached out and turned the doorknob, and her breath caught as the door squeaked open.

They stepped inside and a vile odor blasted them. "Something's not right," she said.

Damon nodded and called the woman's name.

"What's that smell?" she asked.

He frowned. "Blood."

Fear crawled into her. She glanced at the hallway, then around the corner and saw a foot twisted in the doorway, a body sprawled on the floor in the kitchen. Damon unholstered his gun and shoved her behind him. Blood streaked the floor, the walls, the carpet. So much blood.

She covered her mouth to stifle a scream, her stomach clenching. They were too late. Kendra's mother wouldn't be able to tell them anything.

DAMON'S INSTINCTS ROARED, the scent of death so strong that he had to swallow back the bile. He scanned the hall, then spotted a mangled body lying in a pool of blood on the floor and whipped around to Crystal, all the time his senses tuned to high alert in case the killer remained hidden inside.

"Listen to me," he said in a low whisper as he handed Crystal the new cell phone Jean-Paul had given him. "Go to the car, lock the doors and call Jean-Paul. His number is programmed in."

Her glazed eyes told him she'd seen the body. Jesus. He shook her by the shoulders. "*Go*, Crystal. The killer may still be here."

His words registered, and she nodded numbly, clutched the phone and ran outside. He inched to the door to make sure she made it safely to the car, scanned the property in front and breathed a sigh of relief when she slammed the car door shut.

Inside, a noise jerked his head back to the staircase, and he wielded his gun, ready to fire. His lungs squeezed air from his chest as he slowly climbed the stairs, each creak of the step making him pause to listen for an intruder. Upstairs, the windowpane rattled, and he clenched his Glock as he climbed the last step and twisted around the corner.

Nothing.

He slowly crept forward, searched the two bedrooms to the right, then the third one, which must have been Kendra's, as photos of her lined a white bookshelf. The windowpane rattled again, and he finally realized that it was only a bird perched on the ledge pecking at the glass.

Heaving a sigh of relief, he finished checking the upstairs, then inched his way back down and checked out the master suite to the left of the foyer, then the den, and finally he found his way back to the kitchen where Mrs. Yates's mutilated body lay.

Fury raced through his veins as he studied the crime scene. She had been sliced and diced as if she weren't human. Not exactly a copycat of the first Mutilator, but similar to his last crimes.

Still, it was overkill. The sadistic maniac took pleasure in the act.

To hell with the law. This guy deserved to suffer the way he'd caused these women to suffer.

Fury ripped through Damon's gut as he remembered the handwritten number one on the photo the copycat had sent them. Kendra had been his victim.

And now victim two—Kendra's mother.

Would there be another? The Mutilator had killed twelve before being caught. He was joy-killing—harder to create a logic for and trace.

Unlike the first killer though, these victims were related. Mother and daughter, not random victims.

Suspicions mounted. Like Damon, this copycat killer must have thought Kendra might have told her mother something important about her research. Maybe the name of the dirty cop. Or Swafford's location.

But there was no way they could pin this crime

on Antwaun because he was in jail during this second killing.

He contemplated the killer's pattern—if their UNSUB intended to murder everyone who knew Kendra or was related to the case, he might come after Crystal. And if he planned to mutilate her this way…

God, no.

He couldn't let that happen. He'd go back into the dark world of his ops training and kill the sicko first.

A SIREN WAILED in the distance. The dead woman's face was etched in Crystal's mind. As was the photo of Kendra on the wall. And the family picture at Christmas when they were children…

Images bombarded her like small snippets out of a foreign film, a documentary of someone else's life. Only there were mere bits and pieces—the whole story wasn't appearing on-screen…as if clips had been cut from the show.

She buried her face in her hands, trying to put the world back together. She *had* seen Kendra recently. She had known her because…they were related?

She'd joined her at another relative's funeral. *Her* father's…

Grief consumed her, took the air from her lungs. Her father…the car explosion. The man with the wide accusing eyes. The fire eating at his face and body…

*My fault…my fault…my fault…*she'd cried over his casket.

Her mother's scream echoed in her ears. "Jacqueline!"

Sobs racked Crystal's body, and she rocked herself back and forth in the car. Jacqueline—was that her name?

Yes, it sounded right. And Kendra was her cousin, although they'd lost touch.

Until the day of her father's funeral. Then she'd appeared out of nowhere. Pulled Jacqueline aside, warned her that her father had been murdered. That she knew the killer.

And that she might be next on his list.

CHAPTER SIXTEEN

THOUGH HE WANTED DESPERATELY to go to Crystal, Damon first spoke with Jean-Paul, his partner, Detective Carson Graves, and the crime-scene unit outside the house to explain what he had found.

Jean-Paul wiped sweat from his brow. "At least they can't hang this on Antwaun."

"My thoughts exactly," Damon said. "But we need to search the house. My guess is that the killer thought Kendra might have told her mother something important about her investigation. Maybe she even sent her some kind of evidence."

Jean-Paul looked grim as he climbed the porch. "Let's just hope the killer didn't find it first."

Damon nodded. "I need to check on Crystal."

"Go ahead," Jean-Paul said. "I'll oversee the crime scene."

Blue lights swirled against the gray sky, and the heat bore down on him as Damon made his way to his car. His heart pounded with fear. Dammit, he couldn't let another woman down.

Crystal had turned on the air conditioner and sat in the passenger seat, her hands clenched, her eyes staring at the house, a haunted expression on her face.

He opened the driver's door and climbed in, then took her hands in his. "Crystal, I'm sorry you had to see that. Are you okay?"

She turned to him with tears in her eyes. "I…had a memory. Just a flash but…I did know Kendra, and her mother. Kendra was my cousin… We hadn't seen each other in a long time, but recently we reconnected."

Damon's interest perked up. Maybe Kendra had confided something about what she'd been working on. The name of the dirty cop. Swafford's location. Another enemy she might have made. Maybe she'd been researching the original Mutilator case. Crystal looked so fragile, he hated to push her; unlocking the truth might be the only way to keep her safe. "What else did you remember?"

"She came to the funeral." Her chin quivered as she grappled for control over her emotions.

"What funeral, Crystal? I don't understand."

"The car explosion I saw in my nightmares. It wasn't me inside the car, it was my father. His wide eyes, accusing me. The fire, the flames. And then he…died."

He squeezed her hands tighter, wanted her to

know he was there. "He had an accident and you witnessed it?"

She shook her head slowly. "I don't think it was an accident. I think he was murdered. That it was my fault. I heard my mother scream…my name. I think it's Jacqueline." A strangled cry erupted from deep inside her. "Oh, God, Damon, Kendra said she knew the killer—that I was next!"

Damon froze, his adrenaline pumping blood through his veins at an accelerated speed. Crystal knew her first name.

And if Kendra had warned Crystal she was in danger, likely the accident that had stolen her face and memory wasn't an accident at all.

So who had killed her father and why was he after her now?

GUILT CLAWED AT JACQUELINE'S chest. Her father was dead; she knew it in her heart. Worse, she felt she was to blame. But how?

"Were you driving the car that caused your father's death?" Damon asked in a low voice.

"No." She struggled to recall more details but they eluded her. Though she felt they teased at the edge of her mind, within reach.

"What else do you remember?" He smoothed her tear-dampened hair from her cheek.

"I remember seeing Kendra, she was standing

beside me at the graveyard. She insisted we had to talk."

"And Kendra knew who killed your father?"

She nodded, though she was still confused. "She said that I knew him, but I don't remember his name. And I still feel like it's my fault he died, then maybe I deserve to have died, too."

He lifted her chin with his thumb, gazed at her intently. She expected to see disgust, condemnation, but understanding glinted in his hard eyes. "Crystal, Jacqueline... There are all kinds of reasons we feel guilty when a loved one dies. Maybe you and your father had had a disagreement of some kind, a falling out and you hadn't had time to reconcile."

She wanted to believe that was true, but she sensed whatever had happened was much more serious.

"Now, think, *chère*. You see his face. What is your father's name? *Your* last name?"

She closed her eyes, pictured him again. Tried desperately to see the name on the tombstone... But the shadow of darkness that shrouded the lettering felt like death all over again. Only a black wall of pain and grief remained.

Damon's quiet breathing filled the car. She wanted to lean into him, let him help her forget the horror inside her aunt's house. The realization that she might have in some way brought about her father's death. Maybe even her cousin's.

"I need to go back inside, help Jean-Paul," Damon said, cutting into her thoughts. "When we're finished, I'll let you look around. Maybe seeing some of Kendra's things, her room, photos, might help."

She nodded, desperate now for more answers, wanting to fill in that black screen with the story of her life.

"Will you be okay out here alone?" he asked.

She nodded, then squeezed his hand in return. "Yes, go. I want you to find the man who did this to my cousin and her mother. And maybe you're right. Maybe seeing Kendra's things will trigger my memory of our conversation that day."

But a sliver of fear caught in her throat. If Kendra had shared her suspicions or something about the other stories she'd been working on, maybe Jacqueline's own accident hadn't been an accident at all.

Maybe her earlier sense that someone had tried to kill her was reality, and that the shooter who'd run Damon off the road had been gunning for her. Maybe it had been her father's killer, and he wanted to silence her, to keep her from remembering who he was—because maybe she could identify him.

MRS. YATES'S BODY had sustained countless stab wounds. Every inch of her that could be sliced had been. The number of wounds, the depth, and the blood splatters on the wall indicated a highly vicious attack. It was so unnecessary that it sickened him.

Blood pooled beneath her head and torso but also dotted the floor and formed a stream where she'd tried to crawl away from her attacker. Clumps of her hair had been pulled out and lay in the dried blood.

"Poor woman never had a chance," Jean-Paul mumbled.

"No. And this level of overkill has to be a message. We just have to figure out what the hell the killer is trying to tell us." Damon knelt and studied the floor, searching for signs of mud, dirt, a shoe print, anything that might help them pinpoint the perp's identity. Meanwhile, the CSI team was photographing the scene, beginning to dust for prints and searching for trace evidence.

Damon stood and surveyed the room. Drawers had been pulled open and rifled through by the killer, the desk in the corner disturbed, the remainder of the first floor and the den adjoining it obviously searched. He was sure the rest of the house had been as well.

He conducted a preliminary search himself but found nothing, then pulled aside one of the crime techs. "Be sure to bag any notes, messages, computer disks, anything that might have information on it, even if it's a goddamn grocery list."

The tech nodded, and Damon headed upstairs. Jean-Paul followed him, and although it was obvious the killer had already combed the place, they spent the next hour searching the bedrooms, closets and Kendra's room. Judging from the frilly comforter, rose-print wallpaper and collection of photos on the desk, Kendra's mother had preserved her childhood room. Her high-school and college yearbooks filled a shelf along with several copies of the *New Yorker* and books on writing. A photo album of her with friends and family was jammed in the corner, so Damon took it down, deciding to show it to Crystal/Jacqueline and see if it jogged her memory.

Finally, in the lower desk drawer, he found a pink diary that looked like something a teenage girl might have. When he opened it, he discovered it was from when Kendra was only thirteen. Interestingly enough, the entries were written as if she were a reporter, indicating she'd had career aspirations to be a journalist early on.

She couldn't have dreamed back then that her job would get her killed.

He was just about to put the diary in the drawer when a key fell from the inside. He first thought it belonged with the diary. But when he examined it, it didn't fit. It was slightly larger, more like a lockbox or safety-deposit key.

JACQUELINE'S NERVES WERE strung tight as she sat in the outer waiting room of the state prison in Angola. Damon and Jean-Paul had gone in to question Frederick Fenton, a serial killer who had murdered twelve women in the same cruel manner Kendra and her mother had died.

Had Kendra talked to the man herself? Could she have been working on a story about Fenton's past crimes?

And what did all this have to do with Jacqueline and her father's death?

Was her mother still alive? Had she looked for her missing daughter? Did she have any other family she'd forgotten about?

If only she could remember everything she and Kendra had talked about…

Her palms felt clammy as she ran her fingers over the photo album Damon had confiscated from Kendra's house. He'd gotten special permission to remove it from the crime scene.

She thumbed open the book and glanced at the first picture—a shot of Kendra when she was a child sitting in her mother's lap. She skimmed the first section, which held mostly photos of Kendra between infancy and high school. Some of the older shots seemed familiar.

The next section showcased high-school prom, graduation, sorority functions and a wedding that must have been a friend's. Then came photos of Kendra's graduation from college, her journalism awards, a photo of her and the governor of the state after her feature stories on Hurricane Katrina, the aftermath, and heroes she'd discovered during the revival of the city.

Jacqueline scoured the pages searching for other family photos, anything to connect her to Kendra or jog her memory. Stuffed in the lining of the album, she discovered a photograph of a closed casket and a woman bent over it in tears. Roses covered the slick gray coffin in a bed of crimson while the woman seemed stark-faced white in contrast, a picture of grief and remorse.

Her heart clenched. She squinted at the woman's face and realized she resembled Kendra... The woman must be *her.*

This was her father's casket, his funeral, just before Kendra had approached her.

A memory flashed in the darkness that had become her mind, and she closed her eyes, struggling to recall every detail. She'd been sobbing, heart-wrenching cries torn from her gut. Her father was gone. Her hero. Mentor. The man she had adored. The man she'd followed around the world.

She'd been standing by his car, waving goodbye when it had gone up in flames. The explosion had rocked the café beside them, and sent her falling to her knees to dodge the flames and debris. She'd seen his anguished, shocked face as he'd tried to claw the door open, but it had been too late. A second later, flames had consumed the vehicle, the sharp blast of gas and metal exploding into the air, mingling with her screams.

Shell-shocked, she had mourned his senseless loss. Then Kendra had appeared at his graveside to add to Jacqueline's guilt, suggesting it was her fault. The man she'd been dating, the one she'd met at a fund-raiser in Copenhagen with her father, the man whose charming smile and flamboyant attention had seduced her into his bed—he was not the man she'd thought him to be. Kendra said he had used Jacqueline to get to her father.

She pressed her hands over her ears, trying to block out the accusations screaming through her head that Kendra was right. And trying to force the man's name and face in her mind. But it eluded her.

The sounds of male voices in the prison ro sounded through the tumult. The clinking of handcuffs. The prison guards, the police officers, the memory of the fence she'd seen when she'd arrived.

Something about prison…Kendra had said that Jacqueline's lover deserved to go to jail for all the men he had killed.

What kind of monster had been her lover?

BEFORE DAMON AND JEAN-PAUL met with Frederick Fenton, they had a chat with the warden. Rodney Rivera insisted Fenton's mail had been routinely scanned. In fact, he checked the mail and discovered a photo of Kendra's death that the killer had sent Fenton. Thankfully, Fenton hadn't seen it yet.

The hulking, forty-something warden scratched his balding head. "I'll tell my guys to be on the lookout in case he receives anything else suspicious."

"Tell them to ask around inside, see if Fenton's talked to anyone about the Yateses' murders, too," Damon added.

Jean-Paul reviewed the visitor's log for the last six months, but the warden said the only visitor he'd had was some prison groupie who'd become his pen pal through a magazine ad. Fairly common, but they would check her out anyway.

"Does he have access to the Internet?" Damon asked.

Rivera shook his head. "No. Though a few of our guys have earned the privilege, Fenton hasn't. He's too much of a troublemaker."

Damon frowned. "He can pass messages through a third party."

Rivera nodded. "That's possible. The guys trade favors in here for cigarettes, drugs, you name it. They find a way to get it."

Damon was relieved that Rivera seemed cooperative and had agreed to check with a few of the snitches inside. Finally they faced Fenton in a small interrogation room. Damon had pulled up the man's mug shot. Six-one of lean, mean muscle. At the time of his arrest, twenty-five-year-old Fenton had had short spiked black hair, a full beard, a tattoo of a tribal symbol on his left arm and beefy hands. According to his rap sheet, he liked to use his fists on women.

Despite the years, the killer facing them now was just as mean-looking as he'd been when he was young. But he was middle-aged and had put on at least thirty pounds. His hair was scraggly, his beard graying and thin, and jagged scars crisscrossed his face and arms. Damon knew he'd earned those in prison fights.

His shackles clanked as he dragged his feet across the floor, the fierce set of his mouth and narrowed eyes obviously meant to intimidate. But Fenton had no idea who he was dealing with. The Dubois men did not allow criminals to scare them.

"Well, boys, to what do I owe this honor?" Fenton slunk down into the hard vinyl chair across the table from them, dropping his cuffed hands into his lap.

"You've read the news lately?" Jean-Paul began.

Fenton pulled at his chin. "Oh, yeah." As if a lightbulb went off in his head, he grinned, revealing yellowed teeth. "You're here about that woman being mutilated."

Jean-Paul nodded, his body relaxed in the seat. "It looks like a fan of your work has surfaced."

Fenton shrugged. "I guess I've got an admirer. After all, I was a master at the game."

"If you were a true master, you wouldn't have gotten caught," Damon replied deadpan.

Fenton scowled. "So how many has this guy done?"

"Two," Jean-Paul replied.

Fenton's eyebrows shot up. "He do them together?"

Jean-Paul shook his head.

Fenton leaned forward, hands on the table in front of him, fingers flexing. "Shit. That would have been fun. Do one while the other watched." He angled his head toward Damon. "If I get out of here, that's what I'll do. A tag team, mother and daughter together."

"You'll never get out, Fenton," Damon said. "Now tell us, is this guy working for you? Do you know who he is?"

Fenton's eyebrows shifted into a thick unibrow. "What's in this for me if I talk?"

"Depends on what you have to say," Jean-Paul said.

A long hesitation followed, where Fenton acted as if he were chewing over the idea and testing its weight. "Afraid I can't help you boys."

Damon leaned forward this time, his hand slapping the table. "Look, Fenton, we researched your past. Didn't find any real friends you had, no family either. Is there someone we don't know about?"

"No brats if that's what you mean."

Damon clenched his teeth. "Did you have a friend back then? Or maybe you made one inside, he got out and decided to copy your crimes?"

"I don't *need* friends or partners." Fenton shook his head. "I worked alone. No ass-wipe to screw me up."

"What about since you've been inside? Any mail from an admirer? Someone who wanted to boast to you about his newly acquired skill?"

"Nope." Fenton grunted. "But I hope he sends me a picture or something. I'd like to see his handi-work."

So the photo the warden had was the first one the killer had sent. Probably wouldn't be the last. Disgust chewed at Damon's insides and he grabbed Fenton by the collar. "Listen to me, you asshole. If you don't cooperate and we find out you've withheld information from us, we'll charge you with these murders and see that you end up on death row."

Fenton bared his teeth. "All right. Let me look at the crime photos and I'll see what I can tell you from them."

Perverted bastard just wanted a thrill. No way.

Damon made a grunting sound, then he and Jean-Paul motioned to the guard to let them out. Though they hadn't learned much, they'd whetted Fenton's appetite for information on his copycat. Hopefully now if Fenton did hear something from the killer, he wouldn't be able to help himself. He'd brag about it and whoever the warden had on the inside would spill his guts to Damon.

They found Jacqueline sitting quietly staring at the photo album, looking lost and vulnerable.

She clutched the book and stood. "Did you learn anything?"

Damon gestured for her to go outside, and the three of them stepped into the stifling heat. "Not from Fenton. But the warden scanned his mail, and the killer had sent him a photo of Kendra's murder."

"God," Jacqueline whispered. "That is sick."

"Yeah. We'll catch him, *chère*, I promise you that."

Jean-Paul got in to drive, and Damon's cell phone rang just as he opened the back door for Jacqueline. She buckled her seat belt while he connected the call and climbed in front.

"Special Agent Dubois."

"Dubois, listen," said the voice of his partner. "I just got a hit on the fingerprints from that woman who looks like Kendra. We have an ID now."

Damon gripped the phone tighter. "And?"

"Her name is Jacqueline Braudaway."

His mouth went dry. *Braudaway?*

"There's more," his partner continued. "She's the daughter of former Ambassador to Denmark Eduardo Braudaway. He used to work for the State Department and traveled all over the world. But he was killed in a car explosion a little over a year ago…"

Damon didn't need to hear the rest. He already knew what had happened to Braudaway. The ambassador had been murdered by a terrorist. A man the government had been tracking for months. A man the E-team had taken out. It had been Damon's last mission. The one that had fallen apart.

Damon had been responsible for the assassination and setting the explosive himself. But that woman had appeared out of nowhere.

All along they'd wondered how Diego Bolton had gotten to Braudaway.

The hair on the back of his neck suddenly stood on end. They'd suspected he'd done so through family.

Maybe he had seduced Braudaway's daughter… Jacqueline.

Jesus. The woman sitting in his backseat was the ambassador's daughter—and she might have been Diego's girlfriend. She'd said her father was murdered and she was right. She'd also claimed she was to blame for her father's death….

The air in his lungs froze. *Bon Dieu…*

Had she been the woman in Diego's apartment

that fatal day he'd set off the explosive? No...the woman had died in the fire.... Cal had told him she wasn't breathing.

But the photos of Jacqueline's burns, her plastic surgeries, her mysterious appearance in Pace's hospital a year ago, the timing... It all fit.

Except she thought she'd been injured from a car explosion. But what if she was confusing her own near-death experience with her father's car explosion?

What if she'd actually survived the terrorist's explosion, only to be mangled by the one he'd set?

CHAPTER SEVENTEEN

SOMETHING WAS BOTHERING Damon.

Jacqueline saw the strain on his face as they drove back to the police station. As soon as they arrived, Jean-Paul escorted them to his office and got them both a cup of coffee. Damon told her they had to talk.

"Do you want me to leave?" Jean-Paul asked.

Damon shook his head. "No, you need to hear this, too. My partner at the bureau just called." Damon angled his head toward her. "We know who you are, Jacqueline."

She sucked in a sharp breath. Judging from his reaction and the intensity in his expression, he'd learned something disturbing.

"And?" she asked, determined to face whatever he'd discovered. After all, was not knowing any better? Especially since she'd had that flash of a memory in the car.

"Your name is Jacqueline Braudaway."

Jacqueline. So she was right. Yet, there were so

many holes in her mind. Such as why she had Kendra's face.

"Your father was an ambassador to Denmark, Eduardo Braudaway," Damon continued. "He worked for the State Department and traveled abroad."

She nodded, seeing flashes of her travels in Africa and Honduras. That was where she'd learned to speak Spanish.

"And you were right. He was killed in a car explosion last year." Damon tapped into the computer and produced a photo of a tall, regal dark-haired man shaking hands with the mayor of New Orleans and another of him and the president.

Her heart clenched with the realization that this man was her father. Memories teased at her mind. Her father's gruff voice as he addressed a crowd. His caring concern for the people he represented. The trips he'd taken abroad. A thin blond-haired woman in the shadows behind him…her mother? And a little girl tagging behind him, wanting to go everywhere he went. Wanting to be like him, to travel, to help others. Her small hand in his. A time when he'd taken her to a carnival and they'd ridden the roller coaster together. She'd screamed and laughed, and he'd hugged her tight, then bought her cotton candy. Another when he'd surprised her with a hand-carved wooden cross he'd bought in a small shop in Italy. Her high-school graduation, then a trip to Honduras on a church mission trip where they'd worked side by side with the locals, mudding houses, cementing floors and digging latrines.

Tears trickled down her cheeks as other memories crowded her mind. Some fleeting and happy, some reminding her that he'd spent long hours and weeks away from the family. That she hadn't always been able to accompany him.

But he had inspired her to volunteer in developing nations to feed the hungry, and to start a program that sponsored Honduran children for education beyond elementary school.

Damon accessed another photo—this one of the accident that had taken her father's life.

Jacqueline stared at the crushed car, the flames spewing, and remembered the image as the one from her nightmares. A second photo showed the car charred beyond recognition. Grief swelled inside her as if the explosion had just occurred. "It wasn't an accident, was it?" she managed to ask.

"So you remember?"

"Not everything, no. But pieces of the past with him. My father…was a good man." She forced herself to look at Damon, blinking back more tears that begged to be released. "The nightmares I had, the car explosion, the man staring at me through the flames… It all makes sense now." She hesitated, sipped the coffee, then set the mug on the desk. Her hands were shaking so badly the hot liquid sloshed over the side. She reached over to find something to mop it up with, but Damon pressed one hand over hers in comfort, then cleaned up the spill with a napkin himself.

"I'm sorry, Jacqueline."

She nodded, squeezing his fingers. "When you were questioning Fenton and I was looking at the photo album, I had a brief flash of the explosion again." Her voice wavered. "Somehow, I felt like it was my fault."

She studied Damon, searched for a reaction, but his poker face revealed nothing. He looked to Jean-Paul and then back at her.

"Why do you blame yourself?" he asked calmly.

"My cousin," she said in frustration. "She said I knew the killer. I think I was involved with him."

"You weren't hurt that day?" Damon asked, and she shook her head no.

"My accident… It happened later."

"What else do you remember?" he asked.

"Being at the funeral, standing beside my father's casket, my mother crying. And Kendra…warning that I might be next." Jacqueline searched her mind for the man's name, for details of him, for an explanation. "What about my mother? Is she alive?"

"Yes," Damon replied. "But I'm afraid she had a

nervous breakdown after your father's death and is in a rest home. That's why she didn't report you missing."

Sadness washed over her all over again. Her mother… She had always lived for her husband, had been old-fashioned and had supported his political aspirations. And although she hadn't liked traveling to the poorer countries, she had spearheaded charities in the States. What was her mother's condition now?

"I have to see her." Jacqueline wrapped a vise around her emotions, savoring her newfound memories even as pain accompanied them. "Maybe she can tell me what happened, fill in the blank holes." And maybe seeing Jacqueline would help her mother recover….

A second later, a bad feeling tightened her stomach. Maybe her mother wouldn't be happy to see her.

But why? From the brief memory flash, she knew they hadn't been as close as she and her father, but her mother had loved her. Had something happened to drive a wedge between the two of them after they lost her father? Did her mother blame her for her father's death as she blamed herself?

"We'll arrange a visit," Damon agreed.

She nodded, feeling numb, then sensed that Damon was still holding back. Amazing how quickly she'd learned to read the tiny nuances of his expressions, even when he tried to maintain that professional mask. "What else do you know about my father's death? About me?"

Damon gave his brother an odd look—worry? Anger? Distrust? She couldn't be sure.

"Tell me, Damon. Please."

His clipped nod wasn't comforting. "You traveled with your father, taught English in Mexico."

Yes, that was right. No wonder she had connected to little Maria. She was a teacher of sorts.

"Tell me more."

"That's all I know so far."

She stood, gripped Damon's arm. *"Don't lie to me, Damon.* I have to know the truth. What caused my father's car to explode?" She hesitated, then forged on, her chest tight with pain. "Why do I feel like I'm somehow my father's killer? Did I see the man do it? Was I involved with him?" Her voice choked. *"Am* I responsible for my father's death?"

DAMON BATTLED THE WAR raging in his body. Part of him wanted to comfort Jacqueline, hold her, tell her no, absolutely not, there was no way she could be involved in any way in her father's murder.

He knew she couldn't have hurt one of her parents. She didn't have a mean bone in her body, only a loving heart that beckoned him to help her, a heart that was quickly stealing his own....

Dammit, he should have kept his resolve not to become involved with her. She was the kind of woman who could rob a man's sanity. The kind of woman that tempted him to bury himself inside her until he couldn't find his way out.

The kind who ignited his desire to be a better man. To be the hero that his family and the town thought him already.

Even Jean-Paul didn't know the truth about what he had been.

So many secrets… Tell and you die.

The brotherhood of the E-team had lived by that code. To tell Jacqueline the entire truth about her injuries, about Bolton, he'd have to break that code.

An impossible situation. Doing so would endanger others' lives. Jeopardize important government missions.

If she had been involved with Diego in any way, if she had known of his plans for her father, then she was an accomplice to murder. No, he couldn't believe she was involved. The guy must have seduced her, tricked her, used her….

Then again, she might have been different before, might have agreed with Diego's tactics. Would she revert when her memory returned?

"Damon?" Her voice quivered with nerves.

"I don't have all the answers," he said. He had to protect his family, the E-team. And his heart from her.

She sank back down into the hard metal chair and rubbed her temple.

"Maybe seeing your mother will trigger more memories," Jean-Paul offered in a sympathetic voice.

"Will you take me to visit her, Damon?" she asked.

He nodded. "Yes, of course, but first I want to find out more about your father's accident. Give me a few minutes to make some calls, see if the feds know anything."

She nodded, her trusting look wrenching his gut. He was lying now. The feds knew very little because the E-team had covered up Diego's murder, as well as all the evidence they had about the man's crimes, that he might have killed the ambassador. All they knew was that Diego had died.

But there was someone he could call about Jacqueline. His fellow E-team members. Cal and Max had been in the house, had seen the woman and assured him she was dead. Why would one of his friends have lied?

"I'll be back in a few minutes," he said. "Try not to worry, Jacqueline. We'll get to the truth."

He and Jean-Paul left the office at the same time.

"I'll check on Antwaun," Jean-Paul said. "Tell him we're working on the case, that it's moving along."

Not fast enough for any of them, Damon wanted

to say. Especially for Antwaun. He must be going crazy inside, feeling helpless, angry.

Jean-Paul frowned. "I also may have a lead on the dirty cop."

Hope lurched in Damon's chest. "Who? Smith?"

"I don't want to say yet, in case I'm wrong. But I'll fill you in as soon as I know for sure."

They parted, and Damon stepped onto the blistering hot sidewalk for privacy and punched in Max's number, but he didn't respond, so he dialed Cal's, a knot in his throat. While he waited on his old buddy to answer, he prayed that Jacqueline wouldn't know Diego. That she really was as innocent as he thought.

Cal's raspy voice came over the line—his vocal cords had been damaged in a bombing in Kuwait, leaving him with a permanent smoker's voice. "Dubois, good to hear from you. Have you decided to come back to the team?"

Damon shifted. Cal and Max had been furious when Damon had turned FBI. He'd also taken the E-team to a different level when he and Max had gotten out of the service. Now they conducted missions on their own, private contract work for the government that no one claimed to know anything about.

"No, Cal. But listen, I have some questions for you."

"Any way I can help you, buddy. All you gotta do is ask."

Damon sighed. "I guess you read about my brother Antwaun's arrest."

"Yeah, he guilty or what?"

"No, he's not guilty," Damon snapped. "Someone's trying to set him up."

"Whatever you say, man."

"I've been investigating the murder of the reporter he's accused of killing," Damon continued, biting back a barbed reply. "And it's led me down some interesting paths."

"Yeah?"

He explained about Kendra's mother's murder, the photos of the original Mutilator's victims, and his trip to see Dr. Pace. Finally, he wound back to Jacqueline and explained how he'd traced her identity, and that Jacqueline was Ambassador Braudaway's daughter.

"We always wondered if Diego had help on the inside," Cal said with a curse. "Must have been screwing the man's daughter."

Damon gritted his teeth at the very idea that the vile man had touched Jacqueline. Yet he had to know. "It's possible, I suppose. She lost her memory and she's been in the hospital for months." He paused, letting the information register with Cal.

Damon gripped the phone, knowing he walked a fine line. Exposing Jacqueline as the woman who might have info on Diego and their mission was dangerous to both him and Cal. If she remembered, and if she'd seen them, she could blow their secret group all to hell.

Leave no witnesses behind.

And if Jacqueline had been the woman in the explosion he'd set, Max or Cal or a newer member of the team, might feel the need to off her.

"What are you implying, Dubois? That this Braudaway chick was the one in the fire with Diego that day? That she survived?"

"I don't know. Maybe."

"Goddamn it, Dubois. That's impossible. I told you the woman was dead."

Right. Damon closed his eyes, trying to remember that fatal day, the one he'd been trying so hard to forget. He'd panicked when he'd realized a woman was inside the house, had tried to abort the mission, had tried to run in and save her, but Max had dragged him away. He would never have left a potential witness behind. If he'd found the woman breathing, he'd have killed her himself.

"Maybe Bolton had another girl on the side besides Braudaway's daughter," Cal suggested. "There's no way the one in the house survived. I stayed and watched the building crumble to ashes."

The thunderous roar of the house crashing around them echoed in Damon's head as if it had happened yesterday. The wood splintering, glass shattering, flames shooting up in the sky. The burning embers. He'd watched, too. No woman had crawled out....

Although, God knows how many times he'd prayed that she had.

"You're probably right." Damon kicked at the weeds choking the crack in the sidewalk. He must be trying to convince himself that Jacqueline was that woman to assuage his guilt.

Still, the instincts that had kept him alive during the most dangerous of his missions niggled at him— he'd show Jacqueline a photo of Diego Bolton, see if she recognized him.

Find out for sure if she and Diego had been involved. If she was the woman in the fire with him, that damn baby rattle had belonged to her. Which meant that not only had she been involved with the assassin, she might have been carrying his child.

A child he'd killed as well.

LEX VAN WORMER STROLLED the halls of the hospital, struggling for enough energy to give his spiritual form physicality. He understood some spirits could move things, touch surfaces, create noise. He wanted that gift, that power so he could stop Pace from scheming to hurt Crystal and Dubois.

Pace was insane. Lex had heard him mutter that if he couldn't have Crystal, no one would.

Lex had to protect her. Let her and Dubois know that Pace had lied…

Frustration filled him as he remembered the virile soldier he once had been.

A warrior who'd wielded a machete, a machine gun—what he could do with even a goddamn switchblade, if needed. Now he was not only dead but fucking helpless.

He shouted in rage and went to pound at the door with balled fists, but his hands slid through the wood and no sound came from his mouth. Instead, flaky, dry, dead skin fell from his hands and arms like ashes.

He screamed again, knowing that if he was alive, blood might spurt from his cracked skin as he clawed at the wooden door. Dying was worse than he'd expected. It should have brought relief from the unbearable pain of his skin affliction, but a different raw emotional pain had replaced it.

Yet he clung to the gray realm anyway, that invisible bridge between the worlds that left him in limbo. Still in pain, not quite dead, not quite living.

Granted, he deserved this punishment. He'd inflicted suffering on others more times than he wanted to remember, but had justified his actions through the notion of war. He was a soldier for the good and well-being of others.

His one downfall had not been his conscience.

Not like Dubois who'd been haunted by the vile evil of their justified murders.

No, his downfall had been the fact that he'd trusted his own men, the secret soldiers of the E-team. Now, the fiery gates of the world below had a burning stake with his name on it. But a sliver of hope for redemption had stolen into the darkness. Crystal. In the dead zone, she had floated from her earthly body for a bit and they connected in the spiritual realm.

If he had still been alive, he'd have thought she was his soul mate.

Yet his time had already ended, the life had been sucked from him in agonizing currents caused by the chemical that had eaten away his surface. And now as his body lay in the casket six feet under, his flesh was rotting away. Sliding off the bone and crumbling to dirt and ashes.

Yet God had granted him a reprieve by allowing Crystal to see him, which had given him a chance for redemption. He had completed part of his mission. He had kept Crystal alive in her darkest hours. His voice, his encouragement, his whispers that she had hope of loved ones waiting on her had helped her fight for her life. Keeping Crystal alive and helping her find her soul mate was the only way he could redeem his own soul, and avoid burning in hell with Satan for eternity.

Now she was gone, and her fate lay in Dubois's hands.

But what if Dubois failed?

Lex had to find a way to help him.

CHAPTER EIGHTEEN

DAMON'S PALMS FELT SWEATY as he clutched the photo of Diego in his hands. Curses sputtered off his tongue as he mentally reviewed the heinous crimes the man had been responsible for. Not only men's lives taken, but innocent women and children's, and more than once. Diego had dropped a bomb in a village near Beirut and killed thousands. Then he'd wiped out an orphanage in China as a vendetta against one of his enemies. He'd also instigated a plan to attack numerous schools in the States just to remind the Americans of the power of terrorism and the vulnerability of their state. Thankfully, the E-team had intercepted those last plans and thwarted the plot.

The thought that Crystal—Jacqueline—had been involved with a man as coldhearted as Diego, that she might have slept with him, fueled Damon's rage.

The fact that she might have known who Diego was and what he did and had supported him, even loved him, turned Damon's stomach.

No—it was impossible that she'd known the truth about Diego. Jacqueline would not hurt anyone. She had volunteered in Third World countries, had taught kids in need. She could never harm a soul.

She triggered every protective instinct in him, every yearning to be better himself, every desire to be her hero and have the life with her that he could never have.

Because of who he'd been in the past.

He dropped his face into his hands. For God's sake, she might be the woman he thought he'd killed. Might have been burned and undergone months of mental and physical pain, surgeries and rehab therapy because of *him*.

If she knew, she'd hate him.

Steeling himself against his guilt, and the emotions and desire Jacqueline unleashed in him, he strode back in the room. Her pale green eyes searched his, the strain of remembering that her father had died a horrible death evident in her tightly set mouth.

He reined in the need to go to her and kiss those lips until they were soft and pliant against his, until she relaxed and forgot about her grief and could only feel the pleasure he would give her. Pleasure that would never end as his fingers massaged and teased her sensitive skin, as his lips glided against her mouth, neck, breasts, and her hidden secrets.

Pleasure from their bodies joining together until both of their nightmares disappeared forever, until they were fused together as one—

"Damon?"

He forced himself to place the picture on the desk. "This is a photo of Diego Bolton. Do you recognize him?"

Jacqueline bit down on her lip and looked at the photograph as Damon described the man's dossier.

Diego Bolton was a terrorist who killed countless innocents. Silently, Damon added that Diego was a different breed of hired killer than the men of the E-team. Even though they'd used violence as their means, they had fought for justice, to protect the citizens. Diego had no affiliations with any group that wanted justice. No conscience at all.

A strangled sound suddenly escaped her. "God…" Then she clutched her stomach, ran from the office and down the hall.

Damon followed, but paused at the door to the ladies' room.

Her choked sobs and the sound of her violent retching came through the closed door, giving him his answers.

JACQUELINE DROPPED HER HEAD against her arms atop the toilet lid, sobs wracking her body. She'd lost the contents of her stomach but still roiled with nausea.

The man in the photograph—she had known him.

A series of brief flashes invaded the dark spaces in her mind like lightning strikes splitting a cloudy sky. A mental picture of her dancing with Diego Bolton at a ritzy party. Then one of her lying beside him in bed, kissing him, letting him touch her body.

Then a feeling of dawning horror that he was not the man he'd portrayed himself to be. Hints here and there that he might be violent. His hand gripping her arm too tightly. Photos of Diego with suspected terrorists.

The camera in her mind rolled forward in fast motion. Kendra… Kendra meeting her in private. Telling her that she suspected Diego might be trouble, that he might be using her to get to her father. Dear God, had he? And if so, why? Where was Diego now?

"Jacqueline?"

Damon's gruff voice sounded through the closed door. Jacqueline couldn't face him yet.

"Are you all right?"

She swallowed, struggling to pull herself together. "Yes. Please, give me a minute."

Heaving to steady the nausea still rising in her chest, she dragged her weary body up and shuffled from the stall to the sink. She leaned against it, splashed cold water on her face, dampened a paper towel and pressed it to the back of her clammy neck, then rinsed out her mouth and retrieved a breath mint from her purse. She stared into the mirror at her face.

Rather, the face of her cousin.

Like a camera out of focus, the picture bled from Kendra's face to her old one, then blurred somewhere in between.

"Kendra… Oh, God, what did I do?" She lifted her fingers and traced over the delicate new skin, more tears welling in her eyes, blurring her image, yet the face of her cousin still shone through. A strong face that had belonged to a brave, gutsy woman.

A woman who'd been on the verge of exposing a dirty cop and Swafford.

And Diego, her lover.

Why had Kendra needed to die?

Why not her? And how had she wound up with Dr. Pace, a man who'd later stolen her cousin's skin and given it to her?

The fact that Kendra had questioned her about Diego and that Kendra had been murdered seemed too much of a coincidence.

Her lungs constricted.

Wasn't she somehow responsible for her cousin's death?

Guilt clouded her vision again, and the image of her own face returned to float in front of the mirror. Like a slide show of the past, a glimpse of her and Kendra at age five wearing fuzzy bathrobes standing before a Christmas tree, holding identical baby dolls.

Another snippet of them playing tea party when they were six. Then making mud pies in the woods. Stringing beads to make friendship bracelets. And later, as teens, when they'd joined a mission trip to Africa together. Kendra taking notes in her journal, talking about investigative reporting. Her collecting information on the schools and the needs of the children.

Then a frame of her and Kendra beside her father's coffin.

Cousins linked now by a common face and the horror that had ended Kendra's life.

Jacqueline's throat clogged. How could she live like this? How could she go on wearing Kendra's face while her cousin lay in the ground, her life stolen?

She trembled; grief, guilt, fear, anger colliding in a firestorm of determination. If she had caused Kendra's death, she didn't deserve happiness for herself. But she would find out who had killed her cousin if it was the last thing she ever did.

And she'd make sure the killer rotted in jail for the savage violence he had inflicted on her cousin and aunt.

DAMON COULDN'T STAND IT any longer. He knew Jacqueline was upset, probably torturing herself with guilt over her involvement with the man who'd murdered her father. But had she known about Diego or discovered his darker side before she'd been injured?

Had she been the woman in the explosion?

When he got home, he'd send that baby rattle out for testing and see if the prints matched hers. Then he'd know....

He eased the door open, and the sight before him wrenched his heart. Jacqueline stood before the mirror, staring at her reflection as if she'd seen a ghost. Maybe she had—Kendra's.

Forgetting every reason he shouldn't go to her, and ignoring every cop instinct screaming at him to treat her like a suspect, as Diego's possible accomplice, he strode toward her and pulled her in his arms.

"Shh. It's all right."

She fell against his chest, her body trembling, her wet cheeks dampening his shirt.

"Damon, what if I'm the reason Kendra died?"

He rubbed her back in slow circles, inhaled the scent of her shampoo, the scent of the soft spot at her neck that smelled like rain...but also the smell of fear. Her pain bled into his, shutting out his own guilty voice with the need to alleviate her agony.

"Kendra was an investigative reporter, Jacqueline. She knew the risks she took when she looked into Diego, and Swafford, and corruption on the police force. You aren't to blame for the fact that she ended up on dangerous ground. That's what she did, *who* she was, just like Antwaun and Jean-Paul are cops and I'm a federal agent." He gently stroked her hair from her tearstained cheek and pressed a kiss to her temple, then one to her cheek. She clung to him as if she needed his strength, and for the first time since the failed mission, he felt as if he could be a hero again. "And she loved you or she wouldn't have come to you to warn you about Diego."

She turned her angst-ridden face up to him, and licked her lips as if they were parched. His were, too. Dry for the taste of her. For the feel of the sweetness and salvation she offered. For the chance to be a whole man again. A man worthy of being cared for and loved.

"Damon…"

Her gaze locked with his, and heat speared his body, driving his need to a frenzy that robbed him of reason. They needed to escape their pain. Without thinking about where they were or the consequences, he lowered his head and claimed her mouth with his.

Her soft sigh of acquiescence only strummed his desire, and he slid his hands into the tumbling mass of her hair, threading the silky length between his fingers and pulling her closer to his body, so close her breasts grazed his chest. He felt the tight bud of her nipples as they peaked and begged for attention, and wanted her naked and in his arms.

She parted her lips, and he thrust his tongue inside her mouth, tasting and exploring until she sighed and ran her hands around his back and into his hair, drawing him closer as she arched into him. A groan escaped him, and he deepened the kiss, his hunger mounting as she played her tongue against his.

One moment they were kissing and the next, he moved his hands beneath her top. Heat flared inside him as he felt the smooth contours of her flat stomach, the curve of the underside of her breasts, the mounds he wanted to hold in his hands as he took her nipple into his mouth. He released her mouth and bowed his head to find his way to her breast, his hand already loosening the front clasp, her skin grazing his fingers. But the door to the bathroom opened and a female officer walked in. He jerked up, suddenly realizing where he was and what he was doing.

Taking advantage of Jacqueline when she needed his comfort and help.

Disgusted with himself and knowing he might be compromising the investigation by losing his objectivity, he released her and stepped back. "I'll meet you outside."

Avoiding the other woman's eyes, he strode past her, wondering at his sanity and professional reputation as he stepped through the door.

Jean-Paul stood in the hallway, arms crossed. "Is she all right?"

No.

Neither was he. She was so damn hot he wanted to go back to her now. Forget the case and take her home to bed.

But she needed his help, just as Antwaun did. Antwaun, who was sitting in jail. Who'd loved Kendra. A woman whose face Jacqueline now wore.

"She's starting to have flashbacks. I'm taking her to visit her mother. Maybe that will trigger more memories and we can piece together this mess."

"Good. Get back to me. I'm on my way to talk to Antwaun's partner. He may be responsible for framing Antwaun. And the murders."

THE HOWL OF SOME UNKNOWN creature shattered the quiet of the bayou as darkness descended across the swampland. Esmeralda cocked her head sideways listening to the feral cry, reading the signs of frustration and warning of the evil forces at work in the backwoods. The devil's vile breath bathed her neck. The greedy bastard.

She spread her hands before her and began to chant in the ancient language of the witches who had come before her, calling upon the good magic and fairies to draw on their powers, protect the bayou and the good people of New Orleans.

Damon Dubois was one of them, though he would argue that he was not.

He had been lost in the darkness for a while now,

had walked the ledge between the forces many times, as Lex had. But the aura around Damon was shifting now, the black rim tinged with intermittent flashes of gold like heat lightning against a night sky.

Lex was also changing.

All because of the woman.

She needed all of them, but they needed her as well. God had commanded it, and he had chosen well. Even Kendra…the woman with the lost face… was not lost completely.

Sounds of evil warriors erupted in the distance, limbs and brush crackling. The gators surged upward from low-slung resting spots beneath the muddy Mississippi's surface and vented their shrill cry of attack, knifelike teeth ready to tear the limbs off of unseen prey.

The cats arched their backs and snarled, claws bared, ears perched as they surrounded her with their magic protective circle.

Shadows from the swamp rose in the mist, hovering and moving like ghosts through the night, searching for lost souls and innocents, the war between good and evil, a battle that would never end. Someone was out there. The same person who had come for the woman.

He wanted *Esmeralda* now.

But he didn't understand the power of the cats.

Midnight suddenly darted off the porch and ran

into the woods. He had zoned in on the predator and would keep her safe tonight.

She bent low to pet Gorgon. "You must go to Dubois house, call for the others, guard him and the woman."

Gorgon meowed, licked her palm in understanding, then leaped from the porch to do as she bid. She heard a scream erupt in the swamp and knew that Midnight had found the evil one and sunk his claws into the man's flesh.

HE BELLOWED IN PAIN at the cat's attack, furious that the vile creature had caught him off guard. He was a trained sniper, able to get in and out of situations and places that no normal man could, yet the black thing had sneaked up on him, then leaped at his chest like a fucking panther.

Dammit. He beat at the cat, prying its sharp claws and teeth from his chest and arms, plucked it away and tossed it toward a tree. The cat's head snapped backward and a bloodcurdling screech rent the air, but it landed on all fours, green eyes glittering as if it were the devil's own. A vulture soared above, and gators hissed behind him, his feet marring into the quicksand soil as he slowly stepped backward. He had to find a way out.

Reaching inside his pocket, he removed a pack of matches he'd picked up at a strip club on Bourbon

Street, struck a few matches and tossed them into the dry grass. They landed at the edge of the woods, between him and the cat. The brittle blades caught immediately, flames catching the twigs and moss, spreading. The cat crept backward, hair on end, and he took advantage and escaped.

Blood trickled down his chest, dotting his shirt, and he wiped his sticky hands on his jeans as he climbed in his Jeep. Rage exploded inside him as he stared at the old woman's shanty through the fog. Lex had babbled that his grandmother was a witch, and he was beginning to believe it. What if the cat's claws were treated with some kind of poison?

His hands ached, and the wounds on his chest stung like fire. Still, the sight of blood, even his own, stirred his hunger for more.

For a woman's—the one with Dubois. He could cut her up just as he had Kendra.

Suddenly thunder rumbled and a flash of lightning pierced the dark sky, sending rain pouring to drown out the fire he had set, as if God or magic indeed guarded the witch.

Leave no witnesses behind.

Fury raged inside him at his failed mission. Failure was not tolerated. Just as Dubois leaving the E-team couldn't be.

Time to escalate his plan. Send another photo to

the Dubois family. The one Mr. and Mrs. Pierre Dubois would recognize.

The one that would tear the happy little family apart forever.

CHAPTER NINETEEN

JACQUELINE COULD BARELY look at Damon as they drove to the rest home housing her mother. Questions about her past involvement with Diego and Kendra's death nagged at her, along with guilt and grief as she remembered her father's funeral. Her mother had been despondent then, had pushed her away….

Was her father's death related to Kendra's, and to the fact that she'd ended up in a hospital herself? Was it all connected to Diego? Were both their deaths her fault?

"Do you know where Diego is now?" she asked.

Damon cleared his throat. "He's dead."

"You're sure?"

Damon nodded, a grim look in his eyes.

"How did he die?"

He shifted, fingers tightening on the steering wheel. "I can't really discuss it," he said. "All you need to know is that he's gone and can't hurt you, not ever again."

She wondered at his secrecy. "Then it's not him,

but someone else who wants to kill me," she said quietly.

Damon's dark gaze locked with hers. "I won't let that happen."

His quiet authoritarian voice soothed her anxiety, slightly, and she studied the storm clouds outside, noting the gray and black shadows streaking the deserted road, the fingerlike claws of the Spanish moss as it waved in the wind. Any minute she expected ghosts to rise from the ground and shimmy through the bayou searching for their lost souls, or perhaps their salvation.

Lex... Esmeralda said he was gone. Had Jacqueline really seen a spirit caught in limbo?

How about Kendra? Was she hovering in between worlds, faceless and horrified at her fate, waiting for justice?

More images from her past returned in small snippets—she and her cousin jumping rope in the backyard. A birthday party with pony rides and squirt-gun battles. The two of them spying on the boys down the street when they were eleven. Kendra telling her that she was in love for the first time when she was twelve.

And then again...just before she died.

Jacqueline gripped the door handle and glanced at Damon. Kendra had been in love with Antwaun. And now he was accused of killing her....

But it was becoming pretty clear he was innocent; Kendra wouldn't want him to go to jail. Jacqueline touched her face—her cousin's skin—and shivered. She had to be strong and help Damon. She owed Kendra that and so much more, even if she was still disconnected from her old life.

Damon pulled up to a black iron gate with a security stand, spoke to the guard to gain entrance, then they wound down a long secluded drive lined by towering trees. He parked in a guest spot beneath a covered entrance. The stately white building resembled a hotel more than her image of a mental facility, the professional landscaping highlighting dozens of flower beds, a garden area to the side and acres of plush green grass with cobblestone pathways for the residents to stroll. Grateful her mother hadn't been confined to a shabby nursing home and mistreated, she climbed out and walked to the entrance.

A few minutes later, the director of the facility, a stout woman named Geneva Curtis, met them in her office.

"Miss Braudaway, I wondered if you were going to visit."

"I would have come much sooner, but I had an accident and have been hospitalized for months," she explained, feeling chastised by the woman's remark.

The woman jerked her head backward. "Oh, I'm sorry."

"How is my mother?"

Miss Curtis smiled sadly. "She has good days and bad, but her depression continues to plague her. It's almost as if she's grieving her life away."

"Can I see her now? Please."

"Certainly." She and Damon followed the woman to a suite, but the director hesitated at the doorway. "If she becomes agitated though, I'll have to ask you to leave."

Jacqueline nodded, then braced herself. She hoped her mother would recognize her and be happy to see her.

But the harshness of her mother's cry at the funeral taunted her, and told her that she wouldn't.

DAMON WATCHED JACQUELINE AS she approached her mother, hoping to glean some new information from their interaction.

Her mother sat in a wicker rocking chair beside the window, dressed in white slacks and a pale blue blouse, her look glassy, as if she was in a catatonic state or heavily medicated. He'd never met the woman but had seen photos of her and the ambassador. Her once blond hair had tinges of gray in it now, and she had lost weight over the past year, along with any semblance of a smile.

The room smelled like lavender and was simply decorated with a burgundy sofa, coffee table, television and the rocking chair. Magazines about home decorating and antiques were stacked neatly on the table, and several photos of the woman and her husband lined the built-in bookshelf against the wall. Only one photo captured the entire family. Odd.

His own mother had countless pictures of him and his siblings on the walls, tables and bookcases.

"Mom?" Jacqueline's tentative voice jerked him from his thoughts.

A frown marred Mrs. Braudaway's forehead as she glanced at her daughter. "Who are you?"

Jacqueline stooped down to take her mother's hands in her own. "It's me, Mom. Jacqueline."

Shock and anger tightened the woman's mouth. "You aren't my daughter. I'm not blind. I can see, young lady."

Jacqueline winced and bit down on her lower lip. "It is me, Mom. I had a terrible accident, and was burned badly. I had to have plastic surgery."

Her mother reached up and tilted Jacqueline's face sideways. "No. You're Kendra."

"No, Mom—"

"Yes, you are. Why are you lying to me now?" Her mother stood abruptly, letting the afghan in her lap fall to the floor as she gripped the rocking chair arms. "What do you want?"

Jacqueline glanced at Damon, her eyes misting, then turned back to her mother. "I'm not lying. I had surgery and was in the hospital for months. I would have come to see you sooner if I had been able to."

"Where's Jacqueline?" Mrs. Braudaway cried in an agitated voice. "What have you done with her?"

"Listen to me, Mother. I am Jacqueline."

"She ran off with that awful man, didn't she?" Her mother's eyes darted toward him, fear sparking in the glassy depths. "You told me about him, Kendra."

"Mrs. Braudaway." Damon stepped forward and reached inside his jacket for his identification.

Jacqueline's mother panicked and shouted, "He's got a gun! Don't kill me, please don't!"

Jacqueline ached for a hug, to calm her mother, to know that she still loved her. "Mother, please, it's okay. He's with the FBI."

A nurse appeared at the door with a scowl. "What's going on in here?"

Mrs. Braudaway twisted the ends of her hair nervously. "He's got a gun."

Damon held up his hands to indicate he posed no threat. "Yes, I do. But I'm a federal agent. I'm going to show her my identification. My name is Special Agent Damon Dubois."

Jacqueline stroked her mother's arm. "He's helping me figure out what happened to me, Mother, and who killed Kendra."

"Kendra?" her mother screeched. "Oh, God, where is she?"

Jacqueline gave Damon a helpless look, and he flashed his badge. "Mrs. Braudaway, this is your daughter, Jacqueline. I'm afraid Kendra is dead. I'm investigating her murder."

"Murder?" Mrs. Braudaway clapped her hands over her heart and staggered back. "Oh, God, no! Murdered just like Eduardo."

"Mom," Jacqueline said softly, "I need to know what happened."

She turned toward Jacqueline, eyes flaring with emotions. "You know what happened. You killed your father."

JACQUELINE'S HEART CLENCHED in pain.

She closed her eyes, fighting waves of anguish and guilt, trying desperately to see the past, but images blurred and ran together.

"Mrs. Braudaway, that's not true," Damon said.

Dizzy, Jacqueline staggered to the sofa and collapsed onto it, then leaned her elbows on her knees and dropped her face into her splayed hands. She couldn't breathe, although somehow it registered in her muddled mind that Damon was defending her. But why? How did he know she was innocent when she couldn't remember herself?

"Maybe you folks should leave," the nurse suggested, still hovering at the door like an armed guard.

Damon held up a warning hand. "Just give us a

few minutes. Please. Jacqueline needs to talk to her mother. This is important."

The nurse eyed him skeptically, then gave Jacqueline a more sympathetic look. "All right, but if you upset her again, you two have to leave."

She left with a hefty sigh, and Jacqueline remembered her resolve to find Kendra's killer, and gathered her breath. "Mother, I... The accident caused me to have amnesia. All I remember is seeing Dad's car exploding. Then Kendra came to me at the funeral and told me that I knew the killer." She gulped back emotions that threatened to destroy her.

Tears filled her mother's eyes and she sank back into the rocking chair, looking lost. Damon moved forward, knelt and replaced the afghan over her lap. "Please, Mrs. Braudaway. I understand this is difficult. But Jacqueline needs you now. She needs to know what happened to her father. She might be in danger, too."

Jacqueline gave him a silent look of thanks, stunned at his quiet empathy. But her mother stiffened her back and turned to her, a fierce anger in her expression. "I tried to tell you, Jacqueline, not to get involved with that man. Diego Bolton. He was using you to get to your father."

"What made you think that?" Damon asked.

"Eduardo's security team, they had information suggesting Diego was involved with illegal matters, that he was dangerous." She pointed an accusing finger at Jacqueline. "I told you, but you wouldn't listen. And when your father tried to send you away, you two argued so fiercely he feared he'd lose you if he pressed further."

Jacqueline winced, but Damon forged on. "Where did Jacqueline and Diego Bolton meet?"

"At a charity function. Jacqueline…she liked to work with her father. She and Kendra…they always wanted to grow up and travel, and Kendra wanted to be a journalist, and Jacqueline said she wanted to produce photo essays." Mrs. Braudaway knotted the edges of the afghan in her hands again. "Later Jacqueline decided to teach English in Mexico, but she continued her photo essays. She was obsessed with the children and portraying their needs."

"I do like children," Jacqueline said, a slide show of several shots of the starving kids in Africa playing through her mind. "Like Father, I was interested in social issues. I photographed the hungry kids, the ones in need of medication, the poor conditions." Diego had told her he'd admired her work. That he had contacts to help her raise money.

But he hadn't been what he'd seemed….

"You organized several charity events with your shows, and those photos raked in thousands to raise awareness," Mrs. Braudaway added, softening.

"That's where Diego met Jacqueline," Damon

filled in. "At one of those charity functions. He posed as an entrepreneur?"

"Yes, he was charming. Generous. At least he appeared to be." Tears glittered in Mrs. Braudaway's eyes, and she directed her comments to Damon as if Jacqueline were invisible. "If only Jacqueline had listened. Such a smart girl with such a good heart. Yet she was always a fool with men. Always choosing the bad boys, the losers." Her brittle tone cut Jacqueline to the bone.

"And this time, her father died because of it. For that, I can never forgive her."

DAMON BIT BACK A CAUSTIC remark at Mrs. Braudaway's callous condemnation of her daughter. The finality of her unforgiving statement disturbed him, but the raw pain etched on Jacqueline's face bothered him more.

"Mother...I'm sorry. So sorry," Jacqueline whispered. "I wish I could bring Dad back..."

"I'm tired now, please leave." Mrs. Braudaway turned toward the window and stared outside, the glassy, distant look returning to her eyes.

Damon placed a hand along Jacqueline's waist as she stood. He felt the fine tremors in her body and ached to assuage her pain, though only her mother could do that. But she'd cloaked herself in bitterness and grief, and exiled her own child.

Damon thought of his parents and how much they loved each of their children, how they'd never abandon one of their own, how they were sticking by Antwaun now.

But if they knew what Damon had done in the past, what he'd been through, would they still stand beside him? Or would he see the same type of pain and disappointment in their eyes that he saw in Mrs. Braudaway's?

Sweat beaded on his neck as he led Jacqueline outside to the car. She sank into the leather seat, leaned her head back and closed her eyes. A tear seeped down her cheek, and he itched to reach out and wipe it away, but his cell phone rang.

He checked the number—his partner from the bureau—then flipped open the phone. "Dubois here."

"Damon, I got a hit on that key you found at the Yateses' place. It belongs to a safety-deposit box." He relayed the bank address and box number, started the engine, shifted gears and headed toward New Orleans.

"What was that about?" Jacqueline asked softly.

He glanced at her pale face and squeezed her hand, wishing he could do more. "That key we found belongs to a safety-deposit box that Kendra had. We're going there now. Maybe there's something inside that will lead us to her killer."

Jacqueline nodded, then closed her eyes again, and he stroked his thumb along her jaw. "I know your mother's words hurt," he said gruffly. "But your father's death was not your fault, Jacqueline. One day, she'll realize that and you two can talk."

"I wish I could believe that," Jacqueline said in a strangled voice. "But if my involvement with Diego Bolton got my father killed, I don't blame her for hating me."

"She doesn't hate you," Damon replied. "She's just angry and bitter right now. In time, she'll heal." Hopefully so would Jacqueline.

But he understood the blinding power of guilt and how it could destroy a person.

Jacqueline dozed to sleep while he drove back to New Orleans, and he tried not to examine his growing feelings for her, the constant need he had to touch her, to ease both of their pain by making love to her.

An hour later, she stirred as he parked at the bank. Brushing her hair from her eyes, he asked, "Are you all right? I could have taken you back to my house first…"

"I'm fine. I want to see what Kendra put in that safety-deposit box." She lifted her fingers and touched her face. "I have to know who killed my cousin, Damon. She's more a part of me now than ever before. I owe it to her to help find justice for her."

He nodded, and they exited the car. The sky still

hung heavy with gray clouds, the smell of rain and fear surrounding them as they went inside. Damon flashed his identification and explained the circumstances, then one of the bank officers led them to the safety-deposit boxes. Seconds later, Damon removed a large manila envelope from the box and sat down at a wooden table in a private room to examine the contents. Jacqueline joined him, her hands folded, her breath not quite steady.

The files contained Kendra's notes on Swafford. She had discovered that Antwaun was working undercover, and that Swafford had left the country to avoid being caught. Some of her notes indicated that an informant had told her that Antwaun had killed Swafford, but as Damon studied her notes, he realized that she'd questioned the informant's revelations. Was this informant a cop? The one framing Antwaun?

Damon searched but found no name listed. Dammit.

Desperate for more, he skimmed through several pages and discovered his own name in the file. His heartbeat accelerated, and he read on, a sense of dread pitting his stomach. Kendra had uncovered information about the E-team. She'd thought Antwaun might be involved with the group, then had traced it back to *him*.

"What is it, Damon?" Jacqueline asked, her shoulders hunched. "Did you find something?"

"I'm not sure." Panic slammed into him as he spotted notes on three missions the E-team had orchestrated. Three assassinations.

He skimmed further and discovered information on two other kills that weren't his, ones that appeared as if they were direct E-team missions. Some that Cal and Max had undertaken after he'd left?

No. The next page indicated *he* had made the kills.

His fingers tightened around the folder, the hair on the back of his neck bristling. What was going on? Who had told Kendra about the E-team? Had that knowledge gotten her murdered?

And who had named him as the killer in those last two assassinations?

Someone who was setting *him* up in case the E-team was exposed...

Anger surged through him as other realizations followed. Whoever had done so had framed him for murders he hadn't committed. Had betrayed him and wanted him to go down.

You can never escape what you are, Cal had told him when he'd left the E-team. *You're a born killer.*

It was true. Even if he hadn't executed the last two assignments, he had assassinated the others. He had been a hired and trained killer.

So many secrets... Tell and you die.

The only way to save his brother was to confront his past.

If he came forward though, the government's reputation, the other special-ops groups, the country, members of the E-team, his friends, his family—they might all be in jeopardy.

REGINALD PACE STUDIED the sketches of Crystal—Jacqueline—his chest puffing up with pride at the intricate surgical procedures he had performed to piece her back together and give her the finished, polished look of a beautiful woman. He had documented each step and was ready to go public.

But doing so would inevitably bring questions about how he had acquired the skin to transplant onto her face. He weighed his options. Utilizing the powers of his trade and his government connections, he could forge paperwork, signatures, and pull it off. Jeopardizing his position with the government though was a possibility.

But he had to hide all traces of evidence linking him back to Kendra. And then there was the other woman whose face he had removed…

A shadow moved in the waning light, silhouetted in the window of his office like a ghost. Several times lately, he'd felt something odd in the room, as if an ominous presence was near. Sometimes he thought he felt a breath against his neck, smelled the scent of a stranger. No. Not a stranger—the ointment he'd given Lex.

But Lex was dead....

The lights flickered off, then on, then off again, pitching his office into total darkness. He froze, waiting on the backup generator to kick in, but suddenly he felt that breath again. This time closer. It was tinged with a sour, vile odor that turned his stomach.

A second later, a hand gripped his neck, then he felt the pressure of a knife pressed into his throat. He jerked to try and escape, but the sharp point of the knife traced a path along his skin, drawing blood. Fear roared in his head. And he opened his mouth to yell for help, but his attacker shoved the knife in his mouth and cut out his tongue. Pain screamed through him, and his mouth filled with blood, the gurgling sound of it spilling over and dripping down his chin as he slid to the floor to die.

CHAPTER TWENTY

WHAT IN THE HELL had Kendra found out about the E-team?

Damon parked in his drive, glad to be home. Once he'd felt safe and thought he could hide himself from the rest of the world here, yet tonight his world was crumbling apart. Knowing his past was about to catch up with him, he searched the perimeter, his nerves on edge.

Sweat trickled down his back, and the palms of his hands felt clammy. Beside him, Jacqueline breathed unsteadily as if she, too, sensed danger in the darkness.

Ever since that night he'd set the explosion and killed Diego, since he'd seen the woman trapped in the fire, he'd known the day of reckoning would come.

He should feel relieved. If he was outed, he wouldn't have to pretend to be the hero he wasn't. He could skip that welcome at the upcoming Memorial Day parade and honor the men who actually deserved the recognition, instead of lying to the public. He deserved to be punished.

But he'd wanted to protect his comrades in the war against evil, protect his country even if it had meant he'd sacrificed his own humanity. Then later, he'd wanted to protect his family from knowing that their son had fallen from glory.

He hated to see them pay for his sins.

"Damon?"

Jacqueline's soft voice broke through the barrier he'd erected since he'd opened that file. He'd told her that the file held notes of Kendra's investigation into the dirty cop, Swafford and Pace, but he'd omitted the notes regarding his name and the E-team. He couldn't tell her yet, either.

He'd have to talk to Jean-Paul soon. Maybe tomorrow. Time to come clean and get to the bottom of this mess. If Antwaun was being framed because of *him,* he had to confess and face the consequences.

"Let's go inside," he said quietly.

She nodded and climbed from the car, looking weary, and he mentally kicked himself for his self-absorption. She was still weak from stress.

At the corner of his house, he spotted a black cat in the shadows, then a gray one and a fat tabby on his porch. Others appeared out of the bayou, circling his house. Again, the hairs on his neck bristled, but this time he sensed that Esmeralda had sent the cats to protect them.

He didn't actually believe in her magic, did he?

No, but Esmeralda believed and he accepted her eccentricities, felt comforted by this one, at least.

His hand went to the Glock inside his jacket, and he relaxed slightly, relieved he had a weapon.

Jacqueline had been through hell today. No, she'd been through hell for the last few months, mostly because of *him*. He desperately wanted to ease that pain, at least for the night.

He guided her inside, the scent of old wood and the bayou filling the air, the photo of his family and their nearly hurricane-demolished home a reminder of all he had to lose.

But he would have to hurt them to save his brother.

And this woman?

She roused every protective instinct in his Dubois blood, every desire to be a man she could depend on, one she deserved. Every need to hold her and bury himself in her and assuage his own guilt for causing her pain. For leaving her to die.

He might not have the results of the fingerprints from the baby rattle yet, but his instincts told him she had been at Diego's that day. What she'd been doing there, whether or not she was in love with the man, Damon didn't know.

But he was certain she hadn't been a party to his violence.

A thought struck him, and he went to his computer and coaxed her to sit down beside him in the cushy chair next to the ancient rolltop desk.

"Damon—"

"Shh, wait a minute." He Googled her name and watched the results pop up on-screen. A magazine article featured her charity work for the youth of Africa, and another cited a list of her volunteer work in several countries. She'd been an ambassador for the poor herself—had used her father's money to jump-start a foundation to help eradicate polio in developing nations—and had contributed photos to an art exhibit showcasing poverty across the world, raising awareness for her cause and earning her several humanitarian awards.

He studied the images, then turned to see her looking at them with tears in her eyes. "The children… They are the ones who suffer," she whispered in a strangled voice. "I hated to see them so hungry and in need."

He clasped her hands in between his. "Look at all the good you did for the world, Jacqueline."

"Maybe. But look how I destroyed my own mother and father."

God, her pain mirrored his own guilt for what he was going to do to his family.

"You're not to blame," he said, desperate to convince her of the beautiful woman he saw.

He captured her face between his hands and caressed her cheeks with his thumbs. "If you're guilty of anything, it's being good, so loving that you innately trust." He couldn't resist. He pressed a kiss to her forehead, then lowered his hands to her shoulders and massaged her tense muscles.

"Damon, these pictures, they don't make up for hurting my mother. My father…he died because of me, because I was involved with a bad man…" Her voice broke on a sob.

He dragged her into his arms and cradled her against him. "Diego was a terrorist, Jacqueline. He would have found a way to reach your father with or without you. He was a cunning, calculated killer. And he targeted your father because he was an ambassador to a country that supported the war. Nothing you did or could have done would have stopped him." He stroked the sensitive skin of her neck, tilted her chin up so she had to look into his eyes. "You *know* that inside. And your father…he knows you loved him. That you would never have hurt him."

Not the way Damon was going to hurt his own family.

But that was *his* cross to bear. Tonight was about Jacqueline, soothing her pain, assuaging the anguish of her mother's words. Making her feel wanted and needed, and loved.

His chest tightened, and he mentally shook away the thought. He couldn't love her or anyone else, could not allow himself to dream about a family.

Antwaun...

The brothers had always vowed that nothing would come between them, especially a woman. And Jacqueline wore the face of the woman Antwaun loved.

God help him, Damon wanted her anyway. Something about her, the sweetness of her soul called to him as if loving her could offer him salvation from his own evil.

He would pay the price. But he wouldn't let her suffer needlessly. He'd convince her that she was an angel compared to him, and that she deserved forgiveness, even if her mother couldn't give it to her.

JACQUELINE LOOKED INTO Damon's gaze, feeling raw and exposed. Her heart clenched with the need to believe him.

He caressed her jawline with the pads of this thumbs, the gesture so tender that she nearly fell into him. She ached for his understanding and absolution, and hungered for the feel of his lips on her, his hands to strip her, his body to meld with hers until the pleasure robbed her pain and she was mindless with his touch.

His eyes darkened with the same raw hunger, and he lowered his head and claimed her mouth with his, plunging his tongue between her parted lips with a growl of pure male passion. Her tongue reached out to dance with his in a primal ritual, and she lifted her arms and threaded her fingers into his thick hair, urging him closer. One second, they were kissing, and the next he rolled her off her chair, down onto the braided rug in front of the fireplace, and began to devour her.

She arched into him, desperate for the coupling, but suddenly felt afraid.

He removed his clothes and stood naked above her.

He was strong and powerful-looking, and he had scars. A couple from bullet wounds, others that looked like war injuries. Seeing that he'd revealed himself for her, she stood and went to him, traced her finger over each one, kissed the mangled, discolored tissue, then pressed a hand to his chest.

She was so moved by his physical being, his eyes on her, begging for her to trust him, that tears pricked her eyes. "I'm falling in love with you, Damon." She desperately wanted him to love her in return.

Emotions clouded his eyes, and he jerked her to him, fusing his mouth with hers as her admission moved something inside him. His skin felt burning hot to the touch, and she kissed the salty, rough texture of his jaw, his neck, then his chest, reveling in the coarse dark hair scattered across his broad torso. He groaned and laved her neck and the sweet spot behind her ear. Then he flicked his thumbs over her nipples and lowered his head to taste her through the thin material of her blouse. The blouse came off, and he ripped at the flimsy lace of her bra until her breasts spilled into his hands and he kneaded them.

She moaned this time, from deep within her soul, telling him how much she enjoyed his hands upon her. Finally, he kissed the faint scars on her abdomen, just as she had his, bringing tears to her eyes with his tenderness as he lowered them both to the ground again.

With a growl, he kneed her legs apart. She gladly opened to him, cradling his hips, his rigid length between her legs, her senses singing with excitement as he drove himself against her heat. Blinded by desire, she grabbed his arms at the biceps and nipped at his lips with her own, shuddering when he lowered his mouth to take one turgid nipple between his teeth. The pleasure bordered on pain, it was so exquisite. He teased the tip with his tongue, then suckled her hard and long, drawing her between his lips so deeply that she arched and cried out with the torture. Her hips rose to meet his hard sex, and he slid one hand down to cup her mound. But that wasn't close enough either, and he yanked off the rest of her clothes, until she lay beneath him, naked and vulnerable, pleading for more, panting and clawing at him to be nearer.

He rose up, breathing heavily, a fine sheen of perspiration dotting his forehead as he searched her face. She traced a droplet with her finger, then lifted her head to flick her tongue across his nipple. When she sucked it into her mouth, he growled, cupped her head between his hands and pulled her away. Seconds later, he was sucking her breasts again, twisting her nipples with his teeth and fingers, licking his way down her belly. She moaned as he tasted the moist heat between her thighs. His tongue lashes drove her to a frenzied wild madness, and she clutched his arms, begging for him to be inside her.

He used his tongue as if it were his cock though, thrusting into her wet folds, deepening the strokes, lapping at her, starved for the taste of her, feeding on her pleasure. Unable to bear the sweet pressure, sensations splintered her, breaking her world into a million beautiful colors, colors that slashed through the darkness and sprinkled brilliant splashes of hope into the emptiness.

She clung to him, shaking with euphoria and wanting more, wanting him inside her, for the night to last forever.

DAMON SHOULD STOP NOW. Walk away with some pride intact. He'd given her satisfaction, made her come in his arms.

But the heavenly taste of her only whetted his appetite.

She had said she was falling in love with him.

God…he wanted that love. Wanted to be worthy of it. But he wasn't. And if she knew the truth, that he had caused her pain…

He was a condemned man, felt as if he were having his last bit of peace before taking a walk on death row.

His heart pounded, his conscience warring against his burning need to be with her.

God help him, but he didn't have the strength to do the right thing and leave her.

"Damon…" She slid her hands down his back, kneading his muscles, then lower to his hips where she splayed her fingers over his buttocks and urged him to come inside her. The raw need to take her, to make her his, was overpowering, and he grabbed his pants, jerked out a condom, tore it open with his teeth and rose to his knees to slide it on. Her gaze drifted over him, glazed with passion and hunger, crazed with wanting him.

He couldn't resist. He'd wanted her since the moment he'd seen her in that garden at the hospital.

He'd grieved for her when he'd thought she'd died, but by some miracle, she was alive, and he wanted to have this moment with her.

She might hate him tomorrow, but tonight she would know nothing but pleasure.

She wrapped her fingers around his cock and stroked his length, sending his heart ablaze with the fierce hunger roaring through him. She watched him roll on the condom, which only spurred his erection to its peak, making him throb to be inside her. Desperate for her, he cupped her breasts in his hands again, teased her nipples once more until she moaned his name, then he thrust his length between her thighs, rubbing against her folds, teasing her damp center until she wrapped her fingers around his aching member and guided him inside her.

He watched her eyes flare with excitement, felt the tremors of her body as another orgasm built inside her and she clenched her muscles around him. He threw his head back in a roar, and began thrusting in and out of her, first gently, then faster and harder, building the rhythm, sinking deeper each time, forcing her legs wider and her hips higher until he buried himself so deeply inside her body that he knew he was lost forever.

When he groaned his release, she clawed at his back as he pounded himself into her again and again. His body spasmed, shaking with the force of his climax. Even as the tremors of her orgasm began to subside, she pressed kisses to his chest and wrapped her legs around him, begging him not to leave her.

They fell asleep, nestled in each other's arms, their bodies intertwined, his length still embedded deep inside her.

HE HAD BEEN WAITING at Dubois's house, lurking in the shadows of the bayou behind the property, hoping to get a glimpse of Dubois and the woman he'd found in Pace's care, determined to see if she was the same woman with Diego that day. But he had just gotten a better show than he'd imagined.

Dubois had complained of guilt over the woman's near-death at his hands, but like the bastard he believed the man to be, Damon hadn't let it keep him from fucking her. The mere sight of Damon stripping her and pounding himself inside her made him hard, and he'd freed his own cock and sprayed his seed across the bayou.

Behind him a bird squawked and a gator skimmed the surface of the water. He squinted through the towering trees and spotted a black cat combing the edge of the property. Another yellow feline appeared from beneath the tupelo tree, and suddenly dozens of them came out of the darkness, their green eyes glittering as if searching for prey.

Damn cats. Had that witch sent them over here, too?

He quickly zipped his jeans, sweat stinging the cat scratches on his chest. Next time he'd bring a god-damn gun and shoot every one of them. They could not protect Dubois or Jacqueline Braudaway forever.

If this woman had been at Diego Bolton's the day they'd made the hit, she should have stayed dead.

Someone had obviously dragged her from the fire. It had to have been one of the E-team who'd gone back in and rescued her—meaning one of them had betrayed him.

Betraying the men of the team was a crime. Nothing was supposed to come between their bonds of brotherhood.

Whoever had done so must be punished with death. Just as Pace had been.

He smiled, still high on adrenaline from the feel of the man's blood running down his hands. If this woman had risen from the dead, then it was possible that she'd seen them at the explosion site. That meant she could expose them.

She had to die again.

It would be even more fun watching Dubois suffer this time.

His fingers itched to do the job, and he pulled the knife from his pocket, ran his finger over the tip and watched a pinprick of his own blood trickle down his hand. He lifted his head and sucked the coppery droplet into his mouth, craving more.

Her blood. Her life force spilling out between his hands. Her last breath as she gasped and begged not to die.

He'd carve her up into tiny pieces and send them to Dubois. If he'd suffered when he'd thought she'd died in that fire, wait until he saw her body parts mutilated and arrayed on a platter.

She wouldn't come back from the dead this time.

CHAPTER TWENTY-ONE

Need consumed Damon. He'd never felt anything as powerful as the lust that drove him to make love to Jacqueline again and again during the night. He didn't stop to analyze the reason. He'd been dead for so long that for one night he wanted to live.

She had welcomed him with open arms and hungry kisses each time, whispering her love and desires in the darkness as he'd taken her to bed and touched and kissed every inch of her. An hour later, he had pressed her against the bedroom wall, his heart racing as she cried out his name and he'd thrust inside her. Afterward, they had showered and bathed each other, and had made love with the water cascading down their bodies, steam rising in a cloud of mist that obliterated the rest of the world.

Now standing on the porch in the predawn light, he kissed her savagely, lifted her onto his aching cock and impaled her, then dropped his head forward to bite her neck as he ground their bodies together. The sound of his skin slapping against hers, the feel of her moistness squeezing his erection and the scent of her sweet body made him wild. She clawed at his shoulders, threw her head back and moaned, begging for more. He filled her again and again, sucking her tight nipples into his mouth until she trembled with another orgasm that triggered his own release.

Cradling her against him, he dropped into the porch swing, and rocked her back and forth.

Finally they rushed inside and he made omelets. After devouring the food, she looked at him as if the meal hadn't been enough. Knowing his own hunger would never be sated, he flipped her around against the kitchen table, tore off her robe, bent her over and slid inside her from behind. Her hair formed a curtain around her face as she splayed her hands on the table to brace herself for his thick pounding, and together they shook the table as another mind-blowing climax gripped him.

Still shaking from the impact of their coupling, he turned her in his arms and pressed kisses to her neck and face. God, he never wanted to let her go.

His cell phone trilled though, and he silently cursed. Reality intervening meant he had to face the case again. His reprieve had come to an end.

Was this Max confirming his worst fears about Jacqueline?

"I wish you didn't have to get that," she whispered, her hands roaming down his chest.

He nodded, his breathing still unsteady as he kissed her gently. "Me, too, but I have to."

He grabbed the phone off the table and checked the caller ID. Jean-Paul. "Yeah, it's Damon."

"Hey, little brother. We have more trouble."

"I'm listening."

"Some reporter got a hold of a photo of Jacqueline and ran it in the paper this morning, along with a story about the face transplant."

He glanced at Jacqueline, hating the emotional impact the story would have on her. "I can't believe Pace went public." Then he cursed. "He must have figured out a way to cover his ass."

"I don't think so," Jean-Paul said in a gruff voice. "Pace is dead."

"What?"

"It's not pretty. Someone cut out his tongue and left him to bleed to death. One of his nurses found him this morning." His brother paused. "I've got a crime-scene unit there now looking for evidence, and since we're worried about a dirty cop, the bureau has confiscated all of Pace's files including his computer."

"What did you find in that safety-deposit box?" Jean-Paul asked.

Damn. Damon remembered Kendra's files, the ones implicating himself and the E-team, a team Jean-Paul knew nothing about. They might find information on them in Pace's files, or on his computer.

"Meet me at the station and we'll go over everything," Damon said. He hung up and explained to Jacqueline that Pace was dead. She went stark-white and he pulled her into his arms, knowing it might be one of the last times she allowed him to comfort her.

He had to tell Jean-Paul the truth. He couldn't let him find out from another source that his brother had been a hired killer.

Then he'd have to endure watching his brother's respect and admiration turn to disgust and disdain.

But if someone related to the E-team had killed Kendra, her mother and now Pace because they feared some exposure of the truth about their missions, that person wouldn't stop until everyone involved was silenced.

Damon had to be on the hit list, and so did Jacqueline. Jean-Paul would be, too, if Damon breathed a word, but he couldn't protect himself or Antwaun if he didn't know what he was up against. Besides, he'd need his brother to help his parents cope with the truth when he exposed himself as a former killer.

But one thought sparked and lingered in his mind: what did the E-team and their missions have to do with Frederick Fenton? And why would the killer draw attention to himself by using the Mutilator's MO as his own, instead of just quietly offing them?

JACQUELINE STUDIED the photos Damon had accessed earlier on the Internet while he dressed, trying to assimilate everything she'd learned about herself, her willingness with Damon. The intensity of their lovemaking made her senses sizzle, and although she should be sated, her body already craved him again. But he'd acted distant since that phone call with his brother.

Grief for the doctor who'd saved her was tempered by the eerie feelings he'd induced the last few times they'd spoken. He'd seemed so kind in the beginning, so sincere, so determined to help her, but the longer she'd been hospitalized the more it felt as if she'd become some kind of an obsession for him. The fact that he'd taken Kendra's skin without trying to find her family troubled her, too. Had he lied about knowing who'd killed her cousin? Was that the reason the killer had cut out his tongue—because Reginald Pace knew too much, and he wanted to make sure he couldn't talk?

The cell phone Damon had given her trilled. She frowned. Other than Damon, she hadn't given the number to anyone.

Licking her dry lips, she retrieved the phone from her purse and flipped it open. "Hello."

"Hello, Jacqueline," came a low voice that sounded as if it had been electronically altered. "So you decided to return from the dead?"

Her heart catapulted in her chest. "Who is this?"

"Do you know who you've been fucking?"

She clenched the phone and stared outside through the French doors, the sense of being watched making her skin crawl. Had this man watched Damon and her make love?

God…

"You can't trust Damon Dubois." A gruff chuckle rumbled out a malevolent tone. "He's not the hero he appears to be."

"Who are you? And what do you want?"

"Ask him how he knew Diego Bolton. And where he was the night you almost died, Jacqueline. Then you'll know who he really is."

The phone clicked into silence, leaving Jacqueline stunned. Just then, Damon appeared in the doorway. "Are you ready?"

She swallowed hard. She shook her head, hands trembling. What had the caller meant?

"Jacqueline?"

"I just received a strange phone call," Jacqueline said. "A man…"

Damon's jaw snapped tight. "Who was it?"

"I don't know. His voice sounded altered." She stood and crossed to him, but held herself back. "He told me to ask you how you knew Diego Bolton, and where you were the night I almost died."

Damon's mouth parted slightly, then his eyes turned darker. Cold. Empty. The look of death returned, the sated happiness from the early morning lovemaking disappearing completely.

"I knew Bolton from the military. He was a well-known terrorist, and I was assigned to an antiterrorist team. We carried out secret missions that I can't discuss."

She nodded, waiting. Praying he'd say something more to alleviate the anxiety building in her chest.

"Give me the phone when we get to the station, and I'll try to trace that number and find out who made the call and where it came from."

She followed him to the car, the trust she'd placed in his hands when she'd given him her body crumbling. He had just lied to her. She didn't know how she knew that, but she did.

Lied, and now gone completely cold again, as if she meant nothing to him.

THE BABY RATTLE BURNED a hole in Damon's pocket as he drove toward the precinct, the lie he'd told Jacqueline eating away at him. He had to tell her the truth. Better she heard it from him than someone else.

The fact that the man on the phone had used that particular question to taunt her told him that the caller had to be one of the E-team members. But which one? Lex was dead, wasn't he? And he couldn't reach Max, which generally meant he didn't *want* to be reached.

Damon had trusted his life in all their hands. He still did.

Cal had mentioned a rogue agent that was violent....

He couldn't discount the files Kendra had put in the safety-deposit box. Someone was out to destroy him. Frame him for murders he hadn't committed. Frame his brother as well. He must have also sent those photos to Damon's parents to hurt them. And he'd tried to kill Damon and Jacqueline. There was no doubt in Damon's mind that he'd try again.

His lungs ached with the effort to breathe. The thought of anything happening to Jacqueline sent a streak of white-hot terror through his veins.

The euphoria on her face from their lovemaking had been replaced with fear and distrust. She was waiting on him to explain. But he had to talk to Jean-Paul first. Maybe the two of them could pinpoint this killer, and then he'd sit Jacqueline down and confess everything.

Twenty minutes later, he had left Jacqueline having coffee and reviewing more of her own charity photos online while he met Jean-Paul in his office. He'd considered having Jean-Paul's partner and the lieutenant present, but until they discovered which, if any, cop was on the take, he didn't trust anyone but his brother.

First, Jean-Paul showed him crime-scene photos of Pace's death. Apparently his killer had wiped the computer hard drive, destroying all his files. Jean-Paul had also spoken with the bank teller regarding Antwaun's accounts, finding that the account had been arranged over the phone. They needed more evidence to go after Smith. But he *had* learned the man had served in the military.

"I have something to tell you," Damon said. "I think it ties into the murders, Jean-Paul."

His brother narrowed his eyes. "All right. Let's hear it."

As Damon explained about the special-ops unit called the E-team, and lightly sketched out the various missions he'd carried out, sweat trickled down his face and his palms went clammy. He gripped the edge of the desk, turned and stared out the window, unable to look his brother in the face as he described the assassinations.

"Damon," Jean Paul said quietly. "You have nothing to be ashamed of. You were part of the military. The missions…we were all soldiers, did things we hated. Our work was necessary to protect the country." Jean-Paul clapped him on the back. *"C'est la guerre."*

French Cajun for *That is war.* Damon's throat closed. "There's more. This woman, Jacqueline… She was involved with Diego Bolton. He was a known assassin, a terrorist. He killed Jacqueline's father, Ambassador Braudaway. Bolton was my last assignment with the E-team."

"I take it Jacqueline doesn't know that you took out Diego?"

"No," Damon said, swiping a hand across his brow. "You don't understand, Jean-Paul." Damon pivoted to face him, knowing he had to be a man. "We had the explosives set up, the house wired. And then Jacqueline showed up. At least I'm fairly sure it was her." He removed the baby rattle, told Jean-Paul he wanted fingerprint results, then he'd know for sure. "She got caught in the explosion that I set. I tried to go in and save her, but one of the other men said she was dead. I…thought it was too late and left her there to burn."

"Jesus." The breath hissed between Jean-Paul's teeth. "How involved with her are you now?"

Damon fought the urge to lie. But he was tired of all the secrets. "I'm in love with her." A sardonic laugh escaped him. "Pretty twisted, isn't it? When she finds out, she'll hate me."

Jean-Paul's look held both regret and sympathy. "I still don't see how all of this is connected. You, the E-team, Jacqueline, the first Mutilator, framing Antwaun. It doesn't make sense."

"I haven't figured it out either." He rammed his hands into his pockets, then confided about the phone call Jacqueline received. "I'm trying to track down one of the men from the E-team who is missing. Maybe he can fill in the blanks." He paused. "And maybe one of our federal agents can retrieve the lost data."

Jean-Paul nodded and carried the baby rattle to the fingerprint lab, while Damon stepped outside and placed a call to Cal. He had been a true leader, one of the men Damon had trusted most.

"Cal, it's Dubois."

"I heard about Pace."

"The cops are all over it, Cal. And this Mutilator copycat thing…it looks as if the case is coming back to us."

"What? How?" Cal's coarse voice sounded agitated. "And don't tell me you're thinking of exposing us," he barked. "You can't say a word, Dubois. You know the rules."

"My brother is in jail for a murder he didn't commit. Max has disappeared. We have an UNSUB murdering women, and now Pace is dead, his files gone. Someone using a voice masker also called Jacqueline and suggested she ask me about the night she nearly died." Damon's pulse clamored. "The only people who knew about that night are us, Cal. The E-team."

A long silence, then Cal wheezed. "You may be right about Max," he said, voice cracking. "He got caught in an explosion in our last mission and suffered a head injury. Ever since then, he's been having nightmares, memory lapses, emotional breakdowns. I thought I'd convinced him to get help, that's why I didn't tell you."

"Post-traumatic stress disorder?"

"Yeah. The head injury triggered a psychotic break. He claims he hears voices in his head urging him to destroy evil, right the wrongs we did. Pay penitence."

"Then why kill Kendra Yates?"

"She showed up asking questions. I suspect he was her informant, that he told her about us. When I confronted him and reminded him of the repercussions of her exposing us, he freaked. The guy's not stable, Dubois."

There was nothing worse than a brilliant trained killer, except a crazy one.

"I have his new address," Cal said. "Meet me there and we'll talk to him."

Damon agreed and hung up, then went back inside the office to tell Jean-Paul.

His brother gave him a grave look.

"I got the fingerprint on the baby rattle," he began. "You're right. It belongs to Jacqueline."

Damon shifted on the balls of his feet. How the hell was he supposed to tell the woman he'd just made love to that he had almost killed her months ago? That he was responsible for the pain she'd suffered, the countless surgeries, the physical scars, the loss of her memory?

The loss of her own face.

And her child, if she'd been pregnant…

His phone vibrated inside his jacket, and he retrieved it and checked the number. His parents' restaurant. God, what now?

"Damon, it's your father."

Damon didn't like the troubled sound in his voice. "Hey, Papa. Is everything all right?"

"No." His father's heavy sigh shook with worry. "We just received some more photographs."

"More of the Mutilator's victims?"

"Yes." His father hesitated. "Listen, son, there's something we have to tell you. It's about Antwaun and this case."

"What is it, Papa?"

"You have to come over now. We can't talk about it over the phone."

"Does this have anything to do with the secret you and *Maman* were talking about the other night?"

"Yes," his father said. "And I think it might be the connection you need to help find the man who murdered Kendra Yates and her mother."

"Jean-Paul and I are on our way."

THE DUBOISES SHOULD HAVE the photos by now. Soon they would know the vile things their precious Damon had done.

The family and Damon had to see the connection between the Mutilator and their son Antwaun now.

Then Antwaun would finally know the truth as well.

Laughter bubbled in his throat as he watched

Damon, Jean-Paul and Jacqueline Braudaway leave the police station. They were in a hurry, appeared agitated and sped off in the direction of the family restaurant.

Yes, time for things to come to a head.

The Memorial Day parade was the next day. All three Dubois brothers were to be honored. But none of them would make it. They'd still be busy picking up the pieces of their lives instead.

Speaking of lives—time to end one tonight.

Jacqueline Braudaway's.

He inched the white delivery van from the curb and drove toward the Dubois café, his heart pumping with adrenaline as he watched the brothers climb out and hurry to the entrance. Too bad the press weren't present to see the shit hit the fan; they were still circling Pace's hospital and home. But they would get here soon enough. The fireworks would bring them running in droves.

He parked in the rear, near the service entrance, then waited until the Dubois brothers and Jacqueline were inside. He set the timer on the explosive he'd rigged in the kitchen for ten minutes—long enough for Mr. and Mrs. Dubois to confess their secrets about Antwaun. And if they didn't, *he* would when Damon walked into his trap.

Sweet revenge—he tasted it on his lips.

Instead of cutting up Jacqueline and sending the

parts to Damon, he'd decided to let the man watch him slice her bit by bit.

He lit a cigarette, took a drag and watched the smoke curl toward the sky as he began the countdown. In ten minutes, the place would be filled with flames and a fog of smoke. The Dubois family would panic and come scrambling out.

While Damon and his brother tried to extinguish the fire and save their precious family business, he'd grab Jacqueline and disappear.

He reached inside his glove compartment, removed the knife he'd used to kill Kendra Yates, and to cut out Pace's tongue, pressed the tip to his hand, then jabbed the point into his palm. Blood spurted from the cut, and he smiled as he licked the salty, coppery droplet.

Soon, it would be Jacqueline's blood filling his hands and the real fun would begin….

CHAPTER TWENTY-TWO

DAMON ASKED JACQUELINE to wait at the bar area while he and Jean-Paul met their parents in their office. He hadn't wanted to drag her along, but he hadn't trusted anyone at the police department, and he couldn't leave her alone.

Of course if she knew the truth about him, she wouldn't feel safe by his side either. She'd probably run like hell.

His parents both looked ashen-faced and upset, even more worried than they had when the business had been lost after the hurricane. Something was terribly wrong.

"What's going on, *Maman?* Papa?"

His father spread the photos they'd received on the desk, and he and Jean-Paul both moved closer to study them. A red-haired woman, probably mid-twenties, was sprawled on the floor in a bloody mess. Her hands, breasts, legs had been wounded multiple times.

It was the work of the first Mutilator.

Even more disturbing—the woman was obviously pregnant. Killing her would have killed the child. Perhaps that had been his motivation—but why kill the other woman?

His gaze rose to meet his parents' pale faces. His father leaned against the filing cabinet and heaved for a breath while his mother sat with her hands clenched so tightly her nails dug into her palms.

"All right," Damon said, still not understanding the depth of his parents' reactions or what this had to do with Antwaun. "What's going on? And I want the truth this time."

His mother swallowed, a small sob catching in her throat, and Jean-Paul placed a hand on her back. "I know this is upsetting, *Maman*. This man is cruel to send you these photographs."

"We didn't want to believe it," his mother whispered.

"But we have to face the fact that it's all connected," Mr. Dubois said.

"What are you talking about?" Damon asked "You didn't want to believe what?"

"That the reporter's murder had something to do with Antwaun."

A sharp pain clawed at Damon's chest.

"*Maman,*" Jean-Paul said. "You can't think that Antwaun killed Kendra Yates?"

"No," Mr. Dubois said. "But if the truth gets out, it will make him look guilty as hell."

Damon rarely heard his father use profanity. "Why? What is it about the past that you're so secretive about?" A long tense pause took hold where his parents shared a terrified look.

Their father finally cleared his throat, pain in his eyes when he spoke. "We promised never to say a word, to bring Antwaun up just like you boys, that he would never know."

"Know what?" Jean-Paul asked softly.

"That he is not our son," Mr. Dubois said.

Damon clenched the desk edge while Jean-Paul grunted in shock. "What do you mean, *not your son?*" Damon tried to remember their childhood and when Antwaun had been born. But Jean-Paul had been only two, and Damon only one.

Mrs. Dubois pointed toward the picture of the woman in the bloodbath. "That lady, Irene, that was Antwaun's birth mother."

"She was a victim of the first Mutilator," Mr. Dubois explained.

"The man left her for dead, thinking the baby had died, too, but he survived." Mrs. Dubois wiped at a tear trickling down her cheek. "I found Irene… She was a neighbor, a friend. She'd come to New Orleans because she had gotten pregnant and her family threw her out."

Wheels rolled in Damon's head, fingers of unease stirring along his spine as unexpected thoughts began to click into place. "You're saying you adopted Antwaun after this woman died?"

His mother nodded. "Yes. We raised him as our own. We thought it would be better for him if he believed he was our son, if he didn't know that his mother had been murdered."

Jean-Paul frowned and drummed his fist on the desk, studying the pictures again. "So, you think whoever killed Kendra and her mother framed Antwaun to hurt you because you raised this baby?"

Damon's head spun. He'd thought the E-team was involved. That one of his men was trying to get back at him. But someone had a vendetta against the entire family.

Because his family had raised a dead woman's baby? It still didn't make sense.

"*Maman,* Papa, who was Antwaun's father?" Damon asked.

They exchanged another troubled look, then his father spoke in a tortured voice. "Frederick Fenton, the man who mutilated Antwaun's mother, along with eleven other women that year."

Damon tried not to react, but his parents were right. If this leaked out, Antwaun would look guilty as hell.

Dammit. How would Antwaun feel when he learned the truth?

JACQUELINE'S HEAD POUNDED with questions. Who had called and why? What did Damon know about the fire that had sent her to the hospital, and why had Damon lied?

After the heavenly night they'd spent together, and all they'd shared, she wanted to trust him without doubt, but he knew more than he was telling her, and she had a right to the truth. If they were going to have a future together, they had to be honest, let go of old hurts.

But Damon hadn't mentioned love or a future at all.

And what was the family discussing now? Something to do with her?

Outside, the street bustled with activity just as the French Market did. Tourists and locals clamored to various restaurants for lunch. But the Dubois place was empty, a shell of the place it had once been, she was sure—apparently the locals chose not to support the family of an alleged killer.

Suddenly a loud explosion rocked the building, and flames shot up in the kitchen, behind the bar and in the entry to the front door. Smoke mushroomed like a cloud around her, filling the air, and making her eyes and throat burn. Wood crackled and popped, the flames quickly catching the tablecloths and chewing at the walls. The mirror behind the bar splintered, wineglasses and goblets shattered and crashed to the floor, shards stabbing at her arms and face. The building shook and pictures tumbled from the walls into the fire, sizzling as the heat melted the frames and consumed them.

She yelled for Damon, grabbed a napkin, covered her mouth and jumped off the stool to get help. But déjà vu immobilized her.

Memories of struggling to escape the fire months ago seared her brain, and she screamed again. Smoke filled her lungs, and she coughed, choking on the thick plumes. She couldn't breathe. She'd been trapped then. She didn't want to be trapped again.

Before she could run to Damon, someone grabbed her from behind and slammed something hard into her temple. Lights spun amid the fog of smoke, then sparks of fire glittered in the darkness as she collapsed into unconsciousness.

"*MAMAN, PAPA, ARE YOU* all right?" Damon shouted.

The force of the explosion had knocked Damon backward and crashed a bookcase on top of him. His father had thrown himself over his mother to protect her, even Jean-Paul covered them both and pushed them to the floor. Smoke curled through the door, and heat seeped into the small office, the flames burning hot and spreading quickly.

"We're all right," his father yelled.

"How about you?" Jean-Paul shouted.

"Yeah." Damon tore books, photos and pieces of broken wood off himself and pitched them to the side.

"We have to get out!" Jean-Paul yelled.

"Jacqueline!" Pure panic slammed into Damon, stealing the wind from his lungs as he crawled to his knees. His brother was calling 911 on his cell while he felt the door.

"It's already getting hot. Dammit!"

"The back door through the kitchen is closest," his father shouted.

Jean-Paul nodded and inched open the door, checking the growing flames. Smoke seeped through the doorway, creating a thick, blinding haze.

"Get them out," Damon barked. "I have to find Jacqueline."

Jean-Paul nodded and grabbed his mother's arm to help her. She struggled to her feet, sobbing softly, and his father clutched her other arm. "We'll make it, *chère*, just hang on."

Damon's heart squeezed at the way his parents stuck together, no matter what. He wanted that kind of life, a chance to have that with Jacqueline.

God, please let her be alive.

He peered through the door and searched the room. Patches of flames ate at the kitchen and raced into the short hallway to the front dining room. Jean-Paul grabbed a fire extinguisher from the kitchen wall and used it to battle the flames as he guided his parents through a narrow trail that hadn't yet caught fire, yelling for them to watch out for crashing plaster from the ceiling.

"Jacqueline!" Damon found another fire extinguisher and tore it from the wall. Mindless of the heat, he ran the opposite way, weaving through the flames, coughing and yelling Jacqueline's name as he kicked at broken table legs, shattered wood, stepped over glasses and debris. The café consisted of one large room with the L-shaped bar situated in the right-hand corner. Jacqueline was nowhere in sight.

Panic ripped through him again. "Jacqueline!" Fire singed his clothes and shoes as he searched the bar, the space behind it and beneath the ceiling, which had crashed down in the middle of the room. Embers crackled and shot up, flames bursting toward the front door.

Finally a siren wailed in the distance, then roared closer and screeched to a stop. He heard the firemen shouting as they began to douse the flames, and two ran in, masked and suited.

"You have to get out now, mister!" one of them yelled as he grabbed at Damon's arm.

"A woman was in here!" He yanked his arm free, frantic to find her. Sweat poured down his face, and his hands were scalded from tearing away burning wood and metal.

The firefighter traded a hopeless look, then searched the room as well. But Jacqueline was nowhere to be found.

Maybe she had escaped….

But as he crawled over a bar stool, he spotted her cell phone. A foot away, he saw blood trailing outside by the door and had a bad feeling that she hadn't escaped at all. Dammit. The fire had been a diversion.

The killer had Jacqueline.

JACQUELINE ROUSED FROM unconsciousness. A ringing echo in her ears triggered nausea and fear. The smell of blood and death filled her nostrils, her vision blurring with remnants of smoke and memories of the explosion at the Duboises' café. Into the confusion popped flashbacks of the fire that had sent her to Pace's hospital—then her mother's harsh words of condemnation—then the memory of her father's sightless eyes—the photos of Kendra faceless, stabbed and mutilated beyond belief. She closed her eyes against the images.

What had happened?

Think, Jacqueline, think. You have the key to this all locked in your head.

Retrace your last steps.

She'd been sitting at the bar when the explosion had occurred, then the smoke and flames. She'd screamed and wanted to find Damon, but something had hit her from behind. A piece of falling wood?

She blinked, trying to focus, then move, but her hands were bound behind her, and her legs tied to a chair. Panic zinged through her, and she squinted through the darkness, suddenly zeroing in on the fact that she was not anywhere near the café or Damon now. She was in a rotting room with dingy walls painted in blood.

Bile rose in her throat, and she tried to scream, but her throat was so dry from smoke, that no sound came out. God…where was she? Who had brought her here?

She had to get a grip. Figure out what to do, how to escape. How to find Damon…

"I'm sure you're wondering where you are." The smoker's voice intensified her fear. It must be the man from the phone.

"Who are you? Why are you doing this to me?"

"You'll find out, when the rest of our party arrives." His silhouette flickered in the thin light seeping through the edge of the boarded windows. Then the shiny glint of a knife blade flashed in front of her face. He raised it to her neck and she sucked in a sharp breath. He jabbed the point into her skin, then blood trickled down her chest. In spite of the courage she struggled to hold on to, a cry erupted from her, a shrill and pitiful sound amid the silence.

His vile breath bathed her neck. "A taste of what's

to come, sweetheart. Now relax and think about your cousin's face. How pretty it is on you." A nasty laugh followed, rumbling with menace. "You won't have it for long."

He made another slice with the knife across her thigh, bringing blood pooling to the surface.

He laughed again. Then he was gone.

FRUSTRATION AND PANIC TORE at Damon. The firemen continued to pour water onto his parents' café, while his parents huddled in each other's arms. His mother cried softly and his father stroked her back, murmuring soothing words of comfort, her Rock of Gibraltar as always. Just as Damon would like to be for Jacqueline.

Only he'd let her down. And now she might be in the hands of a killer, and he had no idea where to even look for her.

His parents' earlier confession taunted him, and he mentally pictured a whiteboard, jotting down the facts. Antwaun's birth father was the first Mutilator, although Antwaun was completely in the dark. Kendra Yates had been investigating Swafford, dirty cops, and had info on Pace and the E-team. Jean-Paul suspected Antwaun's own partner of setting him up.

Jacqueline had been seeing Diego Bolton, a man who had killed her father as well as countless others. Damon and the E-team had taken him out, inadvertently hurting Jacqueline. Someone had rescued her and taken her to Pace. Then Pace had given her her cousin's face.

But what did the first Mutilator and Antwaun's birth have to do with any of this?

Damon's phone jangled in his pocket, and he grabbed it, praying it was a lead. Cal's voice echoed on the line.

"Dubois, it's me," Calvin rasped. "I thought you were meeting me at Max's."

He quickly filled Cal in on the latest.

"We'll find the woman," Cal said. "But I went to Max's, and looked through his window. You have to come and see it for yourself. I think Max has the woman."

Cal hung up, and Damon's heart pounded. So far, Cal's hunch was the only lead he had. And it made sense. He'd tried to contact Max several times, but he'd vanished.

Jean-Paul had been consulting with the arson investigator, and Damon knew what they would find. He recognized the pattern of the explosives. Hell, he'd used them before to smoke someone out.

He stood and approached his brother, then explained to him about the call. "I have to go. I may have a lead."

His father pressed a hand to his back. "Son…we'll pray you find her. But about Antwaun…"

"I won't say anything yet," Damon said. "But

when this is over, Antwaun has a right to know. This secret…it could kill him if he finds out from another source." Especially the press.

He ran to his car, jumped in and sped toward the address Cal had given. The traffic was abominable, the streets crowded with tourists and partyers gearing up for the holiday weekend. The flags representing the fallen soldiers mocked him as he maneuvered through the throng and honked his horn at pedestrians over-flowing the bars and filling the streets in a drunken haze, oblivious to the urgency that had his blood pressure boiling and his chest squeezing with panic.

It seemed like hours, but minutes later he reached the address, an old brick building that had been reno-vated into lofts at the edge of town in a warehouse district. The tires screeched as he swung into the parking lot, killed the engine and jumped out. Yanking his Glock from the inside of his jacket, he scanned the area searching for Cal or Max. Two kids in their teens leaned against a Jetta necking and a cat trotted across the top of the ledge bordering the walkway. The Mississippi churned and lapped at the shore, and a bateau glided along the river's edge.

He moved slowly toward the building, searching each corner of the warehouse perimeter in case he was walking into a trap. If Max was holding Jacque-line, he might be watching for Damon to arrive.

Behind him, the scrape of a shoe sounded in the

quiet and shells crunched. He pivoted and noticed a homeless man loitering near the garbage cans. Breathing in relief, he inched forward, then slid against the wall, up the stairs. Cal was waiting in the shadows of the overhang and motioned for him to wait while he entered first.

They'd worked together on so many missions that they could read each other's thoughts. Cal twisted the knob and the door swung open. Not a good sign.

Cal stepped inside, swinging his gun in an arc, taking the left while Damon took the right. The stench of blood and sweat nearly knocked Damon off his feet. He gulped back the terror trying to immobilize him, and forced his feet forward. Inside the loft, a one-room unit, he spotted the blood smeared on the wall.

Max appeared from the bathroom right then, and halted in shock as he spotted Cal's weapon and Damon's Glock aimed at his chest.

"Where the hell is Jacqueline?" Damon barked.

Max jerked his hands up.

"He's got a gun!" Cal suddenly opened fire. The bullet slammed into Max's chest. His body bounced backward and he went down, blood spurting from his chest and forming a puddle on the floor.

CHAPTER TWENTY-THREE

LEX HEARD A WHIMPER of fear and knew that Crystal—Jacqueline—needed him.

He had to find a way to help her.

He fell to his knees and raised his hands to the heavens. His body was fading. The skin had completely disintegrated now. He was ready to accept his fate, the burning inferno of hell if needed, but he didn't want Jacqueline to suffer anymore. She didn't deserve it.

Closing his eyes, he begged the gods to save her.

Had he not paid penitence enough to earn a favor? A brief reprieve so he could leave the hospital for where the killer held her.

After all, he had watched the blood drip from Pace's body as his tongue had been ripped from his mouth with no emotions. No bloodlust or the joy that he once might have experienced. He was a more peaceful man.

The raw pain of dying splintered through him as if it were happening all over again, and he wept as he imagined Jacqueline suffering. The fleeting thought that if she died, she could be with him entered his mind, but he banished it. He did not want her at that cost.

A scream of rage filled his throat. Dubois had to find her in time....

Still, there had to be something he could do.

He closed his eyes, trying to speak to his grandmother, to summon her magic....

"No!" DAMON SHOUTED.

Max collapsed onto the floor, blood spurting from his chest. Damon ran to him, dropped to his knees and jerked him by the collar. "Max, where's Jacqueline? What did you do with her?"

Max's eyes rolled back in his head, and blood gurgled in his throat as he tried to talk. Cal stepped up beside him, his gun aimed at Max's head.

Damon shook Max. He couldn't pass out or die yet. He had to talk to them. "Goddammit, Max, where is she?"

Max coughed and tried to lift his hand, but his strength failed him and his arm dropped down to the floor, then he lapsed into unconsciousness.

Fear gnawed at Damon's chest, followed by anger, and he spun around and glared at Cal. "Why the hell did you shoot him?"

"He had a gun, man—he was going to shoot you!" Cal snarled.

"He can't talk if he's dead."

"You don't need him to talk. Just remember what it was like to be on the team, a brother."

"I can't do that anymore."

"Yes, you can. You were born a killer. To find Jacqueline, all you have to do is think like one again."

Go back into the world he'd left behind. To the man he'd begun to hate. He couldn't do that.

But he had to in order to find Jacqueline.

Desperate for another way, he checked Max for a pulse, and found one, low but thready. At least he was still breathing. "We have to call an ambulance."

"Hell, no," Cal barked. "The E-team doesn't work that way. Leave no witnesses behind."

"I'm not with the team anymore, I'm a federal agent," Damon said tersely. He couldn't believe this was happening—one of his buddies and trusted friends nearly dead, maybe after killing Jacqueline, and the other asking him to compromise the investigation and his position at the bureau. He reached for his phone to punch 911, but Cal raised the gun again, this time at him.

"I can't let you call the cops," Cal said.

Damon opened his mouth to assure him he'd think of something to cover his involvement, but the butt of Cal's gun slammed into his head, and he bit his tongue, tasting blood as he crashed to the floor and saw black.

TERROR MOUNTED AS THE seconds ticked by. Jacqueline struggled to untie her hands, but her attacker had secured them so tightly she couldn't budge the cord. Instead the heavy rope cut into her wrists, scraping her flesh raw and sending blood dripping down her hands onto the sticky floor. She tried desperately not to imagine how much Kendra had suffered, but the sight of her cousin's blood smeared on the walls only drove the truth home—her kidnapper had killed Kendra and intended to mutilate her in the same brutal way, then send pictures to flaunt his ugly violence.

She closed her eyes and worked her hands again, determined not to give up. Suddenly she felt a presence near her. Kendra?

No, Lex.

The scent of his ointment mingled with the vile odor of blood and death in the room. Slowly the sweet aroma of a woman's perfume also tinted the air.

Had Lex and her cousin come to stay with her and comfort her as she joined them in death?

She definitely felt Lex nearby and tried to draw courage from his presence. Was that the reason Lex hadn't moved on, because he was waiting on her?

Damon's face flashed in her mind, the memory of his lovemaking replacing the pain, and tears filled her eyes. She thought of the little girl she'd met in the hospital, and how much she wanted children of her own, a family, a man to love her for eternity.

She didn't want to die.

Outside, the sound of a car engine cut through the quiet. When a car door slammed shut, she began to twist frantically at the bindings on her arms, knowing that at any minute the madman was going to walk through the door and begin carving her up.

The wooden chair he'd tied her to creaked as she rocked it back and forth. It was old and rotting, and she managed to pitch herself to the floor, hoping the force would splinter the wood and she could escape. But she slammed her head onto the edge of the door as it swung open, and pain sliced her temple.

The shadow of the hulking man appeared, and a nasty laugh rumbled from him. "Thought you'd get away? Don't think that will happen, princess." He dragged her upright by her hair, and shoved the chair against the scarred wooden wall. Kendra's blood had been painted on the slats, and she knew hers would be, too.

"I have a surprise for you," he said in that coarse voice that grated on her nerves. "Thought you might like some company."

Her head spun as he dragged Damon into the room. His hands and feet were tied as well, and he was unconscious, blood smeared across his forehead.

"Damon?" she whispered. Furious at the man's

sick, twisted games, she turned a raged look toward her attacker. "Why are you doing this? You have me, let him go."

His laughter erupted, even more vile this time. "Oh, sugar, you don't get it. But you will. Soon as lover boy wakes up, I'll explain everything."

"You're a sick man," she shouted. "You killed my cousin and murdered her mother."

"And me," she heard Lex whisper. "He injected me with the chemical that ate away my flesh."

Fresh fury shot through Jacqueline. She had to fight for Damon, for herself, for Kendra and her mother, and for Lex.

The man kicked Damon in the gut, and Damon's eyes jerked open. He looked disoriented for a moment, then his gaze found her, and sorrow and anger tightened his expression. His head whipped back to the man standing over him.

"Cal…" Damon croaked and glanced around. "It was you all along. God…where are we? This is where you kept Kendra—we had it boarded up."

Cal laughed. "Boards. Boards couldn't keep me from such a fitting place."

"Soldiers don't kill innocent women," Damon snarled. "They don't tie them up and prey on them, cut them up like some animal with a toy."

"*You* killed an innocent woman," Cal yelled back.

Then he slanted his wild-eyed gaze toward her. "Oh, sugar, he didn't tell you, did he?"

"Shut up, Cal," Damon yelled. "Let her go. This is between you and me."

Cal's boots pounded the wooden floor as he stalked toward Jacqueline. He flipped his knife out and ripped her top, shredding it in seconds, then he sliced a thin line down her torso, drawing blood. She bit her lip not to cry out, but when he bent and licked his lips along her neck, tasting it, a low sob broke from her.

"Stop it, Cal. For God's sake, stop it now," Damon said between gritted teeth.

Cal aimed an evil smile at Jacqueline. "Your lover boy here isn't the man you think, sugar." He swung around behind her, lifted her hair from her neck, then slid the knife to her throat and positioned himself so he could watch Damon's reaction. "He's a killer just like I am. Part of a special team of assassins in the military."

Jacqueline's heart raced as the knife pricked her skin. Damon's face twisted with rage, but he didn't deny Cal's statement.

"Don't you want to tell her, Damon?" Cal shouted. "Tell her that you're the one who set the explosive that killed her boyfriend Diego."

"Diego killed her father, the ambassador," Damon snarled. "He was a known terrorist. He'd killed countless others, innocent women and children in villages all over the world."

"You were there at his house, Jacqueline, the day we took Diego out," Cal whispered in her ear. "Your lover boy set the explosive, then watched you scream for your life as the flames shot up around you and ate at your clothes and hair."

"I tried to *stop* the bomb," Damon said in a tortured voice. "Jacqueline—"

She shook her head no, pain and denial warring inside her. Damon had saved her from the hospital, had protected her, had made love to her with such emotion. She'd felt connected with him from the moment she'd seen him, had trusted him implicitly.

But the anguished look in Damon's eyes confirmed that the maniac wasn't lying.

"He left you to die," Cal murmured. "Left you in there burning as he stood and watched the building crumble down around you." He grinned toothily at Damon. "But he didn't let that stop him from fucking you, did he?"

"No…" JACQUELINE WINCED. "Please, Damon, tell me it's not so."

He didn't deny it. He couldn't. He'd known his days were numbered, that he had to tell her the truth, just as he did his family. But to have her learn like this, while his old crazy partner sliced up her body in a slow torture…

And Max… Had he been innocent? Cal had shot him to throw Damon off….

He had to save Jacqueline, then call for help for Max. Let Cal kill him, but he could not let Jacqueline die.

He lunged up at Cal and tried to knock him away from her.

Cal slammed his fist into Damon's face and sent him flying against the wall. Boards shattered, and Damon slid down in the grime on the floor, staring at Jacqueline with dazed eyes. God…how could he get her out of this?

Cal whipped around and sliced at Jacqueline's skirt, stripped her until she wore nothing but her underwear. Blood dotted her thigh and torso where he'd cut her, and he jabbed the point of the knife above one breast, grinning at Damon as he carved a small E on her body.

Fury more powerful than he'd ever felt ripped through Damon. He wanted to destroy Cal, tear him apart piece by piece.

But he had to think like a soldier. A killer. Calm. Methodical. Formulate a plan.

Stall. Keep him talking. Maybe Max was alive, would stir and get to a phone. Maybe Jean-Paul would figure out something.

"You sick bastard," Damon growled. "It takes a coward to torture a woman."

"I'm not a coward. You are, you tried to leave the team."

"Only a coward ties up a woman and inflicts pain on her. A strong man battles someone his own size, his equal."

"You asshole!" Anger flared in Cal's eyes, and he dove toward Damon. Just what Damon wanted. Let him take his rage out on him, and maybe he could wrestle the knife from him.

Cal cut Damon's forearm in a quick slice, then pounded the side of his head with his fist. Damon jerked both knees up and rammed them into Cal's stomach, sending him across the floor. Stunned, Cal laughed, sat back and simply stared at him.

"I forgot what a good fighter you are. Just like you forgot the brotherhood of the team and our creed."

"The brotherhood said we could trust each other, but you're the one who broke that trust. You're the one who destroyed our friendship."

"No, you did, when you turned away from the team. When you joined your other brothers in the law-enforcement game."

"You killed Pace, didn't you?" Damon asked. "Why?"

"Because I took Kendra to him so he could use her face in the transplant experiment. I thought it would be kind of funny… Only he didn't tell me that the woman he planned to help was the one I thought died in that fire. Diego's woman. If she remembered us, it would have been bad and you know it. I had to silence her and him."

"What about Max?" Damon asked. "Why did you shoot him?"

"He betrayed me," Cal snapped. "He saved the woman from the fire and took her to Pace."

"No, that was Lex," Jacqueline cut in.

"Lex?" Cal jerked his head toward her. "That's impossible. Lex is dead."

"He died the week after he left me at the hospital. He's here now," Jacqueline said as a wind suddenly stirred through the shanty. The walls rattled with its force, and Cal's eyes went wide.

"He said he carried me to Dr. Pace. Said you injected him with the chemical that killed him."

Damon's stunned gaze shot to Cal, and he saw the truth reflected in his vicious eyes. Remembering the photos Cal had sent his parents, the ones from the first Mutilator, he plunged on. "You hate my family. You framed Antwaun for murder, Cal. Why? Why not just come after me?"

Cal spat on the floor. "Because Antwaun is *my* brother, not yours!" Cal shouted. "But your family took him in, raised him as a Dubois, even though Antwaun was Frederick Fenton's son just like me." Cal stood, sweating as he stalked across the room. Jacqueline stared in stunned silence, fear darkening her pale green eyes, while Damon tried to follow Cal's logic.

"Your father is the first Mutilator? How long have you known?"

"Since I was a kid," Cal bellowed. "I was put in foster care. No one wanted me because I was the son of a serial killer. But your family took Antwaun when he was born. Precious Antwaun had it lucky while I rotted away in the system. Thrown from one abusive home to another. Beaten and shunned by normal kids. That's what made me tough. Helped me join the military, so I could kill."

Damon managed to grab a splintered piece of wood behind him and began to saw away at the ropes binding him. "You found out about Antwaun?"

He gave a clipped, wild-eyed nod. "I thought you were the brother first," he said, his voice raspy as his lungs churned for air. "That's why I joined the E-team. To get close to you."

God, Cal had planned this twisted revenge for years.

"I finally thought *I* had a family. We were brothers, but you deserted us," Cal continued, a wild man's rage showing in his jerky movements. "You chose your birth brothers, even *my* birth brother, the bastard kid of Frederick Fenton, over me." He waved the knife in Damon's face. "But Antwaun is no better than me. He's a killer's son, and now the whole world will know the truth."

Damon flinched mentally. That truth might destroy Antwaun, and his relationship with the family. And Cal… If Damon didn't stop him now, he might kill Antwaun and his parents after he was through with him and Jacqueline.

"Antwaun is nothing like you or Fenton," Damon said, goading him again as he continued working at the knots binding his hands. "He doesn't prey on innocent people. He fights for good, something you've forgotten."

At this Cal spun and stalked toward Jacqueline again, the knife blade gleaming in the darkness. He plunged it into her shoulder, and she cried out in pain. Damon's blood boiled with rage.

He jerked the knots free from his wrists, untied his feet while Cal stared at her blood, and threw himself upright and toward Cal, knocking him to the floor. The knife skittered from his hands and spun across the wood. Blood spurted from Jacqueline's shoulder, but she tried to inch her chair toward the weapon as he wrestled with Cal. The men fought, trading blow for blow, and Damon rolled Cal over, pounding his face with his fists. Jacqueline kicked the knife his way. He grabbed it and brought it down over Cal's face.

"Give it up, Cal!" Damon said between gritted teeth.

"Never!" Cal bucked his body up, kicking Damon

off with his feet. He launched into karate moves then, and Damon jabbed at him with the knife, stabbing his gut once, hard enough that Cal dropped to his knees. A second later, he glared at Damon with hatred in his eyes and lunged at him. The pair rolled toward the door, where Cal managed to grab the knife and stab Damon in the thigh. As Damon gritted his teeth, Cal jumped up, grabbed Jacqueline by the hair and pressed the knife to her throat.

"Move one step, and I'll kill her."

CHAPTER TWENTY-FOUR

"HE'LL DO IT ANYWAY, Damon," Jacqueline whispered. "Get him!"

But Damon froze, pressing his hand against his thigh to stop the bleeding. "Cal, don't do this."

Cal was sweating, his body shaking as he clenched her hair tighter. Jacqueline felt the ropes around her arms being tugged on, loosening. At first, she thought Cal was untying her, but one of his hands was wound in her hair, the other held the knife to her neck.

Lex… She felt his presence. He was here, helping her now. Going to save her and Damon.

The rope slipped free, but, wanting to choose her timing, she held the coils around herself as if she were still bound.

"Maybe we should finish this outside," Cal said in a low growl. "Let the gators taste her blood, then they can finish her."

Damon shook his head no, then she jerked her arms and jabbed upward, hitting Cal with her elbow.

The blow knocked him backward and off balance long enough for her to run for the door. Damon dove toward Cal. If she could make it outside maybe she could get to Cal's car. Find a phone. Call for help.

She was weak from blood loss though, and dizziness swept over her. She wavered and grabbed the wall, felt the blood oozing from her shoulder. But she forced herself on, held the wall until she staggered outside. The musky scent of the bayou assaulted her, the piercing eyes of the gators meeting her in the darkness. Behind her, she heard the men fighting, grunting as they pounded each other. She ran across the wooden bridge over the swampy water to the woods, heaving for a breath as she desperately searched for Cal's car.

Suddenly his strong hands caught her, jerked her hair again, gripped her wounded shoulder and dragged her to the ground. She screamed as pain ripped through her arm and chest, flailing to strike out at him as he dragged her facedown across the rough ground toward the water. She kicked and cried out, using her uninjured arm to jab at his eyes when he rolled her over. He slapped her and pressed the knife to her throat, his eyes gleaming as vicious as a gator's. One flick down her chest, and he ripped her bra away then began to trace the knife around her nipple. Her body quivered with fear and revulsion.

Desperation ballooned in her chest, and she prayed Damon was still alive.

"You're an animal," she panted at Cal. "Go ahead, just kill me." She wanted it over with, did not want to have to endure the slow torture her cousin had.

His pointed smile chilled her heart, then a roar erupted behind him. Damon.

He pounced on Cal's back, dragging him off her. Cal swung the knife, slicing at air, and she pulled herself up, scrambling in the dirt for anything she could use as a weapon. She found a thick branch, raised it and stood on shaky legs, narrowing her eyes to try and see the men. They rolled into the bushes, then onto a wooden-slat bridge. The water rocked against the wood, sloshing onto her feet as she neared them. Cal had Damon beneath him, the knife raised. Jacqueline swung the tree branch and knocked the knife from his hand and saw it fly into the water. Cal punched Damon in the face, then jerked him up and they both lost their balance and crashed into the water. The swamp murk was deeper than Jacqueline had thought, and she lost sight of them as they dipped below the surface, fighting in the dark night.

Sweat beaded on her forehead as she fought to stay conscious, but she feared she might pass out. She crawled back to the place where Cal had assaulted her and ran her hands over the ground in search of her bra. When she found it, she tied it around the top of her arm to stem the bleeding, then tried to crawl back to the bridge. But the woods grew even darker and a gator's attack cry splintered the night. Just before she passed out, a man's cry shot into the night.

She prayed it wasn't Damon, dying.

DAMON DOVE SIDEWAYS AS the gator pounced, its sharp teeth snapping as it caught Cal's arm and bit it off. He bellowed in pain, blood filled the water, and Damon reached out to try and save him. Cal flailed madly, pummeling the water to escape, but the gator lurched again and trapped his leg in its mouth with a sickening crunch of bone. Cal's scream of pain and death echoed through the bayou, and Damon knew it was too late for his former comrade.

He had to find Jacqueline, make sure she was okay. She'd been stabbed and was bleeding....

His own injuries slowed him down, but he slogged through the murk and dragged himself to the wooden structure and crawled on top of it. Behind him, the water gurgled red with blood as the gator finished his feast. Damon searched the bridge and dark foliage before spotting Jacqueline sprawled at the edge of the water. Knowing that more gators might come, he forced himself forward. Every second seemed like an eternity. A snake hissed nearby and another gator surfaced, floating near her. He hurried, half staggering, then dropped beside her and felt for a pulse. Low but steady.

"Don't die, please don't die," he whispered as he moved his hands beneath her and picked her up. "Please, Jacqueline, stay with me. I'm going to get help." He kissed her cheek, then plunged through the swamp to Cal's car. It seemed like miles, but finally he reached it, opened the door and laid her inside on the backseat. Blood, sweat, dirt and filth soaked them both.

He stroked her face gently, then circled to the front seat and searched the interior. Dammit, Cal had to have a phone in here. He ran his hands over the leather and patted the floor, then checked the console and finally found it. His heart pounding, he dialed Jean-Paul's number.

"Damon, where are you?"

"Need help," Damon said gruffly. "Send an ambulance to the shanty where Kendra Yates was killed." He requested another unit to be sent to Max's address.

Hanging up, he removed his shirt and crawled in the back to put it on her, cradling her in his arms. She looked so pale and had lost so much blood that he bowed his head and begged God to let her live.

As he faded into unconsciousness himself, he said another prayer that one day she could forgive him.

TIME BLURRED AND HOURS dragged by as Jacqueline struggled in and out of consciousness. Through the foggy haze of medication, she noticed the scents of the hospital, heard the chirp of machinery, realized that she'd been stitched up and bandaged, and was hooked to an IV.

Where was Damon? Was he alive?

"Don't die, please don't die." The words echoed in her head, the gruff voice belonging to Damon. She winced at the pain in her shoulder and thigh as she tried to turn over, then faintly remembered feeling him pick her up and carry her to the car. Then he'd called for help and held her while they'd waited.

Again in the emergency room, he'd been there, begging her to fight for her life, refusing the nurses' help and insisting they tend to her first. She must have asked about Cal, because she somehow knew that Cal was dead, felt assured that she was safe now.

But her heart was still broken.

Tears leaked from her eyes and trickled down her cheeks. She wiped at them with a bandaged hand. Damon had lied to her, had kept things from her. Had slept with her knowing that he was the one responsible for putting her in the hospital, for the burns on her body and the ruin of her face.

Exhausted, she closed her eyes and fell back into sleep, the pull of death beckoning her. Images of Kendra floated in front of her, then some of Lex as she'd seen him at the rehab facility. He was here now, she could feel him. And so was Kendra, just as she'd felt them in the shanty.

Time wound backward as a dream stole her thoughts. Or maybe it was memories assaulting her. Suddenly she felt herself floating above her body, watching as she lay in the bed tormented and unconscious. Flashes of the past soared around her.

She'd been standing at her father's grave, and Kendra had approached her. First Kendra had explained that she'd gotten involved with a man named Antwaun Dubois, that she was in love with him, but that she thought he worked for Swafford, a criminal she was investigating. Then she'd investigated Antwaun, and discovered he was an undercover cop. She'd first thought he might be on the take, but her research had led to another source—a man higher up with much more authority. And that investigation had led her to Diego Bolton.

Kendra had followed him and seen him meeting Jacqueline. She'd realized then that the man might be using her.

Kendra had warned her that Diego was not what he'd appeared to be, that he was a paid killer. That she suspected he had used her to get close to her father, that he'd killed him, and that Jacqueline might be next.

Denial had swept through Jacqueline. Kendra had to be wrong. She couldn't have been that big of a fool, couldn't have helped set a trap for her father.

But Kendra had shown her files, his modified

picture on the FBI's most wanted list. Jacqueline had been in shock, hadn't wanted to believe that she could have slept with a monster.

Then Kendra had told her she was pregnant, that she might have to disappear for a while to keep the baby safe. She'd given Jacqueline a baby rattle and told her that if anything happened to her, to make sure Antwaun got it. She wanted him to know that she was going to disappear to protect their child.

Knowing she had to confront Diego, Jacqueline had driven to his place. Then she'd rushed into Diego's and heard him on the phone. He'd been planning a hit. When he'd seen her, he'd slapped her in the face. She'd cried out, and tried to run, but he'd caught her, knocked her down, and told her she'd never escape him. Then he'd hit her again, that time so hard she'd passed out.

The explosion had roused her, and she'd woken and seen him fall into the flames, screaming like a madman. The fire had been crawling toward her then, smoke billowing around her, wood crackling and the ceiling and walls crumbling.

"Don't die, please don't die…"

She'd heard the whispered plea but hadn't been able to see the person calling to her.

She jerked awake, panting and sweating, the truth hitting her with blinding clarity. It wasn't *Damon's* fault she had nearly died. It was *Diego's*.

Damon hadn't lied to her. *He* hadn't pretended to love her just to carry out some evil plot. He really had tried to save her.

CHAPTER TWENTY-FIVE

Damon whispered, *"Au revoir, ma douce amie,"* goodbye, my sweet love, to Jacqueline, pressed a kiss on her cheek, then left the hospital at noon the next day, tension knotting his shoulders.

Max was going to make it, thank God. He didn't blame Damon for Cal's actions, and had been concerned about Cal's escalating mood swings since Damon had pulled out of the team. He hadn't contacted Damon because he'd been investigating Cal himself. Max also agreed to use his gift with computers to try to retrieve the lost files from Pace's computer.

Damon's thoughts turned to Jacqueline—the woman he loved.

The woman he had to leave now.

He'd sat by her bedside until she'd started to stir, then he was afraid he'd upset her more, so he'd left, hoping she could find peace now that she had some answers and that Cal was dead.

After getting stitched up himself the night before,

he'd given his statement to Jean-Paul. His parents had rushed into the hospital, hysterical, and he'd assured them that he was alive, then he'd explained what Cal had done.

They were more worried about Antwaun and his reaction to the fact that he was a serial killer's son— and that his father had killed his birth mother—than they were over any fallout from Antwaun's arrest or their business burning to the ground.

Fearing the press might gain access to the truth and print it, they planned to tell Antwaun the story about his birth parents in person. Hopefully Antwaun would realize how fortunate he was to have the Duboises—blood didn't matter.

They were family. They always would be, no matter what.

Now, Damon had to do what was right. He drove toward the town square where the Memorial Day ceremony was to be held. Jean-Paul was meeting with the lawyers to get Antwaun released, and he and the rest of the family were supposed to meet Damon at the courthouse.

Apparently the mayor wanted to honor both him and Jean-Paul for their part in capturing the copy-cat Mutilator.

Decorations glittered with red, white and blue along the French Quarter. Flags waved from houses and street corners commemorating war heroes, and a wall of plaques with names of the fallen soldiers stretched across the market. Another held names of victims of Katrina.

Local artists sold a mixture of craft items, souvenirs, dolls, Mardi Gras masks, beads, voodoo paraphernalia, toy crocodiles, and pictures of the town before and after the hurricane—all with a portion of the revenue going to a fund contributing to the restoration of the city.

A parade boomed through the town with street musicians, colorful floats, balloons, costume-clad dancers, clowns on stilts, and a full band playing a mixture of local jazz and blues tunes blended with patriotic melodies, a true celebration of the culture of the Vieux Carré. A stage had been set up featuring local Dixieland jazz musicians, dancers, magicians, mimes and vocalists, while food booths offered everything from beignets to full-course Cajun jambalaya, and oyster and shrimp po' boys.

Damon arrived just in time to watch the parade, then made his way to the center stage where the mayor waited with a half-dozen soldiers in uniform. Families of the men and women gathered around, and the speech began, commemorating various soldiers who'd died serving the country as well as the ones present. Cheers, clapping and salutes erupted, and Damon congratulated the others. Jean-Paul waved through the crowd and approached, and Damon looked out and spotted his parents. He searched for Antwaun's face, but didn't see him anywhere.

"Where is he?" he asked Jean-Paul.

"He had to clean up first," Jean-Paul said. "But he said he'd be here."

"He knows about the café?"

Jean-Paul nodded grimly. "Yes. And, Damon, Jacqueline called when I was at the station. She was looking for you."

His heart hammered with worry. "Was she all right?"

Jean-Paul offered him a sympathetic look. "Yes. But she claims her cousin confided in her the name of the dirty cop."

Please, God, not Antwaun. "Antwaun's partner?"

"No. Lieutenant Phelps. Internal Affairs has him in interrogation now and has already gotten a warrant for his office and home."

Dammit. "He was so righteous when he arrested him."

"I know. Turns out he was heavily involved in gambling and owed Swafford big bucks. Hopefully he'll lead us to Swafford himself and we can tie up that loose end."

Damon sighed. Maybe the danger was finally over. Jacqueline was safe. And Antwaun...could return to his job.

Damon and Jean-Paul fell silent as the mayor

offered a quick speech, then handed out awards to several soldiers, honoring their bravery. The mayor clapped Jean-Paul on the back, listed his heroic acts during Katrina, his own service experience, then announced that the copycat Mutilator had been caught, giving credit to Jean-Paul, Damon, the local police and Kendra herself.

Jean-Paul accepted the award and shook his hand, then smiled at Britta, who stood to the side of the stage, beaming with pride.

The mayor turned to Damon, listed his accomplishments and reiterated how he'd nearly died getting justice for Kendra Yates and her mother. Damon stepped forward, prepared to dispute his hero status when Jacqueline's face appeared in the crowd. For a minute, he couldn't breathe. He was so damn glad she was alive.

But she hated him, could never forgive him for what he'd done....

All the more reason he had to come clean. He cleared his throat and stepped up to the microphone. "I'm honored to stand here with the true heroes of our war and our city." He gestured toward the soldiers seated onstage. "I personally want to thank them for the sacrifices they've made for us. My prayers remain with them and their families." He pressed his hand to his heart. "But I am not a hero, just a man who has tried to fight evil both overseas and here in the city. But I have made mistakes…"

Jacqueline pushed through the crowd to him and rushed near the front of the stage, an urgent look on her face. "Please, Damon, don't. I have to talk to you."

He met her gaze, shocked at the need he saw in her eyes. Then fear slammed into him. Did she need to tell him something important? Swafford might have resurfaced. What if he'd come after her?

He thanked the mayor, then descended the stairs and pulled her aside.

The band burst into "America the Beautiful" while he zeroed in on Jacqueline's bruised face, the knife wound on her neck, the bandages on her hands. His stomach churned at the sight, while another part of him soaked up her image. He was desperate to hold her in his arms and love her again. "What is it? Are you all right?"

"I remembered what happened that day, Damon. *Everything* that happened."

She squeezed her eyes shut, then opened them. "It wasn't your fault that I almost died in that fire. It was Diego's."

He stared at her in disbelief. "Jacqueline, I set the explosion. I'm responsible."

She shook her head, then gripped his arm. Dammit, he wanted to believe that she'd forgiven him, that they could have a long-lasting love like his parents, like Catherine and her husband Sean, and Jean-Paul and Britta, but he didn't deserve her forgiveness or love.

"It's true," she whispered. "Kendra came to me at my father's funeral, explained about her investigation. She was in love with Antwaun, but thought he was dirty, so she investigated him. Then she found out about his birth father being the Mutilator. She traced him somehow to Cal, then found out about the E-team and Diego. She told me Diego was bad."

Damon gripped her arms.

"I didn't want to believe her, that I could have been so stupid. So I went to see Diego to find out."

He nodded, his chest tight and aching. "That's when I saw you come in the house?"

"Yes. I heard him on the phone discussing a hit. Then I knew Kendra was right. When I tried to turn and escape, Diego hit me and knocked me out. That was before the explosion, Damon." She wet her dry lips, her eyes full of conviction. "He would have killed me, if you hadn't killed him first."

Damon was still haunted by the image of her lying in that fire, of hearing Cal saying she was dead. He felt the cool, fragile plastic of the baby rattle in his hands… "But if I hadn't blown up the damn building, you wouldn't have been burned, been in the hospital for months."

"Diego was a cold-blooded killer who murdered my father, and used me to get to him. If you hadn't blown him up, Diego would have killed me and disposed of my body. You know it's true, Damon." She jerked at his hands, forced him to look at her. "It's not your fault. You got rid of a killer. Diego deserved to die."

She was right, but still, guilt weighed on him. She'd suffered so much, he wanted to make it up to her…. "But how could you forgive me?" he asked. "I found that *bébé* rattle… My God, you were pregnant." He dropped his head forward, sweating, guilt assaulting him again. "I've heard that *bébé*'s cry in my sleep."

She cupped his face between her hands. "That rattle belonged to Kendra, Damon. I wasn't pregnant. She was."

Damon jerked his gaze back to hers. "Kendra was pregnant?"

"Yes, she was going to have Antwaun's baby. She said she might have to disappear for a while to keep the baby safe."

"But Cal killed her first," Damon growled. "Jesus. On top of learning about his birth, knowing Kendra was pregnant with his baby when she died, that will kill Antwaun."

"I'm sorry, Damon."

He slid his hands up to her face. "You have nothing to apologize for, Jacqueline, *ma douce amie.* You were innocent in all this."

"No, I was taken in by Diego. For that I'll never forgive myself."

"He would have killed your father anyway," Damon said gently. "You know that."

She nodded, conceding his point.

He brushed her cheek with his fingertips. *"Sa me fait de le pain."*

She turned her hand into his palm. "What does that mean?"

"It means I'm sorry." Damon's voice cracked. "I wish I could take back all the pain I caused you…"

Tears glittered in her eyes, and she traced a finger down his jaw. The gesture was so tender and sweet that moisture pooled in his eyes.

"I know," she said softly. "But I also know that you tried to save me, Damon. I heard your voice, telling me not to die."

He stroked her arms with his fingertips, aching to kiss her. "I wanted you to live more than anything."

"I'm alive now, and so are you." She twined her arms around his neck. "We can both make up for the past."

He gazed into her eyes, and the pain of the past faded as her love enveloped him. Antwaun might see Kendra's face when he looked at her, but Damon didn't.

"I want that so much," Damon said softly. "I love you, *ma belle*."

"I love you, too, Damon."

He no longer thought of her as Crystal, the faceless woman with no past, or Kendra, a brave woman who'd died trying to expose evil in the town. Jacqueline was a brave, strong woman in her own right, one who offered him trust, love and forgiveness.

Unable to resist, he lowered his head and kissed her with all the passion and emotion that he'd had bottled up for the last year.

He had a second chance with her, and he was going to take it. And just like his parents, their love would last the rest of their lives.

ANTWAUN'S HEART POUNDED as he watched his parents congregate on the square with Jean-Paul and Britta, Catherine and her family, Stephanie, and Damon and the woman Jacqueline.

He was supposed to meet the family here to celebrate his release.

But they were not his family at all.

He gripped the manila envelope holding the file Kendra had on him between clammy hands. His partner had discovered it in Lieutenant Phelps's desk and had handed it to him when he'd been released.

He'd read the contents and had been shocked.

He was not a Dubois at all, but the son of the Mutilator, Frederick Fenton, a cold-blooded serial killer serving life in the state pen.

Damon glanced up through the crowd and spotted him, and their gazes locked. Antwaun shifted and held the folder up, and Damon's face blanched.

So Damon knew his family's secret. Jean-Paul probably did, too. What about Catherine and Stephanie?

Had everyone in the family known that he was the bastard son of a killer except him?

Rage heated his blood. He couldn't go back to the force, not after this past week. And he couldn't join the happy little family who'd lied to him all his life.

Damon started toward him, but he sent the man he'd once called his brother a scowl, then he turned and disappeared into the crowd. He was all alone now. The family he'd once loved not a family at all. The woman he'd wanted to marry…dead, too.

And Jacqueline's face could always be a reminder of the woman he'd loved and lost.

He had no idea where to go, but he couldn't stay here in New Orleans.

EPILOGUE

November, three months later

INSIDE THE HOUSE, he knew the Duboises had gathered for their Thanksgiving feast. There would be heaping bowls of vegetables, desserts, a huge turkey, gravy and all the trimmings. His sisters and his niece, his two brothers and their wives would all be talking at once.

His throat clogged and he swallowed back emotions. Would they welcome him if he knocked on the door, or look at him as a madman's son?

Antwaun parked his car in front of the Dubois homestead, his gut knotted with tension. The last few months he'd struggled with the fact that they had lied to him. That they weren't his birth family. That Frederick Fenton was his real father.

With the fact that Damon's new wife looked like Kendra.

He'd left New Orleans angry, feeling betrayed, wanting revenge for her brutal murder. And for his child's....

And he'd found Swafford.

Then the unexpected.

The woman sitting next to him slid her hand over his and squeezed his fingers in silent understanding. "I'll wait in the car if you need a moment alone with them."

He nodded and tried to smile, but his lips felt glued together. Then he opened the car door, climbed out and went to the front door. Several cats appeared at the edge of the property as if guarding it. For a moment, he wondered if they would sense the evil in him and attack. But one loped up onto the stoop, rubbed against his leg and purred.

He relaxed slightly, but his hands felt sweaty. He wiped them on his jeans and knocked. Boisterous laughter and noise echoed from the other side; then the door swung open and his mother appeared.

God, he'd missed her.

"Antwaun!" She threw her hands to her cheeks and burst into a smile, then grabbed him and wrapped him in her arms. "Oh, my baby, you've come back to us. And you do not knock at your own home. You just *come in.*"

She turned and shouted to the others, and he felt himself on the verge of crying, blinking fiercely. Within seconds, his entire family had encircled him, welcoming him back with hugs and kisses. He hugged them in return, nearly choking as his papa dragged him close and clapped him on the back.

"It hasn't been right without you, son."

His sisters were next, followed by Jean-Paul and his very pregnant wife. Then Damon. Damon was the most hesitant, studying him warily as his wife, Jacqueline, moved up beside him.

Antwaun extended his hand. "Sorry I missed the wedding."

Damon's guarded look morphed into a smile, and for a moment Antwaun's gaze rested on Jacqueline and he saw Kendra. But then she spoke, and the image faded, and he saw her as she actually was. Kendra's cousin, not Kendra.

Finally, when everyone pulled away, his mother tried to usher him to the table.

"Wait," he said, holding up a hand. "First, there's someone I want you to meet."

Puzzled looks met his, and he nearly grinned, knowing they would be as shocked as he had been. But it was a great surprise.

He hurried back to the car, and a minute later, returned with his surprise. The family had been eagerly waiting.

"Mom, Dad, everyone…this is my wife." He grinned at the baby in her arms. "And my daughter, Whitney."

Gasps greeted his announcement. "What?" "When?"

"Tell us more," his mother said.

His beautiful wife stepped forward. "I'm Kendra." She turned to Jacqueline, her voice warbling with emotions. "I'm so glad you survived."

Jacqueline's shock mirrored the others'. "Kendra, is it really you?"

"I know I look different," she said, touching her face self-consciously. "But, yes, it's me."

"I don't understand," Jacqueline said. "How? They said you were *dead*...the fingerprints..."

"I knew Swafford was on to me," Kendra began, "and that he was working with a dirty cop. I'd already traced him to Dr. Pace, the plastic surgeon, and to some financing schemes with Diego Bolton. By then I feared for my life, and when I found out I was pregnant, I decided I had to disappear until the baby was born. I pleaded with Dr. Pace, and he contacted a friend in the WITSEC program who altered my fingerprints and DNA in all the databases. After I had the baby, I intended to enter the witness protection program, maybe even have plastic surgery. So I hid out until Whitney was born."

"She's beautiful," his *maman* said, with tears in her eyes.

Kendra hugged the baby to her. "I know and I wanted to contact Antwaun and tell him everything, but couldn't take the chance. Then when I heard Diego was killed, and that Jacqueline was missing, and I knew she'd intended to confront Diego that day…well…I thought she was dead." She paused and looked at Jacqueline, her heart in her eyes. "I was devastated. But later I found out about a woman being brought into the hospital mysteriously and that Dr. Pace was treating her, and I starting poking around and discovered it was you." She clasped Jacqueline's hand. "I was so glad you were alive, but I had to stay hidden."

Jacqueline wiped at her tears and hugged her cousin. "And I'm happy you're here. I've missed you so much."

Damon frowned. "But Dr. Pace never said a word."

Kendra smiled sadly. "I convinced him that secrecy was the only way to keep me, my baby and Jacqueline alive. In the end, he wasn't such an entirely bad man."

Damon cleared his throat. "But Pace said that Jacqueline received your skin, the skin of a cadaver."

Kendra touched her face again. Antwaun knew she was still getting used to the way she looked, as was he. But he loved her and didn't care whose face she wore. Just knowing all she'd sacrificed to save their child had melted his anger and intensified his love for her.

"I planned to have plastic surgery anyway, in case Swafford's people came after me. Jacqueline had rejected another donor's skin and was near death, so we figured her only chance was a relative. So I let Dr. Pace remove my skin and transplant it on to Jacqueline, then I received the cadaver's face."

"So what about the woman Cal killed?" Jean-Paul asked. "He thought she was you?"

Kendra swallowed hard. "Yes, she was my informant, had worked for Swafford's minions. She was scared and was staying at my place at the time." She shivered, and Antwaun knew she still blamed herself for the other woman's death, as she did for her mother's. "Cal thought he'd killed me, and told Dr. Pace so. Dr. Pace convinced Cal to let him use the cadaver for her skin." She paused again. "He made sure Cal believed I was dead, and that the prints and DNA matched."

The family was gaping now in obvious amazement. Damon turned to Antwaun. "How did you find her?"

Antwaun scrubbed his hand over the back of his neck. "When I first left here, I was angry. Felt betrayed. All I wanted to do was find Swafford and get revenge." His voice grew low. "And I did."

His mother gasped. "Oh, Antwaun..."

He looked his mother in the eye. "It's okay, *Maman.* I found him and planned to kill him, but then I realized if I did, I'd be just like Frederick Fenton, my father."

"*I* am your father," his papa said defensively.

Antwaun gave his papa a grateful look, moved by the conviction in his voice. "And that's what I realized. At least I knew I wanted to be like you. So I turned Swafford over to the authorities."

"We heard he'd been arrested," Jean-Paul said. "But not that you were responsible."

Antwaun shrugged. "My next order of business was to confront Fenton."

His sisters moved up beside him to squeeze his arm.

"Before I could, though, I got a call from Kendra. She'd seen news of Swafford's arrest, told me she was alive and that we had a baby."

Kendra slid her arm around Antwaun's waist, and he pulled her in the crook of his arm, wanting to protect her forever. The baby gurgled and swiped at his hand, and Antwaun let her wrap her chubby fingers around his pinky. He loved his daughter so damn much it hurt to think that he'd missed a single moment with her. But he wouldn't dwell on the past, only the future.

"Kendra explained everything, and I was so happy to know that they'd both survived that we got married that night. And together we went to confront Fenton," Antwaun said. "When I looked at him, I realized he wasn't my father. That I had to come back here." His eyes grew misty. "I know I'm not blood, but I'm grateful to have had you all. And I'd like very much to raise my daughter as part of the Dubois family."

His mother shrieked with joy. "Of course you will."

His father choked on emotion and dragged him in his arms, and the entire family engulfed him and his new family in their arms.

"We have to sit down and eat now!" his mother finally said with a laugh. "I'll set a plate for Kendra."

Antwaun glanced at the table and noticed his usual place was already set.

So they had been hoping he'd come. That meant more to him than anything.

The family hurried to the table, hugging and crying and laughing. His *maman* quickly made a place for Kendra beside him, and his papa grabbed a chair to sit the baby seat in so she, too, would be part of the family.

Then his *maman* waved her hands to quiet everyone and gestured for them to link hands. "Now Papa will give thanks, because we have so much to be grateful for this year."

When they bowed their heads, his father thanked the heavens for bringing them all together again, for the love they shared and for the new additions to the family, the wives and children, and those to come in the future.

Antwaun silently gave thanks, as well. New Orleans was slowly recovering from the storms it had weathered, and so was he.

All because of the love of a wonderful family.

READER GUIDELINES

1. In this story, family issues and loyalties are challenged. If you have brothers or sisters, what kinds of conflicts arise between you? How do you resolve them?
2. The heroine suffers a trauma and has to have plastic surgery, receiving a facial transplant. How would you feel if that happened to you, if the face you saw in the mirror wasn't your own?
3. Have you ever known anyone to suffer memory loss? How did they cope with the problem? Were they able to recover their memories? What special challenges would amnesia pose?
4. The hero served in the military, was assigned to a special-ops team that did secretive government work, and has been commemorated as a war hero. But Damon doesn't feel like a hero at all. Why? What do you think of him as a person, given what he did in the service?
5. Do you know any real heroes? What made them heroic?

6. Keeping secrets is part of this story. Finding the killer in this book means Damon must face the demons of his past and possibly expose the group he has sworn to remain silent about. In doing so, his family will see the questionable acts he committed in the past. He fears his parents will be disappointed and not love him anymore. What do you think? How do the Duboises act when they learn the truth? Would most parents act that way?

7. Are there things in your own past that you don't want revealed? Things that you've done that you would like to change?

8. Have you or anyone you've known served in the military? How did they say that experience affected them? What are your feelings about war? Do you think the end justifies the means?

9. How far would you go to protect a loved one?

10. An elderly woman in the story believes that there is magic and that the magic lies in the cats. Do you believe in magic? Do you think that animals can have special powers, or that there are people sensitive to animals and their thoughts? Have you ever seen any evidence of magic or paranormal elements?

11. What themes do you see as central to the story? Discuss.

12. How does the setting add to the mystery and conflict?

REQUEST YOUR FREE BOOKS!

2 FREE NOVELS
FROM THE ROMANCE/SUSPENSE
COLLECTION PLUS 2 FREE GIFTS!

YES! Please send me 2 FREE novels from the Romance/Suspense Collection and my 2 FREE gifts. After receiving them, if I don't wish to receive any more books, I can return the shipping statement marked "cancel." If I don't cancel, I will receive 4 brand-new novels every month and be billed just $5.49 per book in the U.S., or $5.99 per book in Canada, plus 25¢ shipping and handling per book plus applicable taxes, if any*. That's a savings of at least 20% off the cover price! I understand that accepting the 2 free books and gifts places me under no obligation to buy anything. I can always return a shipment and cancel at any time. Even if I never buy another book from the Reader Service, the two free books and gifts are mine to keep forever.

185 MDN EF5Y   385 MDN EF6C

Name _____ (PLEASE PRINT) _____

Address _____ Apt. # _____

City _____ State/Prov. _____ Zip/Postal Code _____

Signature (if under 18, a parent or guardian must sign)

Mail to **The Reader Service:**
IN U.S.A.: P.O. Box 1867, Buffalo, NY 14240-1867
IN CANADA: P.O. Box 609, Fort Erie, Ontario L2A 5X3

Not valid to current subscribers to the Romance Collection,
the Suspense Collection or the Romance/Suspense Collection.

Want to try two free books from another line?
Call 1-800-873-8635 or visit www.morefreebooks.com.

* Terms and prices subject to change without notice. NY residents add applicable sales tax. Canadian residents will be charged applicable provincial taxes and GST. This offer is limited to one order per household. All orders subject to approval. Credit or debit balances in a customer's account(s) may be offset by any other outstanding balance owed by or to the customer. Please allow 4 to 6 weeks for delivery.

Your Privacy: Harlequin is committed to protecting your privacy. Our Privacy Policy is available online at www.eHarlequin.com or upon request from the Reader Service. From time to time we make our lists of customers available to reputable firms who may have a product or service of interest to you. If you would prefer we not share your name and address, please check here. ☐

BOB07

RITA
HERRON

HQN™

We *are* romance™

www.HQNBooks.com   PHRH0907BL